THE JUSTICE RIDERS

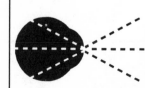

This Large Print Book carries the
Seal of Approval of N.A.V.H.

THE JUSTICE RIDERS

CHUCK NORRIS,
KEN ABRAHAM, AARON NORRIS
AND TIM GRAYEM

THORNDIKE PRESS
A part of Gale, Cengage Learning

GALE
CENGAGE Learning™

Detroit • New York • San Francisco • New Haven, Conn • Waterville, Maine • London

GALE
CENGAGE Learning™

Copyright © 2006 by Carlos Ray Norris, Ken Abraham, Aaron Norris, and The Canon Group.
The Justice Riders Series #1.
Thorndike Press, a part of Gale, Cengage Learning.

Thorndike Press® Large Print Christian Fiction.
The text of this Large Print edition is unabridged.
Other aspects of the book may vary from the original edition.
Set in 16 pt. Plantin.
Printed on permanent paper

LIBRARY OF CONGRESS CATALOGING-IN-PUBLICATION DATA

Norris, Chuck, 1940–
 The justice riders / by Chuck Norris [with] Ken Abraham, Aaron Norris & The Canon Group.
  p. cm. — (Thorndike Press large print Christian fiction)
  ISBN 10: 0-7862-8911-2 (lg. print : alk. paper)
  ISBN 13: 978-0-7862-8911-0 (lg. print : alk. paper)
  1. Large type books. I. Abraham, Ken. II. Norris, Aaron. III. Title. IV. Series: Thorndike Press large print Christian fiction series
PS3614.O7683J87 2006
813'.6—dc22   2006016779

Published in 2008 by arrangement with Broadman & Holman Publishers.

Printed in the United States of America
1 2 3 4 5 6 7 12 11 10 09 08

This book is dedicated to the brave men and women of the United States armed forces who are currently fighting, and have fought, for freedom and justice. Although *The Justice Riders* is based loosely on historical events, our characters are fictitious people fighting fictitious enemies in fictitious battles. But the men and women who have laid their lives on the line so we may live in peace and security are fighting real enemies in real life or death situations. In this small way, we honor them and thank them for being the real Justice Riders.

Chuck Norris
Aaron Norris
Tim Grayem
Ken Abraham

ACKNOWLEDGMENTS

Many thanks to Ken Stephens, David Shepherd, Leonard Goss, Kim Overcash, Jeff Godby, Paul Mikos, and the staff and sales force of B&H Publishing Group for believing in the potential of The Justice Riders series, and for their commitment to producing an excellent product that will entertain and inspire.

The authors also wish to honor the memory of Reily Bonesteel, who perished aboard the steamship *Sultana* in April 1865. A distant relative of Tim Grayem, Reily was only eighteen years of age when he died. It was the discovery of this relative's death that spawned Tim's interest in researching the tragic events surrounding the *Sultana.*

Special thanks to our good friend, Mark Sweeney, for encouraging us to write this story. Without Mark's confidence in us, the Justice Riders may never have "saddled up." Thanks, too, to Mike Forshey for working with Mark to iron out all our contract details. Grateful appreciation is also extended to Felix Saez of Stone Art Gallery in Park City, Utah, for his image of Chuck Norris used to depict "Ezra Justice" in the front cover art.

And thanks to our family members for putting up with us as we've worked on this project.

Most of all, thanks to the Lord Jesus Christ. He is the Ultimate Justice Rider (see Rev. 19:11).

1

Captain Ezra Justice dove for cover just as the vanguard of General Joe Johnston's Confederate Army rounded the bend, coming out of the small North Carolina town of Bentonville, headed northward toward Richmond. Lying on the ground, shrouded by a clump of bushes, Justice stiffened as he heard a sound behind him; his finger tightened on the trigger of his LaMat nine-shot revolver. From behind the bushes emerged a tall, muscular black man, dressed in a Union soldier's uniform, complete with a blue kepi cap and perfectly tied dark blue bow tie. Crouching low, he made his way toward Ezra. Justice relaxed his grip on the LaMat.

Nathaniel York — "Big Nate," as he'd been known most of his life and still was — flopped down on the grass next to Justice. "Everything's in position, Cap'n," he said. "We're ready when you are."

"OK, fine. Good work, Nate."

"Shades of Washington all over again, huh?" Nate pointed down the hillside toward the long rows of Confederate infantry soldiers now coming into view, with the supply line behind them.

"Let's hope so," Justice said, raising his eyebrows slightly and nodding.

Nate understood the look of concern on Ezra's face. The scene below was reminiscent of General Joe Johnston's forces coming to the aid of P. G. T. Beauregard's Confederate army at Manassas in late July of 1861. Johnston's army thwarted the Union forces advancing southward from Washington, not only beating them back but sending them on the run, forcing them to retreat all the way to the Capitol. Had it not been for a dispute between Johnston and Confederate President Jefferson Davis, Johnston may have marched right into Washington and the war may have turned in an entirely different direction.

Davis's badly timed intervention, combined with problems in the supply lines — caused mainly by covert attacks and diversions spawned by Ezra Justice and his band of marauders — stymied the Confederate's offensive action toward Washington and gave the Federal army a much-needed opportunity to regroup and reposition its forces.

Now, more than three years later, with the South reeling from a series of devastating military blows, General Johnston's battle-weary but undaunted troops were threatening to change the course of the war again. And Johnston believed he would succeed in his assignment at all costs.

Equally determined to stop Johnston's army from reinforcing General Robert E. Lee's was a quiet but courageous captain in the Union Army, Ezra Justice. General William T. Sherman had personally assigned Justice and his men — all six of them — to stand in Johnston's way, to slow down an entire army, to do everything possible — anything possible — to interrupt Johnston's northern progress.

More than any man alive, Nathaniel York knew how to interpret the often understated expressions of his enigmatic leader, Ezra Justice. Nate raised a finger to his thin, neatly trimmed mustache as though contemplating some great philosophical truth. "Think we can pull this off, Ezra?"

Justice didn't flinch at the sergeant's familiarity. Most of the other men rarely referred to their leader by his first name, but Nathaniel York was not just a fellow soldier. He and Ezra were best friends, practically family. They'd grown up together on a large, prosperous Tennessee tobacco farm owned by Ezra's parents. Nathaniel York, however, was a former slave, legally emancipated by Abraham Lincoln, but emancipated a long time before that by his friend Ezra Justice. Even as a boy, Ezra had believed that all men were created equal and had defied his family's ironclad rules for relating to "darkies." Against his parents' objections, he had formed a strong bond of friendship with Nate. Now, with both men fighting for the North, that friendship remained intact.

Moreover, Nathaniel York hailed from good roots. His grandfather — also a slave — had gained great respect and admiration as a member of the Lewis and Clark expedition in 1803. For his part, Nathaniel York never thought of himself as enslaved to anybody, despite the fact that his family worked long hours in the tobacco fields and lived in a shack at the back of the Justice property. Bright, articulate, and deeply spiritual, Nathaniel had committed his life to God as a boy and had adopted Jesus' statement, "The truth will set you free" as his motto. When Ezra asked Big Nate to join him in setting other men free, Nate never hesitated. He'd fought throughout the war, a black man and a white man side by side, with his friend Ezra Justice.

Ezra peered down at the seemingly endless line of soldiers streaming out of the town. Getting to the supply line would not be easy, he knew. Getting out with their lives would be tougher still. He spoke to himself as much as to Nate. "We have to stop them, Nate. We have to stop them here."

"Yes, sir. Word from the north is that General Grant has Lee ready to do something desperate."

"It's about time," Justice replied. "That siege at Petersburg has been going on for far too long. For the past ten months, our men have been living in trenches all the way from Petersburg to Richmond. Grant's been puttin' the squeeze on them, and Lee's boys are getting nervous. General Joe Johnston's army in North Carolina is the South's last hope. If we can keep Johnston's troops from reinforcing Lee's, we might be able to bring this war to a close. If we can't . . ." Ezra's voice trailed off.

"If we can't?" Nate pressed.

"If Johnston gets his troops to General Lee, they will be a formidable force against General Grant's army. They may be able to mount an attack that will split Grant's troops and break the siege. If they do that, a lot more men are going to die on both sides."

Nate nodded and proceeded to brief Ezra on the readiness report. "Sergeant Bonesteel has his .44-caliber rifle scope focused on the first ammunition wagon. Sergeant Whitecloud has his own brand of Injun fireworks ready on the other side of town. He can't wait to get into the fight. I practically had to hold him down when he saw those Confederate cavalry boys.

"And the Hawkins twins are itching to try out their new invention they dreamed up for our enjoyment. Some wacky thing they call a 'satchel charge.' " Justice smiled at Nate's sarcasm regarding Roberto and Carlos Hawkins, two of the most ingenious, young explosives experts he'd ever known. Nate would have been content to rely on good old-fashioned dynamite charges, but not the twins. The Hawkins brothers were constantly coming up with seemingly ridiculous new methods to destroy something, and Ezra learned long ago not to be so cynical. The twins' crazy inventions usually worked. *Usually.*

Nate interrupted Ezra's ruminations. "And O'Banyon wants to go down and try

14

to talk them into surrendering."

Ezra's mouth hinted at a smile as he thought of Shaun O'Banyon, the lovable, impetuous Irishman who in the past had preferred a bottle of good whiskey over fighting any day. Shaun O'Banyon believed that he could talk his way out of most any situation, and he often did. But this would not be a day for talk.

"Pass the word, Nathaniel. When the church bell strikes three, let 'er rip. There's no way the seven of us can stand a chance against their entire army. Our goal is to slow them down by taking out their supplies. Try not to get involved in combat with their troops any more than necessary. Otherwise we will lose our element of surprise. We have to hit them hard and fast. Get in quickly and get out. If we take more than a few minutes, we're all dead men."

Nate rose to his knees. "Got it, Cap'n." He halfway stood up, brushed himself off, and repeated the command. "Start the attack right after the bell strikes three. I'll meet you back at the camp. God be with ya, Ezra."

Ezra nodded but didn't look around as Nate slipped away. "Here's hoping."

General Joe Johnston's troops never knew

what hit them. One moment they were trudging through town, complaining about their aching feet and how much farther they had to go before meeting up with General Lee; the next moment, just after three o'clock, when the church bell tolled for the third time, the earth erupted. Preset dynamite charges blew dozens of soldiers closest to the supply train sky high. Many of the multiple sticks of dynamite tied together and buried just below the ground exploded almost simultaneously due to some long fuses rigged before sun-up and now ignited by Harry Whitecloud. Huge craters ripped open in front of the supply train bringing it to a halt.

From his concealed location in the hills, Reginald Bonesteel squeezed the trigger on his Henry .44-caliber repeating rifle. The butt of the high-powered rifle kicked hard against Bonesteel's shoulder, but the British-born marksman kept on firing. A moment later, an enormous explosion blew the first ammunitions wagon into a ball of flame. A second concussion followed, creating several more deafening blasts. By the third and fourth rounds, bits of fiery wood were flying through the air, landing on the ammo wagons following behind, igniting the canvas atop the arms wagons, turning that section of the road into an inferno as well. Satisfied with his work, Bonesteel mounted his horse and kneed it toward the fire. With a double set of holsters strapped on the front of his saddle and another double set of guns behind the saddle, Bonesteel swept through a line of Confederate officers at full gallop, firing incessantly in every direction as he crossed the road. Men in gray uniforms who had been maneuvering the troops, in their efforts to fend off the attack, dropped in Bonesteel's path. A piece of shell winged the brazen Brit in his shoulder, but it didn't slow him down a bit. His steed's powerful legs stretched out as though in a race for dear life, and Bonesteel disappeared into the forest on the other side of the field.

The sky around the supply train turned a gritty brown laced with orange. The acrid smell of burnt gunpowder permeated the air. The flames and smoke created so much chaos and confusion in the Confederate ranks that nobody noticed the lone rider racing toward the water wagons. When a soldier finally caught a glimpse of the rider wearing a blue jacket and a wide-brimmed hat, it was too late. The man on the horse blew the soldier into eternity. He flipped a lever on his specially designed LaMat, and the single shot pistol became a blazing rapid-firing repeater. Good thing, too. Ezra Justice needed all the fire power he could get. Three or four Confederate soldiers converged on him, but Ezra eluded them. Justice felled several more gray-coats as he dodged the musket balls whizzing by his ears. He took comfort in one of his own favorite sayings that he used often with his men: "Don't worry about the lead you hear. If you hear the bullet, it's already gone by you. It's the one you don't hear that you have to worry about."

Ezra knew that merely upsetting the wagon carrying the large barrels laden with water wouldn't be good enough. He wanted to destroy General Johnston's water supply. An army can survive a long time without food but only a few days without water. Even if the troops kept moving northward, they'd have to stop for water before long, giving General Grant more precious time to drive toward Richmond.

At full gallop, Ezra reached the water wagons and started firing, not at the soldiers nearby but at the barrels containing the water. One by one, streams of water poured out of the barrels as, too late, the Rebels realized the true targets of Ezra Justice's bullets. With his gun barrel hot, Justice danced his horse through the maze of dead bodies, mangled wagons, and other equipment. Getting to the supply line was one thing; getting clear of it would be quite another.

Ezra veered hard to the left, attempting to avoid several Rebs running back toward the supply train. His horse obediently leaped over a pile of rubble as Ezra pulled up hard on the reins. Just as he went airborne, he saw the soldier in the dirty gray coat, kneeling on the ground straight ahead of him, aiming his musket right at Justice. Ezra tried to duck, but it was too late. He heard the sound of a rifle blast.

The kneeling soldier crumpled to the dirt as the hoofs of Ezra's horse touched the ground. Ezra looked behind him and saw Nathaniel York coming alongside, smoke still curling from the barrel of his carbine. "Thanks, Nate. That was a close one."

"Glad to be of service!" Nate yelled as he galloped by toward the chow wagons without breaking stride. Nate pulled a sawed-off 12-gauge shotgun out of his saddle holster and blasted his way toward the food supply. Confederate soldiers scattered or dropped to the ground as the feared shotgun sprayed pellets in a wide swath. The shotgun blast gave Nate just the opening he needed to get close to the mess wagons. He lit a torch on the way by and tossed it onto the top of one of the covered wagons carrying the food supplies.

Whooosh! The wagon burst into flames.

Shaun O'Banyon had worked his way to the rear of the supply line where the extra horses were in tow. His job, although relatively easy in the midst of the chaos, was one of the most dangerous. He wanted to set the horses free, to stampede them hopefully in the opposite direction of Richmond, so even if the Confederates were able to round them up again, the time it took to track down and capture the horses would disrupt the army's forward progress.

While the confusion raged up ahead at the front of the supply train, O'Banyon raised his head up out of the ditch in which he had been waiting impatiently. He spotted the horses about to come by, roped to several feed wagons. Taking careful aim from his position, O'Banyon picked off three men struggling to keep the horses calm that were pulling the feed wagons. He then quickly mounted his wild-eyed Appaloosa horse, which had been hidden behind a thicket. Before anyone saw him coming, O'Banyon came out of nowhere and boldly made for the horses.

Pulling up in front of the feed wagon, O'Banyon couldn't resist commiserating with the animals. "Such a pity to be agitating these fine animals," he said, as he slashed the reins previously securing two large beauties to the wagon. "Get on, now! Go south." O'Banyon slapped the rear flanks of the biggest horse. "Go now! You've seen enough of this kind of fightin'. You've served these Johnny Rebs for too long. Today, I'll be giving you your own emancipation proclamation. Go, Big Fella! Go, Sweet Lady. Go visit General Sherman or just go find a wee bit of green." One by one, O'Banyon went down the row of horses, slashing the reins, offering a few words of encouragement or a friendly pat to each animal before slapping it on its way southward. When the last horse had been freed, O'Banyon spurred his own animal, which reared slightly and took off through the haze of spherical lead balls flying all around him.

Meanwhile, Ezra Justice headed toward the twelve-pound round-shot howitzers, each with its own large ammo box being pulled on the same wagon wheels as the huge gun barrel. Ezra ducked just as a hot piece of shrapnel flew by his head. He heard a sickening thud as the metal seared into a young Confederate lieutenant, hitting him chest high, shredding his upper shoulder, and mangling his left arm. Ezra Justice flinched as he saw the boy fall on his face. Ezra hated this war, with its senseless maiming and killing; but there was nothing he could do but hope that by doing his job well, he could help bring it to an end soon.

Ezra glanced in the direction of the front lines. Time was running out.

Although only a minute or two had passed since the first shots had been fired, by now, Rebel infantrymen and, beyond them, the Cavalrymen had realized the true nature of the attack and were doubling back to help their fallen comrades. The Confederate soldiers had been caught with their guard down, but those who had survived the initial blasts were scrambling to defend the supply train with any weapon available.

Pulling two sticks of dynamite from his saddlebags as he rode, Justice was about to light the fuse and toss it toward the howitzers when a soldier on the ground grabbed a shovel, hauled off and swung the blade at Ezra's midsection, walloping Justice right in the stomach, knocking him off his horse, and sending him tumbling to the ground face first. For a moment Ezra's world went dark; then he felt the dirt and blood in his mouth. Holding his side, Ezra thought sure that a rib was broken. *No time to worry about it now.* He spit out some blood and staggered to his feet, just in time to elude the soldier diving toward him, bowie knife in hand. Undaunted, the soldier came at Ezra again.

Ignoring the pain in his side, Ezra pivoted on his left foot. Instantly, he whirled around a full 180 degrees and launched his right leg at the man's face, connecting his right foot squarely with the soldier's jaw, flipping him backward in the air and landing him on his side with a grunt, right next to a dead Confederate soldier. Ezra's attacker raised up, leaning momentarily on his left hand, sliding his right hand over the dead soldier. Still a bit groggy himself, Ezra almost didn't see the Rebel snatch the dead man's revolver off the ground, fumbling to aim it at Justice. In a flash, Justice's strong right arm chopped down, the straightened side of his rigid, bare hand connecting firmly on the side of his attacker's neck. Ezra stood over him, waiting to see if he was going to retaliate. The soldier didn't get up; he was out cold.

That's when Ezra saw Mordecai Slate for the first time.

Off to Ezra's left a Cavalry officer sat on a black horse, amidst the burning rubble, smoke, and dust of battle, the blackened remains of a supply wagon behind him. Dressed in full, clean Confederate regalia, while his soldiers wore filthy, tattered trousers and shoes with gaping holes in them, the officer was ruggedly handsome yet possessed a nearly palpable sense of malice at the same time — the type of man that men feared and women could not resist. Although he had never met him, Ezra recognized the officer immediately. He'd heard about Mordecai Slate, a leader who preferred to fight out front with his men, rather than remaining in safety, behind the artillery lines. Known as a ferocious and merciless soldier, Slate was the commander of a regiment detached from the rest of the Confederate army, a regiment that nobody on either side of the Mason Dixon line wanted to claim — "the Death Raiders" regiment as they were known.

At one time, the band of thugs under Slate's command may have been honorable soldiers of the South. At one time . . . maybe . . . but not anymore. Mordecai Slate had slowly but surely transformed his regiment from noble men fighting for a cause they believed in to murderers who enjoyed killing for no reason or any reason. They took no prisoners, preferring to shoot anyone they captured rather than bother with having to feed, house, and/or transport the enemy.

Slate sat high on his horse, his revolver aimed at Ezra's chest. "Justice!" he called. "How about some of Mordecai Slate's brand of justice?"

Ezra looked up and saw Mordecai Slate pull the trigger and felt the bullet slam into his chest. The impact of the bullet sent Justice reeling backward onto the ground. His body didn't move; his face was expressionless.

Mordecai Slate let out a hideous laugh, spinning his horse and galloping back to the fracas.

Charging at full speed, Roberto and Carlos Hawkins streaked down the supply train, one on each side of the row of howitzers. Attached to the boys' saddles were two large satchels. Roberto's horse jumped, and Roberto's arm raised high, revealing a long knife in his hand. His arm slashed downward, toward the side of the saddle, and the bag dropped to the ground, landing just under the howitzer's ammo box.

No sooner had Roberto's horse landed in stride, the first satchel exploded beneath the howitzer. The force of the explosion sent cannonballs flying in all directions, as well as igniting fires all along the supply line. A moment later Carlos delivered his first satchel charge, his horse leaping a cannon on a dead run. Carlos whacked the satchel away from his saddle directly above the cannon. He knew he had only a second or two before the charge went off. The back legs of his horse barely touched the ground when the bag exploded — fortunately in the opposite direction from the one in which Carlos was jumping. The Hawkins boys crisscrossed the artillery lines, delivering two more satchel charges and leaving a trail of death and destruction behind them as the Confederate ammunitions supplies went up in smoke.

Harry Whitecloud was racing by, shooting fire arrows into the canvas-covered ammunition wagons when he spotted Ezra Justice lying deathly still on the ground. Harry sprang off his horse, and the well-trained animal came to an immediate halt. Harry ran to Ezra, praying that his captain was still alive but expecting to find him dead. He knelt down and rolled Justice over on his back. Ezra's face was caked with dirt and blood. Harry's worst fears were realized when he saw the ragged bullet hole that had pierced Ezra Justice's jacket just above his heart.

Whitecloud had seen death many times, but something about Ezra Justice caused

Harry to regard him as invulnerable. *This can't be happening. This man is indestructible,* Harry thought. "I'm not going to leave you here, Captain," Harry said aloud. The strong Indian grasped Justice by the shoulders, preparing to hoist Ezra onto his horse. As he did, he heard a low groan emanating from the captain.

"You're alive!" Harry cried.

Ezra struggled to sit up. "Yeah, barely," he said hoarsely. He reached inside his breast pocket and pulled out a gold pocket watch. Lodged dead center in the watch was a flattened .44-caliber slug.

Whitecloud looked at Ezra in amazement. "Captain, you are shot full of luck."

"It's more than luck, Harry," as Ezra slowly stood to his feet. "Now let's get back to the cabin."

Ezra looked around and saw destruction and dead bodies everywhere. The stench of war, burning flesh, and acrid smoke burned his eyes. The one man Ezra did not see was Mordecai Slate. Somehow, in the rain of lead and cannon, and the haze of dust and smoke, Mordecai Slate had disappeared. Ezra's stomach churned. He had a feeling he'd meet Mordecai Slate again.

Ezra whistled for his horse, grabbed onto the saddle horn, and pulled himself onto his mount. He winced at the pain in his chest as he straightened up in the saddle.

Harry leaped onto his horse and looked back over his shoulder at Justice. "A guy could get hurt around here," Harry dead-panned. Without breaking stride, they maneuvered their horses through the smoke and fire, past the remaining supply depot guards, and toward the safety of the forest across the field.

A few moments later Harry and Ezra were out of harm's way. Ezra turned around long enough to look back at the devastation he and his rogue band of soldiers had caused. All along the supply train fire and smoke filled the air, and burning debris littered the ground. Harry and Ezra slowed their stallions to a trot, and Ezra reached into his coat pocket and pulled out the gold pocket-watch his father had given him as a young man. Ezra flipped open the watch's lid and smiled. Mordecai Slate's bullet had stopped the timepiece at barely seven minutes past three.

One by one, Ezra's men picked their way through the woods and made their way back to their previously agreed upon meeting spot. Harry and Ezra were the first to arrive at the camp, an abandoned cabin deep in the North Carolina forest. They were followed shortly by Reginald Bonesteel.

"How'd you make out, Bonesteel?" Ezra asked as he helped the always particular Englishman unload the four holsters from his horse.

"A most enjoyable afternoon, Captain." Bonesteel dismounted and pulled his rifle out of a side pocket on his saddle. He stroked the .44-caliber's long barrel as though he were caressing a pet. "Henry here was magnificent."

"Come on inside, Mr. Bonesteel. Let's see how bad that wound is. I'd hate to see you get any more blood on your uniform." Ezra smiled as Bonesteel gazed in surprise at the dark blue spot on his coat, where blood was oozing from his shoulder. Ezra correctly guessed that Reginald Bonesteel had nearly forgotten that he had been winged during the fracas.

"Sit down over there." Ezra nodded toward a stool in front of the fireplace. Bonesteel shed his double-breasted coat and shirt, revealing his muscular upper body and hard-as-a-rock chest. As a former member of the Queen of England's personal bodyguard, Bonesteel had been selected to that honored position as much for his striking good looks and powerful physique as for his uncanny skill with a rifle.

Justice poured some water into a cracked bowl and brought it over to Bonesteel. "Sit still. Let's see where that bullet is." He wiped the blood away from Bonesteel's wound, and with a small set of tongs he pulled the lead out of Bonesteel's shoulder. Bonesteel winced but didn't say a word. Fortunately, the musket ball hadn't penetrated too deeply. Justice found an old bedsheet and ripped it into strips of cloth that he used as bandages to stop Bonesteel's bleeding.

"We're both very fortunate today, Reginald."

"Let's hope it stays that way, Captain."

Nate came through the cabin door next. His usually immaculate uniform was soiled and torn, but otherwise the big man was intact. "Those Rebs are going to be stuck here for quite a while, Captain. Even if they do get to Richmond, General Grant will have plenty of time to get ready for them."

Ezra glanced up from where he was still working on Bonesteel's wound. "That's what we wanted to accomplish, Nate. Good work. And thanks for saving my life out there."

"Aw, it was nothin', Cap'n. You'd do the same for me."

Justice looked his friend in the eyes. "That goes without saying, Nate."

The Hawkins twins were laughing in youthful enthusiasm as they turned their horses toward the cabin. "We've never come up with any weapon quite like those satchel charges," Roberto said, shaking his head. "Were they amazing or what?"

"Maybe so," Carlos replied. "But next time, let's allow another second or two before the charge goes off. That last one singed the hair on my neck."

"Ha, you're lucky that's all it did," Roberto fired back. "I hope there's something to eat and drink in this place. I'm starved!"

Inside the cabin Ezra Justice and his soldiers heartily embraced, locking arms in an expression that said more than the words they spoke. "Glad you made it back OK."

The twins stretched out on the floor while Nate and Harry sat at a dusty old dining table that may have at one time, long ago, been surrounded by the sounds of happy children eating breakfast. Bonesteel relaxed on a makeshift bed made of old rags and blankets. They rested, laughed, reviewed the escapades of the afternoon, and filled each other in on their encounters with the enemy. As the afternoon light began to fade, only one man was missing. "Has anybody seen O'Banyon?" Ezra asked.

"Last I saw him, he was talking to some horses," Carlos said.

"Typical Irishman," Bonesteel said with disdain.

"He's probably off somewhere dancing an Irish gig," Harry Whitecloud offered.

"Do you mean an Irish jig?" Roberto howled.

"Gig. Jig. However you white men say it," Harry answered. The other men chuckled at Harry's mistake. Educated in some of the finest schools in the Northeast, Harry nonetheless occasionally made a mess of his adopted language. When he did, the twins were quick to let him know it.

"Hard telling where that free spirit might have wandered off to," Carlos said as he shook his head and grinned. "If he was en-joyin' the scenery, he might be halfway to Richmond by now."

"Especially if someone told him there was a Blarney stone in that direction!" laughed Roberto. "Wherever he went, he better get back here pretty soon, or he's gonna be all alone out there behind enemy lines."

"Naah, O'Banyon's never really alone," said Nate, his lips turning into a smile. "The Lord's with him and watchin' out for him."

"I sure hope so," Ezra said.

A few minutes later, the men in the cabin heard a horse neighing outside in the woods. Then another.

"Cover the windows!" Ezra commanded. "Reginald, take the front door." The men were already pulling their carbines while Ezra barked rapid-fire orders in a firm but quiet whisper. "Carlos and Roberto, get upstairs. Nate, cover the back door. Nobody fire until I do."

Sounds of several snorting horses could be heard thrashing through the brush outside, their riders making no attempt to conceal their actions. Justice increased the pressure on the LaMat's trigger.

"Wait. Don't shoot!" Carlos called from upstairs. "It's O'Banyon! And he has half a dozen horses with him, as well."

"What?" Ezra looked out the window and saw Shaun O'Banyon approaching the cabin with five or six horses in tow. Justice couldn't believe that Shaun would jeopardize his life to bring the horses through the thick woods to safety. But that was the kind of man Shaun O'Banyon was. Always thinking about how he could help someone, even if the *someone* was a four-footed animal.

Ezra opened the door and went outside

on the porch as O'Banyon tied the horses to a nearby tree. Justice stood on the porch, his LaMat revolver in the holster on his hip. "Shaun O'Banyon, what on earth are you doing with those horses?"

"They are such fine specimens, aren't they, Cap'n? They were much too lovely to simply let go. After all, they might mistakenly wander back to the Johnny Rebs. And we couldn't have that; now could we?"

Ezra stepped off the porch and patted one of the stallions. "They are beautiful animals, Shaun. I'm just not sure what we're gonna do with them. We already have horses. But it was good of you to save them."

"Ah, my Lizzie would have it no other way. She would wallop me sure enough, if she were thinkin' I left these beauties in the devil's hand," O'Banyon said as he pulled a small locket out of his breast pocket and flipped it open. Inside was a picture of his wife, Elizabeth O'Banyon. "Lizzie loves animals of all kinds but especially these big fellows. And she has just the right touch with them. She can shoe a horse better than I can." O'Banyon looked at the photo in the locket. "She's a dear one, she is." He snapped the locket closed and replaced it in his jacket pocket.

With O'Banyon back in the camp, Ezra

could finally relax. All of the men loved Shaun O'Banyon, even Bonesteel, though the hard-nosed Brit would never admit it. Nevertheless, he maintained a grudging respect for the Irish O'Banyon as a courageous soldier, a man willing to lay down his life for his brothers, and as a man of utmost integrity.

O'Banyon nearly drove Ezra crazy at times with his rambunctious behavior, but Justice saw the good in O'Banyon and loved him as his own brother. Shaun O'Banyon was one of the first men Justice had recruited. Ezra sat down on the floor, leaned back against the wall, and looked around the cabin at the valiant men in his squad, each one an expert in his field. Ezra smiled as he recalled how he had brought this unusual assortment of men together.

2

Although Ezra Justice had been involved in covert operations for the Federals since the beginning of the war, it wasn't until the first week of September 1864 that he received the terse message from Washington: *Report to General William T. Sherman immediately.*

Sherman was camped outside Atlanta, the Southern jewel and the Confederacy's primary railroad hub and industrial center. Dressed in rumpled, dusty blues, his unkempt beard looking more scruffy than usual, Sherman was in a somewhat relaxed mood when Justice arrived. And why not? Sherman had finally succeeded in taking Atlanta after a long siege through the hot summer of 1864. For months prior to Justice's visit, the wily white Tecumseh had played cat and mouse with Confederate General Joseph E. Johnston, with Johnston repeatedly retreating in the face of Sherman's superior numbers. A military conservative, Johnston was too smart to clash directly with Sherman any more than necessary, but his reluctance to throw his men into battle with little chance of winning cost him his job. Jeff Davis replaced Johnston with General John Bell Hood on July 17, 1864, and a few days later Hood launched a futile and foolish attack against Sherman's army at Peachtree Creek. Soundly defeated with nearly nine thousand casualties, Hood desperately held on to Atlanta for six more weeks. During that time, Sherman laid siege to the city and allowed his artillery to take target practice even on the civilian population while he sent out raids to cut off the supply lines coming into the city. Finally, on September 2, Sherman's troops swarmed into Atlanta. Hood ordered a hasty retreat, pulling his troops out to positions north of town, burning some of the South's most valuable supply depots, and turning large sections of Atlanta into an inferno rather than allowing the ammunitions to fall into Sherman's hands.

Sherman telegraphed Washington: "Atlanta is ours, and fairly won."

Then he sent for Ezra Justice. Sherman liked Justice because, much like the general himself and unlike many Union commanders, Ezra Justice was not afraid to take quick, risky action to accomplish a mission. The two brilliant military tacticians met in an ornately appointed Southern antebellum home that had been recently confiscated by the Federals.

General Sherman greeted Ezra robustly and led him into the parlor. "Come in, Captain. Sit down." The General nodded toward two high-backed chairs in the heart of the room.

Ezra Justice glanced at his dirty uniform. "Perhaps I'd better stand, sir."

"Nonsense. We own this house now and everything in it. Sit. Sit. Care for a drink?" Sherman motioned to a bottle of brandy on the table next to him.

"No thank you, General."

Sherman raised his left eyebrow slightly as he stared at Justice. "Suit yourself. Good liquor is hard to come by these days. If you don't want it, General Grant will be glad to have it." Sherman chuckled, sat down in a chair opposite Ezra, leaned back a bit, and crossed one leg over the other. He got right to the point.

"We need to bring this war to a close, Justice. If the Rebs get one major victory at this juncture, it will boost their spirits and make them even more determined. People in the cities up north are calling for us to make a truce with Jefferson Davis. A truce! Can you imagine that?" The general's gravel-toned voice raised in pitch and intensity. "We don't need a truce; we need a total victory. The Rebels have taken some losses, but they still have a powerful, potent army out there in the field. General Grant and I believe that the only sure way to end this war quickly is to cause the Confederacy's strategic, economic, and mental capacity for war to be decisively broken. Understand?"

"I think so, sir."

"As soon as we're done here in Atlanta, I plan to move toward the sea. We will scorch the earth, burning crops, killing livestock, destroying railroads and civilian property as we go. And we will free the slaves. The Confederates are deeply committed to their cause, so they will not give up unless we force them to do so. Our goal is to break the Rebels' will to fight and hopefully hasten the end of this hellish conflict."

A native Tennessean who had made his living off his family-owned plantation, Ezra recognized how that sort of devastation might impact people's lives for years to come. He carefully broached the question to Sherman. "With all respect, sir, won't that create an enormous amount of ill-will among the Southern people once the war is over and we try to put this nation back together again?"

Sherman's head snapped straight up as though Justice had spoken words of treason. The General glared at Justice for a moment, and then his expression softened slightly. "It probably will, Justice. But we can't be worried about that right now. We'll leave it to the politicians to apply the bandages and help with the healing. Right now, our job is to stop the killing and bleeding."

"Sir, why did you call for me?"

"Because you can help me end this war. Hood is moving northwest toward Tennessee, probably somewhere around Nashville. I don't plan to let him get there. We have George Thomas and his army moving in that direction right now, and I am hoping he will cut Hood off somewhere around the town of Franklin, Tennessee. Meantime, I want you to infiltrate enemy lines and cause trouble in their ranks — tear up their supply lines, interfere with their communications. Wreak havoc. Blow up some train tracks. Do whatever is necessary to demoralize the Confederates."

Justice was intrigued but puzzled. "Yes, sir. That's what I've been trying to do since you first commissioned me to your special services. I'm a little confused, however. What do you want me to do that I am not doing already?"

"I'm authorizing you to form a group of elite soldiers. Pick your men, Justice, and pick the finest. Keep it a small group, five or six; seven is a good number. You can draw them from our ranks or enlist your own men. Do whatever is necessary. But understand this: If you get caught, you are on your own. You'll be hung as a spy. The United States Army or the government of the United States or I myself have no knowledge of your doings."

"I understand, General."

"I'll send you your orders, but how you accomplish your missions will be up to you. Any questions?"

"No, sir. When do I start?"

"Yesterday. Now get going."

Ezra stood to his feet and saluted the general. Sherman snapped a sharp salute in return, and Ezra turned toward the door when he heard Sherman's gruff voice.

"Captain Justice."

"Yes, General?"

"May God be with you."

"And with you, General."

The mid-September weather was already

41

turning cold when Ezra Justice stepped off the train in Boston, looking for his first recruit. A brisk wind sent a batch of leaves rustling around his legs, and the chill that enveloped his entire body threatened to reach his soul. Ezra pulled his scarf up around his neck.

He made his way to "Paddy Town," a slum section of Boston in which thousands of impoverished Irish immigrants had settled. The Irish brought with them few possessions from their homeland, and those who survived the arduous six weeks traversing the Atlantic Ocean, crammed aboard a rat- and lice-infested ship, disembarked with only what they could carry in their hands. They landed in Boston and literally started life over from scratch.

Fleeing the famine and disease in Ireland caused by the blighted potato crop, by the mid 1800s, twenty to thirty thousand more illiterate, destitute Irish immigrants were landing in Boston each year. With virtually no money and few skills other than farming, drinking, and fighting, the newcomers were an explosive population just awaiting a spark to set them off. Justice could almost feel the tension as he walked through the shantytown, dark, filthy, refuse-littered streets, lined with one row of shacks after another. Small fires burned here and there, each with as many desperate people gathered around them as possible, all trying to keep warm.

"I'm looking for a man," Justice said to anyone whose eye he'd catch. "O'Banyon's his name. Do you know where I can find him?"

"Hmmph."

"O'Banyon," Ezra said to the next man. "Ever hear of him?"

"There's lots of O'Banyons around here, mate."

"Shaun O'Banyon. He's a pretty good fighter. A young man in his mid-twenties, maybe early thirties. Do you know where I can find him?"

"Aye, yes. I've heard of that O'Banyon. He's been around here. Wounded at Gettysburg, wasn't he? My guess is that you'll find him either in a church or chatting in a bar."

Ezra found a small bar open for business and crowded in with the rough looking men and a few not very attractive women. The locals eyed him suspiciously as he stepped up to the counter.

"What'll ya have?" the bartender asked.

"Nothing right now. I'm looking for a man."

"Got lots of men around here. Those that

aren't off to war, that is."

"O'Banyon. Shaun O'Banyon. Do you know where I might find him?"

"Why do you want him?"

"I have an offer from General Sherman that I think he might be interested in."

The bartender cocked his head and looked at Justice for a long moment, as though trying to decide whether he could trust him and, more importantly, whether he should give him any information or not. "Sherman, huh?" He picked up a rag and wiped the bar while he spoke quietly, his eyes focused on his cleaning, without looking at Justice. "Right over there," he nodded toward the doorway. "Cross the street, and go in the back door of the ironworks building. Some rich folks have a sporting activity going on. You'll find O'Banyon there."

"Thanks."

"Don't mention it."

Ezra caught the message. "I won't," he said, touching the brim of his hat with two fingers as he nodded at the bartender.

The noise in the warehouse section of the ironworks was so loud that nobody noticed Ezra slip in the back door. The torch-lit room was hot, stuffy, and rancid; the smell of smoke and perspiration hung heavily in the air. Dozens of men — some dressed in business suits, others in military garb, and some in dingy working-class clothes — crowded around a roped off square in the center of the room. Inside the ropes, a large black man wearing only brown drawstring slave pants, and a much smaller, but handsome, youthful-looking Irishman — also naked from the waist up, but wearing army-issued blue pants — were engaged in a bare-fisted boxing match. At least, it looked to Ezra that the men were supposed to be boxing. In fact, it seemed more like a street brawl. Both men's skin glistened with sweat, reflecting the glow of the torches like tiny lights on their bodies. Blood dripped from the big man's mouth, and the smaller man had a nasty cut above his eye. With every blow landed by one or the other boxer, the spectators in the room erupted. "Hit him again!"

"Give it to him!"

Justice sidled up next to a round-faced, boisterous man wearing a black suit and a top hat. He nodded toward the smaller man in the ring. "O'Banyon?" Ezra said above the din.

The man in the top hat turned to look at Justice for a moment. "Yeah, that's O'Banyon. At least, that's what's left of him.

The darkie is giving him quite a beating."

Just then, the big man in the ring connected with a powerful blow to O'Banyon's midsection, much to the delight of the crowd. Ezra winced as O'Banyon doubled over in pain, staggering backward trying to elude the stone-like fists of the black man. Too late. O'Banyon was still bent forward when the big man swung an uppercut that looked as though it started on the floor and flew up to O'Banyon's jaw. The punch landed with such a loud thud, even the calloused men in the ironworks gasped.

O'Banyon's head snapped back, his body catapulted through the air and slammed into a pole holding up the ropes that formed the ring. The Irishman slid down to the floor and sat there looking up in a daze, as though he were watching the clouds go by. Then his head jolted forward, and he fell over sideways, unconscious.

A roar went up from the crowd as the men converged on the big man, slapping him on his wet back, and then heading to the cashier to divvy up their winnings or to the pub across the street to drown their sorrows. Others milled around the ring, arguing over the highlights of the bout. Meanwhile, O'Banyon lay motionless on the floor.

Ezra Justice pushed through the crowd,

found a bucket of water and a sponge, and knelt down next to the dark-haired, young Irishman. He plunged the sponge in the water, filled it to capacity, and then squeezed it over O'Banyon's head, letting the water drip down his face and chest. O'Banyon stirred slightly, so Justice doused him again. O'Banyon blinked, and then flinched, as the blood dripped into his eyes. Ezra poured more water on him.

"Are you OK?" Justice asked.

"Do I look OK?"

Ezra laughed. "No, you look awful. Come on; let me help you up. Take it easy."

Ezra reached behind O'Banyon, wrapping his arms around his chest, and pulled him off the floor. O'Banyon staggered momentarily, then caught his balance. Ezra kept one hand on O'Banyon's arm as he stepped around in front of him. "OK?"

"I'll be feeling a wee bit better in a while," O'Banyon said as he tried to smile.

"I doubt that, but come on. Let's get out of here."

"Who are you, anyhow?" O'Banyon asked.

"The name's Justice. Captain Ezra Justice. I'm on special assignment from General Sherman, and I'm looking for a few good men."

"General Sherman?" O'Banyon's eyebrows raised slightly. "Aye, he was a brigade commander when I served under him just a few years ago in New York. Now he's running the whole show, I take it."

"That's right. General Grant has put him in charge of the entire western front."

"And you are considering me as one of the few good men?"

"He told me I could pick the best. And he said you were one of the best."

"For what?"

"I'll explain later. Let's go someplace where we can talk." Ezra handed O'Banyon his shirt and a blue, nine-button Federal army coat.

O'Banyon slipped on the clothes. "Glad I didn't get any blood on my uniform," he said with a twinkle in the eye that wasn't swollen shut. "There's a pub across the street. We can talk there."

A haggard, red-haired waitress approached the small square table in the corner of the room where Ezra and O'Banyon sat down. "What will you have?"

"Just coffee for me," Justice said to the woman.

"Irish coffee?"

"No, just plain, if you don't mind."

"Whatever makes you happy," the woman

replied. She looked at O'Banyon. "And what about you?"

"Just plain coffee for me, too, ma'am."

Ezra eyed O'Banyon. "I expected you to drink something a little stronger than coffee."

"I did in my young and wild days, but then I met my Lizzie. Now, she allows me one drink per day. And I think I'll take it right now." O'Banyon reached into his pocket and pulled out a small silver hip flask. He took a quick swig and placed the flask back in his pocket.

O'Banyon faced the wall to avoid the stares and derisive comments from some of the men who had been in the ironworks warehouse and had now retired to the pub. Justice sat looking out toward the front door.

"So what's this all about?" O'Banyon asked.

"First give me some background. I don't really know much about you," said Ezra, "just that you come highly recommended."

"Recommended for what?"

Ezra ignored the question. "How long have you been back in Boston?"

"Just a couple of weeks, really. I'm supposed to catch up with the 69th regiment next week. Commander Meagher sent me up here to recruit some boys for our unit. We're down to about two hundred men, and we need some reinforcements. Meagher wanted to come himself, but General Grant said he needed him with the Army of the Potomac. So the commander sent me."

"Looks like you're about to have a change of orders. How'd you get here in the first place?"

"Do you mean how'd I get to Boston?"

"Yeah, something like that. How'd an Irishman get involved in an American war?"

"Ha!" O'Banyon chuckled. "Lots of us have. My parents and I came across on one of those floating morgues they called freedom ships about twenty years ago. I was twelve years old at the time, and the potato crop in Ireland had been destroyed by blight. Nobody had any food. Disease was everywhere. The landlords burnt down our house to get rid of us, but there was nowhere to go. Thousands of people fled the country to America, hoping to get to Boston or New York. It took about six weeks for the boat to make the trip. My father — God rest his soul — didn't make it. He gave what little rations he had to my mother and me, and I think his resistance just got low. He died of cholera the third week, and the sailors tossed his body into the sea. They wouldn't even try to give him a decent burial."

Ezra nodded his head in understanding. "Did things get better for you when you got to Boston?"

"Goodness no, man! Er, sorry, Captain. Don't mean any disrespect. But the answer is no. My mother and I lived in squalor. The conditions in Boston were worse than what we had left behind in Ireland. But she was a God-fearing woman who always said that God would not give us more to endure than we could handle. And she taught me that this great nation had received us with open arms when we had nothing to offer in return. Even though there was no pot of gold on every street, there was a hope for the future, which is more than we had back home."

"So when did you join the army?"

"Right after Fort Sumter. Soon as President Lincoln made his first call for volunteers. I started with the 69th New York Militia. That's where I first fought with Sherman. We did well together at Bull Run. Then we returned home, and for some reason they mustered us out. So when I heard about the Irish Brigade forming under General Thomas Meagher, I signed on with him; and I knew I'd found my niche."

"Meagher? He is a bit of a wild man, isn't he?"

O'Banyon smiled. "That's what I like about him. The man isn't afraid to speak his mind. Of course, that's what got him in trouble in Ireland. He despised the British rule, and eventually the queen exiled him to Tasmania."

"I thought Tasmania was just a place in stories," Justice said with a laugh.

"It was no fairy tale to Meagher," O'Banyon said as he sipped his coffee. "He fled to the United States and stayed active in the Irish independence movement. I honestly think part of the reason he got involved in this war, raising the Irish Brigade, was to rally the troops to fight for independence in our homeland. We've all heard the rumors that Britain is supporting the Confederacy, so anything that Britain is for, a lot of Irish folks are against."

"Mmm, maybe so," Justice replied, stirring his coffee. "Is that why you signed up?"

"Maybe a little, but mainly due to the fact that my mother instilled such a sense of gratitude in my heart for our adopted nation. Despite the hardships we Irish have experienced in America, anything that threatens the stability of the Union threatens me, so I wasn't going to stand by while they tore this country apart."

"What about the slave issue? Where are you on that?"

O'Banyon's brow wrinkled. "Well, that's a tough one. I know President Lincoln means well, but I'm not sure he realizes what he's done by flooding the workforce with all those freed slaves. When the Irish first came to this country, they were willing to work for meager wages under the worst of conditions. That created a lot of anti-Irish sentiment among some people. A lot of my countrymen have been surviving by doing menial jobs that nobody else wanted to do. Now, many Irishmen feel betrayed because of the large number of colored workers pouring into town, taking away what little work opportunities they had. Anti-Irish prejudice is everywhere. I saw a sign advertising for workers the other day that said, 'Any country or color except Irish.' If we can show people that we are as American as anyone else by fighting and bleeding for our country, maybe some of that prejudice will disappear. And maybe we'll see less of those 'No Irish' signs."

"I sure hope so," Justice said. Ezra looked O'Banyon directly in the eyes. "Tell me something, O'Banyon. Can you work with a colored man? Or will your Irish heritage get in the way?"

O'Banyon didn't blink. "I'm an American, Captain. Not an Irish-American or a Federal American. I'm an American. Period. I don't judge a man by the color of his skin. And I sure don't judge him by where he comes from. Lord knows, I've experienced enough of that sort of hatred myself. I can work with a person of any race. Like I said, I'm an American."

"You mentioned Lizzie. Is she your wife?"

"She sure is!" O'Banyon reached inside his coat and pulled out a locket. He flipped it open and showed Ezra the picture inside of a beautiful Irish woman with long reddish-blonde hair, a finely sculptured face, with smooth pale skin, and a fire in her eyes. "This is my Lizzie," O'Banyon said with obvious pride.

"She's a stunning woman," Justice replied.

"Yes, she is," O'Banyon said, "and she's strong, too. A real fighter."

"Where's she at now?"

"Back home in Missouri. We have a little farmhouse at the foot of an old abandoned gold mine. Sets back in the trees, up against the hills." O'Banyon snapped the locket shut and placed it back in his interior breast pocket. "She watches for me to come home every day. One of these days, I'm going to surprise her."

"I heard you almost didn't make it at Gettysburg. That you took a musket ball right close to your heart."

"Yes, that's true. The Rebs thought they had me there! But I fooled them. I survived. Although, when that big fella back there in the boxing ring caught me a few times right near the wound, I wasn't so sure. That last punch really got to me; he socked me right where the bullet struck me. And by the time I could catch my breath, he nearly disconnected my head from my body."

Justice smiled. "I know, I was there, remember? Where else have you been in combat?"

"Well, the Irish Brigade has been pretty active. We mixed it up with those Rebs at Fredericksburg a couple of years ago. Then we were right in the middle of things at Antietam in '62. That was awful. Over there on Miller's Farm the rifle fire was so intense it cut every corn stalk to the ground. It looked as though someone had gone through and harvested the corn with a knife. A lot of good men were cut down in that cornfield, too. Twenty thousand men died that day at Antietam." He paused with a faraway look in his eyes. "We took some serious losses there, and even worse in a wheat field at Gettysburg. I've got a few miles on me."

"The men I'm looking for — I want them to have a few miles."

"Well, you're looking at one. I'm an old soul already, thanks to the destruction and killing I've seen."

Justice nodded. "Aren't we all?" Ezra guzzled the last of his coffee. "OK, O'Banyon. Here are my orders." Justice pulled out the handwritten orders from General Sherman and tapped the papers against his hand. "These orders come directly from General Sherman. He's given me a mandate to form an elite squad of soldiers to work on special covert assignments. I think you can be of help to us. From what I understand, you are one of the best soldiers in the Irish Regiment, a scrapper, a man who is not afraid to try anything once." Justice paused to let his words sink in and then said, "And I've heard that you're not a bad boxer, too." Justice smiled broadly.

"Guess I messed that up, huh?"

"Not a problem. Look who you were fighting. That took a lot of guts."

O'Banyon smiled. "OK, enough about building me up. What do you want me to do?"

"You've heard General Sherman say that war is hell?"

"Yeah . . . he used to say that all the time. Actually, he said it the moment he heard that the South had seceded."

"Well, we're going to pay hell a visit. We will be going right into the midst of the fire. We'll be pulling off raids that the boys in Washington say are impossible. We're going to sabotage the South's supply lines, obtain crucial intelligence information, snatch and grab prisoners, and possibly assassinate a few top Confederate officers. We'll be taking chances every day from now till the end of this war. You'll still be a Federal soldier, but you will be directly under my command, nobody else's. You don't have to accept this mission, but if you do, there will be no turning back. Today will be your last day as an ordinary soldier in the Union army. Do you understand?"

"Aye, yes, Captain, I do. It sounds downright exhilarating! Count me in."

"Oh, I forgot to mention one little detail: If we get caught, we're on our own. Nobody will come to our rescue. It will be as though we don't exist. Do you still want to join up?"

"Yes, Captain, I do. But can I wire my Lizzie to tell her why I'm not in Boston any longer?"

"I'm afraid not. This is a top-secret operation. If we do well, she'll find out what a hero you are soon enough. If we don't . . ." Ezra stopped short.

"If we don't?" O'Banyon probed.

"If we don't, she may find out where you are buried, and she may not. Nobody will know for sure whose side you are on from this day forward."

"I see," O'Banyon said quietly. "Captain Justice, do you really think we can help bring this awful war to a halt any sooner by what you plan to do?"

"I am completely convinced of it."

"Fine, then. Where do I sign up?" O'Banyon's eyes sparkled with excitement.

"You just did. Go get your satchel. Bring your best, cleanest clothes and meet me at the train station in half an hour."

"Yes, sir. And where might we be going?"

"To a New York ball."

"A ball?"

"A dance."

"But Captain, sir, I don't know how to dance."

"Neither do I, but we're gonna learn."

3

Captain Ezra Justice and Sergeant Shaun O'Banyon looked as though they had just posed for a photograph in the *New York Times* as they walked up the stairs of the Manhattan mansion where the ball was being held. "You clean up pretty well," Justice said to O'Banyon.

"Thank you, sir. And you are looking quite the gentleman tonight, as well."

Dressed in their blue military uniforms, buttoned all the way to the collar, with just a trace of white shirt and bow tie revealed, boots shined, and faces freshly shaven, the two handsome men caused heads to turn as they entered the chandeliered ballroom. Several women dressed in elegant evening gowns stopped and stared openly as Justice and O'Banyon passed by. "Did you ever feel like you were on display, Captain?" O'Banyon quipped. "Not that any of these fine ladies could compare to my Lizzie, but

I can't help noticin' that these women are noticin' us."

"Don't let it go to your head. They're used to seeing a bunch of very old men at these things. Most of the young guys are off at war, except for a few wounded soldiers or men on leave. Just keep walking, Shaun," Justice said while looking straight ahead. "Act as though we belong here. Let's head over toward the punch bowl."

The soldiers casually picked their way around the periphery of the ballroom floor, carefully avoiding several couples who were waltzing gracefully to the music of an eight-piece orchestra playing in the corner of the room. At the punch bowl, a group of older gentlemen dressed in fine suits greeted Justice and O'Banyon. A sophisticated-looking man with silver-gray hair spoke on behalf of the group. "Welcome, Captain. Good evening, Sergeant. How goes the war in your ranks?"

"Very well, sir," Justice replied. "Since Gettysburg, things have turned in our favor more often than not. With a little luck and God's help, we can bring this war to a close soon."

"Welcome to the ball. Glad to have you here," another man said enthusiastically.

"Thank you, sir." Ezra nodded, as he

shook hands with the man. "Senator Kline suggested that we stop by for an evening of refreshment before heading back to the front."

"A well-deserved interlude, I'm sure," said one of the more distinguished looking gentlemen. "Enjoy the dance, my good man. No doubt there are some pretty ladies who would be delighted to share a waltz or two with you."

"I'm not much of a dancer, but the punch is good and the scenery is quite pleasant." Justice nodded toward several attractive women smiling in his direction from the far side of the room. The older gentlemen laughed and patted Justice and O'Banyon on their backs.

"Indeed it is, boys. Indeed." The businessmen moved off to talk with others in the room, while Justice made eye contact with one or two of the women.

"Excuse me, Cap'n," O'Banyon's voice brought Ezra back to reality. "I know we are on a mission, but what exactly are we doing here?"

"We're observing, Sergeant. We're looking for two young men. You'll recognize them when you see them."

"I will? How?"

"They're twins."

"Twins?"

"That's right. Roberto and Carlos Hawkins were raised right here on the streets of New York. Their father was an English gentleman who fell in love with an exotic gypsy woman. Unfortunately, their father died when the twins were young, so his wife — Angelica Hawkins — taught her boys the mysteries of gypsy life as well as how to function in more sophisticated society."

"They're gypsies?" O'Banyon's mouth was agape.

"Let's just say that they know how to skin a man of his wallet in more ways than you or I can imagine. But they're smooth. Good-looking boys, with friendly personalities and good hearts, they are a potent combination of playfulness, charm, larceny, and lethal instincts."

"What was their business before the war?"

"They were both card sharks and con men. They have an uncanny ability to make the cards appear and disappear in a deck just as they need them. I've watched them play poker with men twice their ages and take them for every dollar on the table."

"And why are we interested in these two hooligans?"

"They are also two of the foremost experts on explosives in the world. They can blow up a wagon, a house, or a bridge with equal ease. Inventors, you might call them. They're always coming up with some new way to destroy things."

"Ka-boom!" O'Banyon said quietly. "And why will we find them here?"

"Because they never pass up an opportunity to attend a gathering of rich and charming women."

"How will we find them in this crowd?"

"Just look for the prettiest ladies. The Hawkins twins love women, and women sure love them."

Just then a handsome, dark-haired soldier and a beautiful brunette woman swirled by so close that Justice and O'Banyon caught the scent of the woman's perfume. "I presume that's one," O'Banyon said.

Justice nodded his head. "I have a hard time telling them apart, but I believe that was Roberto."

Right behind the first Hawkins twin came a second young man, with identical dark, handsome looks, and with equal ease on his feet. The young man twirled the lovely lady with whom he was dancing, caught her in his arms and guided her right back into step, making the move look almost majestic.

"You're right, Cap'n," O'Banyon said with a smile. "They are smooth."

"Keep an eye on them, and you'll see just how smooth," said Ezra.

They watched as the Hawkins twins whirled effortlessly around the dance floor. At the end of the dance, the young men bowed to their partners and joined the crowd of partiers in a round of applause. "Oh, pardon me, sir," Roberto Hawkins said to a man he had bumped as they exited the dance floor. "I'm so sorry to have jostled you."

The man nodded in appreciation and continued applauding as they walked off the floor to the edge of the crowd. He never felt Roberto's hand remove his billfold from the side pocket of his coat. The action went undetected by everyone except O'Banyon and Ezra Justice.

"I see what you mean," O'Banyon said.

"Where's Carlos?"

"He's over there talking to those two ladies."

Justice had noticed the two women earlier. "Wasn't that woman in the beige dress wearing a set of pearls when we saw her previously this evening?"

"I believe she was, Captain. Do you think she lost them? Or perhaps she was uncomfortable and she simply removed them?"

Justice looked at O'Banyon incredulously.

"Oh, I see," O'Banyon said as he noticed Carlos Hawkins touch the woman's arm.

"Come on. We better get those boys out of here before somebody calls the police," Ezra said. "Besides, we have work to do." Ezra and O'Banyon moved onto the dance floor, just as the orchestra began the next number.

"Oh, my! Are you coming to ask me for this dance?" a lovely woman with blonde hair pinned atop her head asked Ezra, as she stepped in front of him so closely that Ezra nearly banged right into her.

"I'm afraid not, ma'am," he said, his eyes never leaving Roberto Hawkins who was engaged in conversation with another woman across the room. "Please pardon me. I was just leaving."

The blonde woman turned and caught sight of the woman to whom Roberto was talking. "I'm much more interesting than she is," she said.

For the first time, Ezra stopped to notice the blonde in front of him. He looked her right in the eyes. "I'm quite certain you are, but she's with my friend, and I must get him back to camp before reveille."

"A pity to depart so soon."

"Yes, ma'am. It is a pity." Ezra sidestepped the beautiful woman and headed toward

Roberto Hawkins, who already had his eye on a broach the woman in front of him was wearing. Justice and O'Banyon reached Roberto's side just in time to hear the twin say, "My, what an exquisite piece of jewelry. It is a piece of art, is it not? Yes, it must be. May I see it more closely?"

The woman reached to remove the broach from her dress, when Justice grabbed Roberto by the arm and nudged him toward the door. "No, you may not."

"Whaa . . . ? Hey, what's going on here? Who are you? What are you doing? The fine lady and I were having a conversation I'll have you know."

"And I'll have you know that unless you want to be placed under arrest you will keep moving toward the door. O'Banyon, get Carlos and meet us outside."

"Will do, Cap'n."

Justice gripped Roberto's left arm as the two men walked toward the exit. "Just keep smiling, Sergeant Hawkins. We're having fun, aren't we?"

Roberto Hawkins glanced quizzically at the man steering him toward the door. The pressure on his arm told him that the captain was not one with whom he wanted to tussle. "Yes, sir."

They had no sooner walked out the door

and down the front steps of the mansion, when they heard Roberto's brother Carlos complaining to O'Banyon. "Would you mind telling me what this is all about?"

"It's kaboom time," O'Banyon replied. He and Carlos quickly descended the steps.

Once outside away from the crowd, Ezra released his grip on Roberto's arm. Justice guided the men to the livery stable on the side of the main house. "Have a seat," he motioned toward some bales of hay. "We can talk here."

For the next half hour, Ezra Justice explained General Sherman's instructions to him and how he wanted the Hawkins twins in his squad. The boys picked up on the adventure aspect of the mission immediately.

"Are you in?" Ezra asked after a while.

"I'm in."

"Me, too."

"Excellent. We'll leave for West Point first thing in the morning. Meet us at the train station at eight sharp. Be on time."

"Yes, sir," Carlos said. "Eight sharp."

"Right on time," Roberto added.

"One more thing."

"Yes, sir?"

Justice looked Roberto in the eyes. "Go

back inside and return the billfold that you took from that gentleman's pocket."

4

"Duty, Honor, Country" was more than the motto of the United States Military Academy at West Point. It was the creed by which Ulysses S. Grant and Robert E. Lee — both West Point graduates — conducted their daily affairs. Although Lee may have adhered to the teachings of the Bible much more closely than did Grant, both men concurred with the basic values they'd learned at the Academy.

Located about fifty miles north of New York, the Academy was set on about sixteen hundred acres of land adjacent to the Hudson River. The train trip from New York City to West Point had taken most of the morning. By the time Justice and his men arrived, the cadets were already engaged in rifle drills on the firing range. O'Banyon and the Hawkins twins gawked openly as an impeccably dressed army cadet ushered Ezra Justice and his group into the Academy's central post area.

"Please follow me, gentlemen," the cadet intoned. "Mr. Bonesteel is teaching a class on the firing range this very hour. I'm sure he will be delighted to have guests."

"I'm sure he will," Justice whispered to O'Banyon.

The cadet performed a perfect about-face and began walking briskly toward a flat-topped hill with targets set up in the shallow valley beyond it. Justice and his men hurried to keep pace with the young cadet. As they approached the hilltop, O'Banyon was the first to see the strange sight. "Cap'n, I'm not believing my eyes!"

"O'Banyon, straighten up," Justice ordered.

"Yes, sir. Sorry, sir. But look at that egomaniac."

"I said straighten up."

"Yes, sir. I apologize, sir."

"What's that guy trying to prove?" Carlos asked. "What kind of outfit is that?"

"Yeah, doesn't he know we're in a war?" Roberto said. "He looks as though he's in a parade."

Indeed, the man teaching the rifle class was not dressed as a typical Union soldier. He wore a bright red military coat with brass buttons, over blue trousers with a red stripe down each side. On his head sat a tall, black, bearskin cap, with a fiery red plume on the right side. The cap seemed to rise a full twelve inches above the man's forehead. Across his chest he wore a white shoulder sash, and on his arm sleeve were the embroidered words: "Second to None."

"It's the uniform of the Coldstream Guard," O'Banyon explained. "Dirty Brits. And he's probably one of the dirtiest. The Coldstream Guard is part of Her Majesty the Queen's elite regiments. They have a battlefield history that dates all the way back to Cromwell, but more recently they are best known for keeping the Queen from stubbing her royal toes."

"What kind of gun is he carrying, Captain?" Roberto asked.

"That's a Henry .44-caliber repeating rifle," Justice said, as he watched Reginald Bonesteel turn around quickly and hit seven targets in rapid succession. Bull's-eyes, every shot. "And Mr. Bonesteel there is one of the best sharpshooters in the world."

O'Banyon looked at Justice impertinently. "Captain, please; you don't mean to tell me . . . Captain Justice, the man is from England, of all places!"

"I know, Shaun. But he's the best."

"Cap'n," O'Banyon protested. "You didn't

tell me I'd be fighting alongside one of the Queen's loyalists when I signed on with you."

"You didn't ask," Justice replied. "And besides, you said you could fight alongside anyone. But don't worry, Shaun. You and Bonesteel will get along just fine. He's got a tart tongue, but he's a good man on the inside. I'm not saying you'll ever be best friends, but I know you will work well together."

"Captain!"

"Sergeant O'Banyon. That's enough."

"Yes, sir."

"Take a seat, men. Watch and learn." Ezra nodded to a fence behind the firing area that was close enough for them to hear Bonesteel teaching the cadets, yet safely out of the line of fire. O'Banyon and the twins propped themselves up on the fence and listened as Bonesteel launched into a tirade about the foolishness of a soldier having only single-shot weapons. "I'll give you a three-day leave if you can reload your single-shot musket and fire once before I can score three of those targets down there." He pointed to the targets about a hundred yards away in the valley. "Ready, set, go!"

The cadets fumbled with their muskets as three shots rang out and three targets fell over down in the valley. Not a single cadet had gotten off a round.

Ezra Justice smiled.

For the next hour, Reginald Bonesteel lectured about weapons and demonstrated various techniques to use in battle. He seemed especially fond of a four-holster harness that could be slipped over a saddle, providing for four guns while engaged in battle on horseback. "Why should you face the enemy with one gun that has to be constantly reloaded when you can have four guns loaded and ready?"

At the conclusion of the session, Bonesteel came back to meet Justice and his men.

"Pretty impressive," Justice offered.

"Impressive? No, not impressive. Rather convincing, I'd say, wouldn't you?"

"Yes, that is a better description," Justice said.

"Ah, yes. But I see that you have skeptics in the choir." Bonesteel nodded toward O'Banyon and the Hawkins twins still seated on the fence.

"They're a little more cynical than I am," Justice said. "But once you get to know them, you'll get along fine."

"And why would I want to get along with *them?*"

"Because you're going to be spending a

lot of time with them."

"I beg your pardon, sir, but I have important matters to which I must attend."

"I'm sure you do, Mr. Bonesteel. But nothing quite as important as what I have for you. The name's Justice. Ezra Justice. I'm under direct orders from General Sherman. And those orders involve you."

"Meeeh? Whatever are you talking about, my good man? How could your orders possibly have anything to do with me? I am here as a special guest of the United States Military Academy."

"Did that request arrive before or after the queen gave you the boot?"

Reginald Bonesteel stiffened as he looked Ezra Justice squarely in the eyes. "That, sir, is none of your business." Bonesteel whirled on his heel and started to walk away.

"Oh, but it is my business," Justice called after him. "Especially since it seems that your dismissal from Her Majesty's elite force was under a bit of a cloud. Something about a woman, I heard."

Bonesteel stopped cold in his tracks. He stood facing away from Justice for a few moments, then whirled around and came back. He stood close to Justice as he hissed, "The woman was fully of age. The fact that she was a member of the Royal family was irrelevant. She was a consenting adult who appreciated my talents."

"And what talents might that include, Mr. Bonesteel?"

"What exactly do you want, Captain . . . what did you say your name was? *Justine?*"

"Captain Ezra Justice. Learn it. You're going to hear it a lot. Let's you and I take a little walk. We have important matters to discuss."

By the time Ezra and Bonesteel returned from their walk, the British sharpshooter was a member of Justice's elite squad. Ezra introduced Bonesteel to the others. "Reginald Bonesteel, these are the Hawkins twins, Roberto and Carlos."

"Good to meet you," Roberto said, extending his hand to shake with Bonesteel.

"Welcome to the party," Carlos said with a laugh, shaking hands.

"And this is Shaun O'Banyon, pride of the Irish Regiment," Justice said, standing between Bonesteel and O'Banyon and stretching out his hands in an obvious gesture meant to bring the two men together. O'Banyon and Bonesteel glared at each other as though they were two rattlesnakes ready to strike.

"I have despised everything Irish since my

childhood," Bonesteel said flatly, "but Captain Justice tells me that you are quite the soldier. We'll see, I suppose." Bonesteel reluctantly stretched out his hand to O'Banyon.

"And for the life of me, I could never imagine myself fighting next to a member of the Queen's Guard," O'Banyon said, spitting on the ground. "But if you're good enough for Ezra Justice, you're good enough for me. Maybe there is one good Brit alive after all." He extended his hand and grabbed Bonesteel's in a firm clasp. The two men held their grip as they looked into each other's eyes. "This could be great fun, you know," O'Banyon said, a hint of a smile creasing his lips.

"Agreed," Bonesteel said.

"Alright, great. Let's go," Justice said. "I hate to break up this lovefest, but we need to be in North Carolina tomorrow night."

"Isn't that area still controlled by the Rebs?" Carlos asked.

"Yes, it is. Is that a problem for you?"

"No, sir. Just looking forward to a little excitement."

"You'll have plenty soon. Right now, let's pick up Mr. Bonesteel's equipment and get moving. Sergeant Bonesteel, I've already informed the Commander here at West

Point that you will be coming with us."

"Sergeant? I was a captain in the Coldstream Guard. Not only must I fight with men of questionable lineage, you want to demote me as well?"

"Welcome to the U.S. Army, Sergeant Bonesteel. Let's get moving. Oh, and don't you have anything less colorful you can wear?"

Bonesteel looked at his red jacket and removed his bearskin cap. "The Coldstream Guard does have an informal uniform. Perhaps that may be more conducive to combat."

"I'm sure it must be," Ezra said.

Ezra waited outside while Bonesteel went in to one of the West Point dormitories to change his clothing. When the sharpshooter emerged, he wore a dress brown uniform with brass buttons and a white belt. Beneath the brown coat, Bonesteel wore a beige shirt with a brown neck tie and a white shoulder sash. On his head was an odd-shaped, safari forage hat with a pointed brim in the front and a white band around the cap.

"Oh, that's much better," Justice said, as he shook his head.

O'Banyon and Bonesteel traded blistering remarks throughout the long night as the train clacked along from New York to Washington. By the time they got to Fredericksburg, the two bitter enemies had become allies. Barely tolerable allies, but men who could be friends nonetheless.

In Fredericksburg, Justice and his men picked up fresh horses and then took another train as far as they dared. From there, they rode by horseback into North Carolina. Each night along the way, the Hawkins twins crept into one Confederate camp or another, planted booby traps, land mines, and other explosive devices and then set them off when the Rebels were trying to rest. The explosives did marginal damage to the troops and equipment, but the toll they took on the gray uniformed men's morale was devastating. "How can somebody come right into our camp in the middle of the night and operate undetected like that?" they wanted to know.

Spooky sorts claimed the Hawkins twins' work must have been done by phantoms or ghosts. More battle-worn soldiers feared that their night watches were getting slack due to fatigue and lack of food or sleep. In either case the result was a lowering of morale among the troops, just what Ezra Justice had hoped for.

Bonesteel and O'Banyon got in some

licks, too, with Bonesteel's marksmanship causing several wrecked ammunition wagons, and O'Banyon's courageous and scrappy sabotage efforts resulting in havoc among numerous Rebel camps.

Moving deeper into North Carolina, Justice and his men arrived near Fort Fisher, a fiercely held Confederate garrison along the seacoast in New Hanover County. O'Banyon and Justice went out on a reconnaissance mission, gathering vital information for a planned Union thrust against the fort, to be followed by an advance against Wilmington, one of the last open and functioning seaports of the Confederacy along the Atlantic coast. From there, all five men traveled to Cherokee, a densely forested area at the base of the Appalachians, near the Tennessee border, on the edge of the Great Smoky Mountains.

"How much further do we have to go into this thick stuff?" Roberto asked, pushing a tree limb away from his face, then allowing it to snap back just in time to swat Carlos coming behind him on his horse.

"Hey, watch it, will ya?" Carlos complained.

"We're nearly to the top," said Justice. Ezra's horse picked its way through a clearing in the trees.

"And we're really going to find somebody waiting for us up here?" O'Banyon wanted to know.

"That's right, Shaun. We're meeting Harry Whitecloud at the summit, then we'll keep moving west into Tennessee, hopefully in time to prevent Hood from making a fool of himself and costing a lot more lives. He's still smarting from the beating General Sherman gave him in Atlanta, so he might be more reckless than usual."

"And what pray tell is so marvelous about this Whitecloud fellow?" asked Bonesteel.

"Harry's father was a white man and his mother was a Sioux Indian," Justice answered. "As a boy, Harry was educated at some of the finest schools in the East; but when his father was killed over a land squabble, Harry's mother packed up and returned to her people. Harry lived among the Sioux out west and was educated in the warlike ways of the tribe. Growing up, he developed outstanding tracking abilities. He can follow a trail for miles and tell you not only where your enemy has been but also where he's going. Some people say he could track an eagle in flight if he had to."

"Is he a good soldier?" O'Banyon asked.

"Let's just say that before he joined the army, he was practically a legend out west.

His exploits with a Bowie knife were the subject of conversations in smoky saloons from Missouri to Texas. As a young man, he also learned the mystic arts of the medicine man in his tribe; then as an adult, he returned to the East and was studying to be a doctor at Princeton when the war broke out. He joined the Union army at Philadelphia, and he's been one of the best scouts in the entire Federal army."

"Sounds like an interesting fellow," O'Banyon said.

The men reached the summit of the mountain and dismounted in a clearing. "Look at that!" O'Banyon shouted. "It's amazing!" He pointed at the panoramic scene below them, the lush green forest covering the land as far as the eye could see, all the way down the other side of the mountain, into the valley and beyond to the Great Smoky Mountains in the distance, all under the panoply of a bright blue sky. The natural beauty was awe-inspiring, even for jaded soldiers such as Bonesteel and Justice.

"It is a sight to see," Justice said matter-of-factly.

"I never saw anything like that growing up on the streets of New York," Carlos added.

Just then a rustling in the bushes caught

the men's attention. They instinctively pulled their carbines but quickly relaxed as they saw the ruddy-skinned Indian dressed in a Union soldier's coat, a Confederate soldier's trousers, and knee-high buckskin boots emerge from around the rock cliffs covered by brush. With long black hair dangling from under his U.S. Army-issued cap, and piercing dark brown eyes, Harry Whitecloud looked like a cowboy's worst nightmare. His muscular body seemed to move with the agile grace of a mountain lion.

"Captain Justice, I presume." The Indian spoke English with perfect diction and enunciation.

"That's right, Sergeant Whitecloud." Ezra stepped forward to shake Harry's hand.

"It is a pleasure to meet you, Captain. I'm honored to have been selected by you, and I'm looking forward to serving our country together with you."

"I'm glad to have you with us, Sergeant Whitecloud. Do you have any belongings out here?"

"No, I'm traveling rather lightly." Whitecloud patted two cases on his belt. "Just a few tools of the trade."

"Meet the other men. That's O'Banyon, there. The Hawkins twins, Roberto and

Carlos, I'll let you figure out which one is which. And that fellow leaning up against the tree over there is Bonesteel."

Bonesteel nodded. "Are you really as good with a knife as they say you are?" Bonesteel called.

"Better," Harry replied. "If you need convincing, stand right where you are. Don't move now. Keep your shoulder wedged firmly against that tree." Harry pulled out a large Bowie knife from the sheath. Without aiming, he reared back and hurled the knife in Bonesteel's direction. Even with his quick reflexes, Bonesteel never saw the flashing blade coming. It ripped through his odd looking hat, skinning the white hatband off the hat and pinning it to the tree.

"Hey, there. That's my good hat, chap! Are you insane?"

"Well, you did ask about my ability to throw a knife. Would you care for a further demonstration?"

"A mad Irishman and a crazy Indian," Bonesteel grumbled, as he stomped off toward his horse. "What have I gotten myself into?"

The other guys laughed aloud as they shook hands with Whitecloud. "Incredible!" Roberto gushed. "How do you do that?"

Whitecloud replied, "It's all in the wrists."

"Glad you're aboard, mate," O'Banyon greeted Harry. "If that boorish Brit gives me any trouble, I'm calling on you for help."

"Ha! I think he has been convinced. What's his problem anyhow?"

"Oh, he's OK," O'Banyon assured Harry. "He's just a little . . . how would you say it? *Aloof?*" O'Banyon mockingly attempted to muster a most proper British accent.

"Alright, men, let's mount up," Justice interrupted. "We have a long ride over some rugged terrain. And we need to pick up one more man before we head off General Hood."

For the next several days Justice and his men worked their way across Tennessee toward Chattanooga. A cold, dreary rain followed them across the state, leaving a misty haze hanging in the air. They encountered the Tennessee Colored Battery, a regiment of Negro troops commanded by General George H. Thomas — a white man — camped alongside the railroad tracks in a barren burned-out area near Murfreesboro. The unit, made up entirely of freed slaves, except for its commander, possessed ten large-barreled cannons pulled by wagons. A loading dock built next to the tracks allowed the Colored Battery easy access to transportation any time they were called upon to defend the supply lines between Nashville and Chattanooga, which was often. Seven men stood guard over the loading dock at all hours.

The camp itself was desolate. Remains of large charred trees dotted the periphery of the camp, but there was little foliage on the trees. The entire area looked like one gigantic target range for the big guns.

Justice and his men rode into the camp and tied their horses near a double row of gray tents. While the men watered the horses and checked on supplies, Justice presented his orders from General Sherman. "I'm looking for Nathaniel York," Justice told the commander. "Most people call him 'Big Nate.' "

"You're in luck," the commander replied. "He just got back in camp. Hood is moving northwest toward Franklin, and Nathaniel York was on a raid to slow the Rebs down. You'll probably find him over by the big guns."

Justice trudged through the mud toward the cannon area in front of the loading dock about a hundred yards away. Before he got anywhere near the train tracks, however, Nathaniel York recognized his old friend and began running toward him. The two men met in the middle of the muddy field. Nathaniel threw his arms around his childhood friend and former owner and hugged him so hard Justice could barely breathe.

"Ezra! It is so good to see you. I had heard that you were involved in some dangerous missions, and I feared the worst. I prayed for you often. How are you?"

"I'm fine, Nate; thanks," Ezra said, "but I'd be much better if my lungs could work."

"Oh, I'm sorry," the big man said with a laugh. "I'm just glad that you are alive and well."

"Me, too, Nate. I'm glad to see you are doing well. I've heard good things about your unit."

"Yes, sir. These men are all fighting for their lives," Nate said. "If the Union loses the war, they have no future. So they are not afraid to take risks and do whatever it takes to keep the railroad lines open."

"Sounds like the Colored Battery has been getting you ready for my squad."

"What do you mean?"

"General Sherman has given me a mandate to pull off some tricky maneuvers, and I need your help. You'd be part of my command, if you don't mind leaving your men here."

Big Nate looked around at the camp.

Several men stood with rifles ready, guarding the tracks. Others were repairing and cleaning the cannon. Still others were gathered in small groups in front of their tents. "These are my people, Ezra. They need me here."

"I need you, too, Nate. And if we do our jobs well, maybe these men can go home to their families and begin a real life of freedom. I won't force you to come, but I'd be honored to have you with us."

"Us?"

"I have a small squad, six of us at present. We're working in covert missions, attempting to sabotage Confederate lines and generally cause all the chaos we can for the enemy. I've already cleared your transfer with the commandant."

Nate rubbed his neatly trimmed mustache. "You and me again. Working together, fightin' the Rebs? How could I miss that chance? Of course, Ezra. Let's do it. Tell me more."

Justice filled in Nate on more of the details of their mission as they walked back to Nate's tent to gather his belongings. The other men were stretched out resting in a tent when Ezra brought Nate in to introduce him. The men all stood to shake hands with their new member. "Sit down. Take the load off your feet for a while. You'll be needing your energy later on. Besides, I want you to meet my best friend in the world. This is Nathaniel York," Ezra told the squad. "We've known each other since we were children. I used to have to protect this man all the time."

"Oh, was that the way it was?" Nate laughed.

"Well, I'm only telling part of the truth," Ezra said as he sat down on a cot. "When we used to go swimming out at the local lake, Nate, here, sometimes had a little trouble with the young thugs in our town — white kids who enjoyed reminding Nate that he was a slave. They'd come after me, too, saying such things as, 'What are you doin' swimmin' with that colored kid?' Then they'd start abusing Nathaniel, pushing him around, shoving him, spitting on him, that sort of thing.

"Well, Nate was a tough guy even back in those days, and he could have licked the whole bunch of those boys single-handed; but I knew if Nate so much as threw a punch at one of those boys, old Rosco Johnson would come running with a 16-gauge shotgun and would shoot Nate and his family, too."

Several members of the Colored Battery

sitting in the tent nodded in agreement. "Ummm-ummh. I know dat's right," an older man said.

"So even though Nate could take care of himself, I had to handle the ruffians for him, much to his consternation and frustration. Isn't that right, Nate?"

Nathaniel scowled at Justice and then slowly allowed his expression to turn to a smile. "Yep, you 'bout got the livin' daylights beat out of ya a few times, now didn't ya?"

"I sure did!" Ezra laughed. "Meanwhile, he'd be off to the side watching me get the stuffin's kicked out of me. He wanted to fight so bad, and I had to keep telling him, 'Don't, Nate; you just can't do that or you're a dead man. And your family members are all dead, too. You just stay put, and let me tend to this matter.' "

"I used to get so angry," Nate agreed. "There I was, a big boy, wanting to fight my own battles, wanting to be free, but reality pinched at my idealism. I just had to wait for my opportunity. And trust. And pray.

"One time that bunch of hoodlums jumped me from behind when Ezra wasn't around. One of them had a knife and stabbed me while the other guys took turns beating on me. I was a bloody mess. Had it not been for Ezra coming along and carrying me on his back all the way back to the plantation, I'd have been a goner for sure. Captain here saved my life, and I've never forgotten it."

"You give me too much credit, Nate. Much more than I deserve. I have to stop over at the commandant's office for a few minutes. You men just go on and get better acquainted. I'll be right back." Ezra left and the conversation continued.

Roberto Hawkins looked at Nate and asked, "Did Captain Justice really own you as a slave on his plantation?"

"Sure 'nuff," Nate replied. "But Ezra Justice treated his slaves differently than most other plantation owners."

"Really? How?" Roberto probed.

"He never treated us as slaves," Nate said. "He treated us as hired hands and actually paid us a wage to work on his plantation. Truth is, his mother and father didn't do things that way. They were typical slave owners, who regarded a slave as a piece of property. But Ezra never did. He used to tell me, even as little boys, 'We're equal, Nate. I'm no better than you, and you're no better than me just because of the color of our skin.' That was a radical concept for a kid born in the South to have back then."

"It still is in many places," Reginald suggested.

"Right. Absolutely right," Nate said. "Ezra was a Christian — I was honored to introduce him to the Lord myself — and he believed the Bible's teachings about us all being equal. He respected our Constitution and the Declaration of Independence when the founders of our country declared that God created all men equally. But those beliefs cost him dearly."

"Why? What do you mean?" Carlos asked. "Captain Justice never mentioned anything about it."

"Naah, he wouldn't," Nate said. "He was only sixteen years of age when his parents died of cholera. He took over the plantation and started doing things differently. Treating the slaves as human beings was part of that, and it sure ruffled some feathers with his neighbors and fellow townspeople. Many of them were resentful that Ezra treated his workers so fairly and wouldn't rule his blacks with an iron fist. Mr. Justice just said, 'You run your plantation, and I'll run mine.' "

"How did the neighbors respond?" Carlos Hawkins asked.

"They said, 'But they're slaves!' And Ezra Justice said, 'You consider them slaves, but

91

they are not slaves to me. They are fellow human beings.' His parents had owned a large group of slaves — maybe about eighty, I'd guess — so when Ezra Justice started paying us wages, it cost him a lot of money. He treated all of us so well. But as a Christian man, he felt that's what he was supposed to do."

"Was Ezra snubbed by his friends for his beliefs?" Roberto wondered aloud.

"Some respected him for standing up for what he believed in, but a lot parted ways with him and wouldn't do business with him. But the one that hurt Mr. Justice the most was his own wife."

"Was she unfaithful to him?"

"Not as an adulteress, if that's what you mean," Nate replied. "But maybe in a far worse sort of way she didn't believe in him anymore and tried to undermine his values."

"What do you mean? Why would she do such a thing?" O'Banyon asked. "I can't imagine my Lizzie working against me on anything."

"When Ezra was about twenty-five," Nate went on, "he married Chelsea Richmond, a beautiful and sophisticated Southern belle, but unfortunately she was steeped in the slave culture. Her family all owned slaves; and as the new wife of a large plantation owner, she couldn't understand why Ezra was so radically opposed to slavery. She bucked him on that issue all the time. She was totally against treating the darkies with such dignity. She felt that blacks should be kept in their place as slaves. I used to hear her say to him, 'Why are you treating those darkies as equals?' And he'd say, 'Because they are equal, Chelsea, in God's eyes, even if they aren't equal in the courts or in certain parts of the country.' They argued over slavery all the time. It was sad to watch and hear because I'm sure Ezra loved Chelsea more than any other woman he's ever known. Eventually, the slavery issue became so divisive for Ezra and Chelsea that it destroyed their relationship, and she refused to bear him children. But he would not compromise the truth.

"That's why when the war broke out, Ezra Justice decided to fight for the North, and Chelsea went home to live with her parents."

O'Banyon whistled softly. "No wonder Captain Justice fights so passionately and is so adamant about seeing this war come to a close quickly."

"It sounds as though you men have some real history," Reginald Bonesteel said. "I'm glad you're back together."

Nate looked at Justice, who had just

returned to the group. "Yeah, me, too. It's my turn now to stand up for Captain Justice."

"We're all in this together, Nate," Justice said. "I've handpicked each of you men after receiving recommendations from your commanding officers and some from General Sherman himself. I'm convinced we have one of the finest groups of fighters ever assembled. But we better get some shut-eye. Tomorrow we are moving over toward Franklin. From the scouting reports I've received, it looks as though we're going to have our work cut out for us."

5

Elizabeth O'Banyon gently fingered the heliograph, a tintype sepia-toned photograph of her husband and her. In the picture she wore a long, flowing work dress — not one of those prissy dresses like the rich women wore but a simple working-class garment that despite its common style nevertheless accentuated her slim, shapely figure. Her long, reddish-blonde hair swirled around her face and shoulder blades, highlighting her smooth skin and edging her high-buttoned neckline. A natural beauty, her fiery, bright hazel eyes seemed to draw people to Elizabeth like a magnet. She looked at the world with the intelligence, dignity, and grace of a woman who knew that she was competent on her own — with or without a man in her life — and intrinsically valuable. Elizabeth O'Banyon was comfortable with herself and pleased with how she looked. She knew her husband was, as well.

Elizabeth smiled as she thought of her husband, Shaun. Clothes didn't mean much to him. She'd had a tough time getting him to dress up for the photograph. Though he wasn't the most handsome man she'd ever seen, something about him drew Elizabeth to his side. She was shorter than he was — about five-six — and the top of her shoulder fit snugly beneath his arm when he pulled her close to him. For all his roughness, Shaun O'Banyon possessed a certain gentleness, a kindness that exuded through his confident gaze. Dressed in well-worn boots with a thin layer of dried mud that seemed to cling perpetually to his heels, Shaun had worn a white short-sleeved shirt, revealing tanned muscular arms and hands that were accustomed to a hard day's work. The calluses on his palms had been there for so long, he wouldn't feel right if they ever disappeared. Of average size, he was nonetheless the type of man who attracted attention, both from the men who grudgingly admired his strength and skill as a fighter and the women who wished that they could know him as Elizabeth did. But what endeared people to Shaun O'Banyon most readily was his enormous heart; he didn't know how to live with anything less than unbridled passion and couldn't understand anyone who did. Shaun O'Banyon's only fault was his unwillingness to back away from a fight.

O'Banyon exhibited the perpetual twinkle in his eye and the faint hint of a smile playing on his lips as he looked far beyond the camera lens into some place only the two of them knew.

At Elizabeth's insistence, they'd stood for the photograph right before he'd gone off to war. Shaun had insisted that the photographer take a second picture of Elizabeth alone. In the photo, she exuded a radiant beauty, looking into the camera as though she were looking directly into her husband's heart. She trimmed the stunning picture, placed it in a small gold locket, and the night before Shaun left to join the Irish Regiment, she gave it to her husband. "Take this locket with you, and hold it close to your heart. If you can — when it's safe and you're not fighting the Rebels — some time during each day, pull out the locket and think of me. You can be sure that I'll be thinking of you any time of the day or night that you look at the photograph. And I'll be asking God to watch after my Shaun." Elizabeth had laid her fingers on his face and whispered, "You be careful, now, Shaun O'Banyon, and come home to me soon."

She could almost hear him playing down the danger. "Oh, Lizzie," he said, throwing his head back and laughing. "You know those Rebs are no match for our Irish blood. I won't be lettin' none of them gray coats get near to me anyhow, now will I?" Then, more seriously, he looked at her with that impish grin that made his eyes twinkle all the more. "Besides, Lizzie, you and I have got a lot of livin' and a lot of lovin' to do yet." He pulled her close to him, and she playfully pushed him away. She loved it when he called her Lizzie. It was his way of saying "I love you," without even saying the words.

That had been more than three years ago. Now as Elizabeth held the heliographic photo in her hands, she let her fingers trace the lines on her husband's face. She missed him so badly. She cursed the war that had separated them for so long. But she smiled at the quiet strength in the man looking back at her in the photograph. She recalled again her words to him the night before he left. "You be careful Shaun O'Banyon . . ." Elizabeth felt the tear trickle from her eye. "And come back to me soon."

Shaun O'Banyon packed up his mess kit and put it in his knapsack. "Which way are we heading, Cap'n? Now that General Joe Johnston and his boys have been slowed down, are we going to keep chasing them, trying to distract them like we did Hood's infantry and Nathan Bedford Forrest's cavalry back in Franklin a few months back?"

Justice nodded as he recalled how his men had slowed down Forrest's forty-five hundred horsemen approaching Spring Hill, a small town twelve miles south of Franklin, Tennessee, giving General John M. Schofield's Union army time to slip out of Forrest's grasp overnight. "We sure fooled them that time, didn't we?" Ezra said with a laugh. "It's hard to believe that you six men succeeded in convincing Forrest that there was a large Union cavalry out there in front of him somewhere."

"Ha, and what about your exploits, my good Captain?" Reginald Bonesteel called from across the cabin. "How you ever got inside Hood's command tent and replaced his reconnaissance with phony maps is beyond me."

"Well, I didn't replace all his maps, and the ones that I swapped just had a tiny bit of misinformation," Ezra said.

"Yes, especially the map showing Columbia, Spring Hill, and Franklin," Carlos crowed. "That was perfect! Hood was so confused, his troops didn't get to Spring Hill until three o'clock that afternoon, and by that time Schofield and his boys were long gone, setting up breastworks in old man Carter's backyard in Franklin."

"Yeah, a lot of good boys died in that hundred yards or so between the Carter's house and their cotton gin across the field." Ezra's expression turned serious. "I'd never before experienced such vicious hand-to-hand combat as we engaged in that day. I can still picture it in my mind. I don't think I'll ever be able to forget those awful sights of human bodies being torn apart by close-range musket shots, the thunderous roar of so many cannons, and the smells — the awful stench of blood and death all around us; wave after wave of the Rebels pouring over those breastworks at the Carter place, and men dying on top of one another, both blue and gray uniforms."

O'Banyon shook his head. "I remember it, too, Captain," he said. "It was worse than Pickett's charge up at Gettysburg."

"I agree," Harry Whitecloud offered. "I've never seen such brutal and savage fighting as I saw at Franklin. Men firing on one another at close range, and if they didn't have any more ammunition, they started clawing, clubbing, punching, stabbing, or choking one another."

"The smoke was so thick from the cannons and guns," Roberto said, "I couldn't tell friend from foe."

"Men were bayoneting and bludgeoning one another to death," recalled Ezra. "We were lucky to get out of there with our lives, much less a victory." Ezra got up and looked out the cabin window. "But to answer your question, Shaun, no; we won't be chasing General Johnston. From all our reports it looks as though General Sherman is moving up through the Carolinas, and it seems like it is only a matter of time before he overtakes Johnston's troops. As fine a tactician as General Johnston is, I don't think he can do much more than annoy General Sherman at this point."

"Do you think the war is almost over, Cap'n? That I'll be goin' home to my Lizzie soon?"

"Well, I wouldn't plan any homecoming parties yet, but it does appear that some good things are happening. Just this week I received news that the Confederates are exchanging prisoners of war with the Federals at an astonishing rate. Two of the largest Confederate prison camps, one at Cahaba, Alabama, and one in Andersonville, Georgia, are exchanging the men who are incarcerated there for Southerners. That's where we're heading next. General Grant wants us to make sure the prisoner exchange goes smoothly."

"Sounds like a waste of our talents, Captain," Bonesteel huffed. "Are you certain they need our assistance in such a mundane matter as prisoner exchanges?"

"It won't be as easy as it sounds, Reginald. We'll be traveling through dangerous Confederate territory most of the time, moving from Georgia, down through Selma, Alabama, then on to Vicksburg, Mississippi, where the Rebels are gathering most of the prisoners of war to be sent north by steamboats traveling in a straight shot to Memphis and on to St. Louis and some to Cairo, Illinois. We will help with the exchanges and will maintain the pressure on the Rebs to make sure the exchanges go off without a hitch."

"As I said," Bonesteel said with a yawn, "how boring."

Ezra shook his head. "We'll see, Mr. Bonesteel. I hope you're right."

6

In late March 1865, General Robert E. Lee mounted a desperate attempt to punch through the siege laid against his Army of Northern Virginia at Petersburg by General Ulysses S. Grant's forces. At first, it looked as though Lee's troops might have a chance, but the enormous numbers of well-supplied Union soldiers simply overwhelmed the proud Virginians. A few days later, in early April, Grant was ready to deliver the death blow to Lee's army. Union soldiers broke through Lee's lines at Petersburg, and Lee finally was forced to evacuate the town. Richmond, the Confederate capital, fell in short order, with fires and looting breaking out all over the city.

On April 3, Union troops entered the city and raised the Stars and Stripes. To the south, General William Sherman was pushing northward through the Carolinas bearing down on General Joe Johnston's troops.

When Lee knew that all hope was lost of joining his army with Johnston's and mounting an attack against Grant, the gallant Confederate general realized that further fighting would be futile. He sent out a lone, young officer on horseback, carrying a white flag. On April 9, 1865, Lee and Grant met at Appomattox Court House, a small town in Virginia, and Lee surrendered.

Spontaneous celebrations broke out in Washington; but because communication lines had been cut, the news of Lee's surrender was slow in reaching many of the troops in the deep South and in the West. It was more than a week later before General Johnston surrendered to Sherman in Durham, North Carolina. Many skirmishes and several full-scale battles took place even weeks after Lee and Grant met face-to-face at Appomattox. Nevertheless, for all intents and purposes, the moment Lee surrendered to Grant, the war was over.

But for some people, the war would never end.

One such man was Mordecai Slate. A tall, strong man in his early thirties, Mordecai Slate was handsome in a quirky sort of way. Though he often appeared as an agent of light, helping men and women achieve their goals, he possessed a strange darkness to his personality. He had grown up in a wealthy, elitist Southern family, on a beautiful plantation. As a young man he attended West Point, where he distinguished himself for his cunning and cutthroat behavior. Shortly before Fort Sumter was attacked, Mordecai Slate was expelled from the Academy for a series of treacheries that revealed his lack of honor and integrity. Returning home without a sign of remorse, Mordecai soon discovered that his father had squandered away the family fortune by gambling. While he once had great pride in his family, now even that was destroyed. Hatred, bitterness, blame, and resentment seethed in his heart and mind.

When the war broke out, Slate signed on with Jefferson Davis and had no qualms about turning his guns on some of the same men with whom he had spent several years in training at West Point. Throughout the war, Mordecai Slate operated under the authority of various Confederate generals, yet only to the extent that he chose to do so and only insofar as the needs of the Confederacy fit into his own agenda. To Mordecai Slate, the world revolved around him.

A charismatic leader at the war's end, Slate gathered about fifty malcontents around him, soldiers who had grown so accustomed to fighting and killing that they didn't want it to stop. They enjoyed killing for the thrill of it; they didn't flinch in the face of a fight; they relished it. Some of Slate's men maintained a misguided notion that the Confederacy would rise again — that the peace was an unstable interlude allowing the South time to rebuild and reinforce its army, and soon the war would continue to rage, this time with the Yankees being pummeled into submission.

Others sought revenge for the North's humiliation of the South and vowed to carry on subversive actions any way they could to thwart the efforts to pull the nation back together and bring healing to America's soul.

Still others simply had no place else to go. They were lured into a life of perverted power, robbing, vandalizing, raping, pillaging of people who were already vulnerable after more than four long years of war.

Mordecai Slate's band of thugs came to be known as the Death Raiders. Each member of the troop wore a distinguishing red hatband or headband, as well as a red neckerchief. They made for an ominous sight as they rode into a town, striking fear in the hearts and minds of the populace.

Slate and his men were near the

Mississippi–Alabama border during the closing days of the war, fighting ferociously to break out of the siege at Fort Blakely even as Lee and Grant drew up the terms of surrender in Virginia. Mysteriously escaping Fort Blakely just as the Union army forced the surrender of the nearly thirty-seven hundred men inside, Slate and his men headed east, plundering as they went. Although they didn't know it, they were traveling on a collision course with Captain Ezra Justice.

"Ezra! Have you heard the news? Oh, God, please help us."

"What's wrong, Nate? What are you talking about? Are you OK?"

"Oh, God, please protect us." Nate dropped to his knees and buried his face in his hands. Ezra realized that Nathaniel York was praying, not simply being dramatic. He stepped over and placed his hand on the big black man's shoulder.

"What is it, Nate?"

"He's gone, Ezra. They shot him. Our best hope for peace, and the maniacs assassinated him!"

"What? Who? Nate, what in the world are you talking about?"

"President Lincoln. They shot him while

he was attending a play in Washington. The nation is in an uproar. Andrew Johnson is the new president. Ezra, what is this world coming to?"

"I don't know, Nate. Are you sure it's true?"

"It's true, Ezra. The war is finally winding down, and now this! Oh, God, have mercy on us."

Ezra's mind was racing. Without President Lincoln, would the "Emancipation Proclamation" stand? Would the slaves remain free? Would Nate be a marked man because of the color of his skin? Ezra understood well Nate's concerns. That was one of the reasons he had joined the Union army rather than the Confederates in the first place. Although born and raised in Tennessee, Ezra Justice disagreed with his own parents' political views — especially in regard to slavery — to the point that he would alienate himself from his family to fight for the equality of all men and women.

Now, he wondered, *what is our nation going to do?*

Lincoln's death, sad as it was, did not negate or alter Ezra Justice's orders. He and his men were still to assist in the prisoner exchanges. As part of the terms of

Johnston's surrender to Sherman, the prison camps at Andersonville and Cahaba were to be emptied of the men in the stockades and sent to Union facilities where they could be sent home. Actually, the prisoner exchange had already begun.

For several weeks prior to Lee's surrender, the Confederates had increased the exchange activities, hoping to get back some of their own soldiers by cramming Union soldiers on board trains and shipping them in every direction.

"Prepare for a prisoner exchange," the Confederate authorities at Andersonville said. For many of the Union soldiers incarcerated in the camp, those were the sweetest words they'd ever heard. With no fanfare, and barely time to gather what little personal possessions they might have, the first group of prisoners filed out through the prison camp's gates, accompanied by several young, shotgun-toting Confederate guards.

Once they were beyond the stockade walls, some of the men paused long enough to pray, thanking God that their deliverance had finally come. Others hugged, some laughed through their toothless gums and gaunt faces — poor nutrition had long since caused many of their teeth to come loose and fall out. A few more exuberant men actually sang as they hobbled along toward the railroad line in Montgomery, Alabama.

Many men had to be helped by their stronger prison mates. With eyes nearly popping out of their skulls and bones protruding through their tattered clothing, the men were nothing more than thinly covered walking skeletons, every face showing the horrors of suffering they had endured. Mile after mile they trudged until they finally made it to a train that would transport them to Vicksburg. Prior to the end of the war, the Confederate Office of Exchange had agreed to transfer all prisoners east of the Mississippi River to the Union-held city in the heart of the south for shipment back north to their homes. The prisoners were housed at Camp Fisk, about four miles from Vicksburg, until they could be boarded on steamboats to take them up the mighty Mississippi River and home.

Making it onto a train was no guarantee of freedom. One train derailed three times before it finally arrived in Vicksburg. Many soldiers who had survived the camps died aboard the crowded trains. At every stop, dead Union soldiers were carried off the trains. Now Ezra and his men were on a train heading south.

The train lurched to a stop somewhere

near Americus, Georgia, and Ezra and his men got off in the midst of a dense forest. The mid-April air was laden with a sweet balsamic scent of pine trees. Wild flowers dotted the landscape, and springtime offered a hope of a new beginning for both the North and the South.

Ezra had wired ahead to arrange for fresh horses, and a young Yankee private had them waiting nearby. Much to Shaun O'Banyon's delight, the animals were magnificent, especially considering how long the war had dragged on.

"Look at these beauties, Cap'n," O'Banyon gushed as he brushed down each horse with a soft cloth. "Absolutely gorgeous."

"I asked for some strong horses," Ezra said, "and I'm glad to see the army came through. We have a tough trip ahead of us."

Justice and his squad mounted up and started north along an eerie desolate road. The only sound was the occasional snort of a horse and the soft crunching of hooves against pine needles. The men had traveled about ten miles when they first caught sight of their destination, a huge prison camp covering more than 26 acres, enclosed by a 12-foot-high stockade of hewn pine logs. Within that enclosure were two more walls, one appearing about 16 feet high, and the innermost wall that looked to be about twenty feet tall. Justice brought his horse to a halt and, for a full thirty seconds or more, simply stared at the fortress. The other riders gathered around him.

"What is it, Cap'n?" O'Banyon asked.

"Andersonville," Justice replied. "Hell on earth for more than forty-five thousand Union soldiers." Justice continued staring at the massive wooden gates with heavy iron hinges and bolts. He spoke quietly but with strong emotion. "Inside those walls, more than thirteen thousand of our boys have died from disease, malnutrition, or exposure to the elements, not to mention those who were hanged or shot by the Rebel prison guards. This is one of the largest prison camps the Rebs had. And it's time to set our men free. Let's go."

The huge gates, now manned by a few Yankee privates, swung open as Justice and his men approached. Big Nate and Ezra led the way. But not even an experienced soldier like Ezra Justice was prepared for the sight that met his eyes. Thousands of dirty, disheveled, emaciated men huddled together inside the stockade. Several dead bodies lay exposed. Row after row of makeshift tents lined the camp, and thousands of other men

— in all sorts of tattered clothing, and some with no clothes at all — lay in their tents or on the cold ground. Most of the men appeared to be sickly. Many looked like walking skeletons. Some did not have enough strength to raise their heads when Justice and his men rode into the camp.

The air inside the stockade reeked, partially from the foul smells from the polluted stream running through the camp, and partially from the horribly unsanitary conditions. Moreover, the high-walled stockade did not lend itself to fresh breezes that might blow the stench in another direction, so the atmosphere itself seemed clogged with human waste.

Justice shook his head as he stared at the nearby swamp and accumulated excrement that made habitation almost impossible. "It's hard to imagine that human beings could treat other human beings so horribly," Justice said. "Killing men in battle is one thing, but what they have done to these men is an abomination."

Nathaniel York looked at Justice, then back at the prisoners, and nodded. "The Good Book says there are none righteous, Ezra. None of us. We've all messed up. There's no limit to how low a person can go when he forgets that men and women are all made in the image of God."

"I suppose so, but it sure seems like some sink a lot lower than others."

"How many men are living here, Captain?" Nate asked.

"Last count was more than thirty thousand, but nobody knows for sure. Looks to me like most of these men have less than a few square yards of living space. No wonder they've had such problems with malaria, typhoid, smallpox, scurvy, and gangrene. And some of these men have been here or at other Rebel prisons for several years."

"Where are they supposed to go now?"

"Most will want to go home, I'm guessing. The Rebels have agreed to send some to Florida and others to Vicksburg. Then it's up to the Union government to get them back wherever they belong. By the looks of it, though, I'm wondering if most of these guys can even make it to the train. We're supposed to help facilitate the exchange of prisoners and transfer men to Vicksburg, where the government is paying for their passage aboard steamers that will take them back home to the North."

Ezra felt something tugging at his leg and was about to shake it off when he realized that a frail old man wearing the remnants of a Union soldier's uniform had gotten to his knees and was reaching up to him as he passed by. "Moses!" the man called out. "Moses, you've finally come to lead us out of Egypt."

Justice dismounted carefully, trying not to cause the feeble soldier to fall over. He reached his arms around the man and lifted him to his feet. As he did, Ezra noticed something that looked like a puff of smoke rise from the man's hair. Looking more closely, he realized the man's head was crawling with lice.

"I'm not Moses, old man, but we're gonna get you out of here." Ezra eased the man back to the ground. "You hold on, now; don't give up. You've made it this far."

Justice and his men moved on into the camp and up to a section that looked as though it might have been the commandant's office area. Once inside, however, they realized it was the camp hospital, if it could be called that. "They must come here to die," O'Banyon whispered to Nate as the men stepped inside. Dozens of naked prisoners lay in contorted positions on the floor. There were no cots or beds. Many men moaned in pain.

In the corner of the room, a young man in a Confederate uniform was taking a bandage off one man and using that same soiled bandage on another man. "Are you a doctor?" Justice asked.

"No, sir," the young man replied. "I've had to cut a few legs and arms off, due to the gangrene, so the commandant ordered me to work here."

"Why did you stay when the rest of the Rebels took off?" Justice probed.

"I may not be a doctor, sir, but I'm all these men have."

Justice nodded. "Harry, can you help him out here? Do we have any clean bandages he can have?"

"Yes, sir. I'll go get some right now." Harry Whitecloud knew the ways of the Sioux medicine man as well as the medical practices at Princeton, but he also knew there was little that could be done for the men languishing in this pit. Still, they had to try.

Ezra found the man in charge, a low-ranking Confederate officer who had been hiding out since Lee's surrender in fear for his life. He needn't have worried too much. Most of the men at Andersonville were too weak to mount much of a vengeful attack. Captain Henry Wirz, a former doctor himself and the man who had run the prison for the past year and a half, left when he knew the war was lost. Eventually he was caught and taken to trial. When later questioned in court about the appalling conditions at his camp, his answer was, "I was merely following orders."

Justice and the officer in charge signed the appropriate papers, and the camp was officially closed although the officer agreed to stay on the premises until the men could be put on trains to Vicksburg.

The scene and conditions at Cahaba prison, a much smaller camp along the Alabama River not far from Selma, were no better. About the best that could be said about Cahaba was that it was about a tenth of the size of Andersonville. But into that tiny area, the Confederates had crammed more than three thousand men who subsisted on bug-laden soup and a few kernels of insect-infested cornmeal.

Again, Justice and his riders did their best to alleviate any suffering they could, and rectify the immediate situations they could help with, but the needs were enormous. All they could do was hurriedly get the prison closed and the prisoners headed toward Vicksburg by train or on foot. One group of Union soldiers, most of whom were barefoot, walked more than thirty miles to Camp Fisk outside Vicksburg. With their last burst of energy, the men threw their hats in the air and started running toward the American flag they saw waving in the wind, flying high above the fort.

"I haven't seen the Stars and Stripes in several years," one man said. "I didn't think I could take another step, but when I saw Old Glory, something spurred me on, and I knew I could make it."

Once Justice and his men had made all the arrangements and had set the prisoner exchange in motion, they headed by horseback toward Vicksburg, hoping to arrive in time to help get the men on their steamboats to freedom. "The trip to Vicksburg should be relatively uneventful," Ezra told his men, as they pulled out of Cahaba, "but stay alert. From what I understand, the Rebels in Alabama have not surrendered yet, so we may bump into a few skirmishes here and there."

"Nothing we can't handle," Carlos Hawkins said with a smile.

"Shall I even load my dear Henry .44?" Reginald Bonesteel quipped, rolling his eyes.

Camped in a small town not far from Vicksburg, Mordecai Slate spun the chambers on his revolver, caressed the long-barreled gun, and grinned.

7

"Listen!" Harry Whitecloud demanded. His ear was to the ground, his body stretched out flat on the surface, his face intent, as he waved back the other riders. "It's something bad, and it's not too far away." Harry snapped to his feet in one smooth motion. He turned to Ezra Justice who was still in his saddle. "I can't tell for sure, but it sounds like heavy gunfire to me."

"OK, thanks, Harry." Justice rose up in his saddle and turned to the other riders. "Alright, men. Let's head in that direction, but stick to the ridge. If it is a skirmish and our guys have it under control, we may pass right on by. But have your guns loaded just in case they need us to get involved."

Ezra led out toward the ridge, with the riders following two by two behind him.

A few miles further and there was no more question about the sound. It was gunfire, alright. But whose? Where? And why?

"Let's go!" Ezra called out. "Ride to the sound of the gunfire. Let's find out what's going on. But stay high on the ridge. Don't anyone go down into the valley until we know what we're facing."

Seven strong horses carrying seven strong men galloped across the top of the ridge, stirring up a plume of dust on the dry Mississippi horizon. A few more minutes and the riders could see smoke in the valley below, as the loud gunfire resonated off a nearby hillside. Ezra pulled up hard on the reins; and his horse came to an abrupt stop, the remaining riders following suit alongside him.

"This doesn't look good," Justice said, dismounting and moving to the edge of the cliff, crouching down low for a better view of the tumult below. One by one the other riders joined him.

"Looks like trouble to me," Nate agreed, standing above Justice and looking through a pair of field glasses.

"What's going on, Nate?" Roberto asked. "What do you see?"

"Seems like those Confederates have some Yankees trapped in a sort of boxed canyon down below. The Union guys are up against the high, sheer cliffs, and there's nowhere for them to go. A number of men are already dead or severely wounded. Looks like their only defense is that breastworks sort of fence that they've turned into some kind of makeshift ramparts. They're pinned down and firing hard from behind that barrier, but it doesn't look like they're gonna be able to hold off the Rebs much longer."

"The first lesson of warfare," Reginald Bonesteel muttered. "Never allow yourself to be fenced in on three sides."

"Somebody needs to tell those Johnny Rebs that the war is over," O'Banyon said.

"Good idea, Shaun," Carlos said jokingly. "Why don't you go down there and do just that?"

"Well, maybe I will."

"Calm down, men," Ezra said. "Let's figure out a plan. We can't charge down into that boxed canyon. The seven of us against an entire regiment; we wouldn't stand a chance. But we can't let those Union soldiers be slaughtered either."

Ezra didn't have to say any more. The men looked at one another silently; then without a word they simply pulled out their guns and began double-checking their ammo.

"Alright. Let's think here," Justice said, still crouched down but turned now to face the others. "Any suggestions?"

"We could try to draw their fire away from

the guys behind the ramparts by hitting them with dynamite from above," offered Roberto.

"Yeah, that might work for a few minutes," Ezra agreed. "What else?"

Nathaniel York rubbed his mustache as he often did when he was thinking. "Ya know, in the Bible, there's a story about a fella named Gideon. Anybody remember that?"

"Sure, Nate, but this is no time for a church meetin'. We gotta come up with a plan," Carlos said.

"Hang on, Carlos," Ezra said. "What do you mean, Nate?"

"Well, Gideon was going up against a powerful enemy army with only three hundred men, so he divided his troops into three companies surrounding the enemy, but he told them to stay extremely quiet until a given signal. He gave each man a trumpet, an empty water pitcher, and a torch inside the pitcher. On Gideon's signal his soldiers jumped up, blew the trumpet, smashed the pitchers revealing the torches, and they yelled out, 'A sword for the Lord and for Gideon!' The enemy was so surprised and confused, they started fighting among themselves and running away. Gideon's guys won a great victory against overwhelming odds."

"So what you are suggesting is that we attempt to give the impression that we are an entire army," Bonesteel said. "Is that correct?"

"Precisely," Nate replied, gently mocking Bonesteel's British formality.

"I like it," Ezra said. "What do you think, Harry?"

"We need to create a sense of ambush," Whitecloud replied. "With a little luck and these dry shrubs, I think I can make this hillside come alive with fire. If I add some bullets to the fire, it will sound as though we have a much larger force."

"We have enough dynamite in our saddlebags that we can make it sound like an entire regiment is coming over the ridge," Roberto concurred.

"OK, good," Ezra said. "Bonesteel, you stay right here and keep that .44 hot. With that high-powered scope of yours, you should be able to pick off a few Rebs from here. If nothing else, they'll at least be aware of firepower coming over their shoulder."

"Carlos and Roberto, you come with me. We're going to swoop down behind the Rebs. We'll give 'em our best shots and a few more. I want you to make them think that there are a hundred of us. Keep the firepower coming. Keep moving. If you have any more of those satchel charges, now would be a good time to pull them out of your bag of tricks.

"Harry, light up those hills on either side of them if you can. Nate, move around to the left flank and hit them with the strongest stuff you have. Keep moving across the top of the hill. Don't let them pin you down, or you're done for.

"O'Banyon, head around behind those Johnny Rebs. Get on the other side of them, and cover our backs. Don't let anyone come up behind us. It may take you a few minutes to get there, so I'll give you a head start. But hurry. Those boys down there behind the barricade must be running low on ammunition; they aren't going to last much longer."

"Aye, Captain," O'Banyon saluted. "I'll see you on the other side."

"Be careful, Shaun. You're going to be all alone out there. Don't take any unnecessary chances."

"Oh, I'm not worried in the least," O'Banyon said almost jovially. "I've got my Lizzie right here close to my heart." He patted the pocket where he kept the locket with his wife's photograph inside.

Justice nodded. "Alright. Get moving. I'll wait until I see you in position before sounding the attack."

O'Banyon headed out by horseback, keeping below the top of the ridge to avoid being seen by the Confederate forces in the valley. Justice watched him go for a minute or two, then turned to the Hawkins twins. "Are you guys ready?"

"All set, Captain," Roberto responded. Carlos finished hooking two satchel charges to his saddle. "I'm set, sir."

Turning to Bonesteel, Ezra said, "This area is all yours, Mr. Bonesteel. Give us rapid-fire support from this hillside. I'm going to attempt multiple shots myself. Accuracy won't be as important as the impression that there are a lot of us." Ezra pulled out his LaMat and slid the lever to the multishot position. "And keep an eye on O'Banyon if you can. You're probably too far away from where he's going to be hiding to offer any cover fire, but he's our first and only line of defense on our backside. If he gets in trouble, head in that direction."

"I understand, sir," Bonesteel said with a respectful salute.

"Remember, Nate, don't fire until you see us shoot. Then turn that ridge into a shooting gallery."

"Got it, Captain. May God watch over us."

Ezra looked Nate in the eyes. "He's done a pretty good job so far, but it doesn't hurt to keep asking."

"You're absolutely right about that, my friend." Nate waved and hoisted himself into his saddle.

"Alright everybody," Ezra said, "let's move out. We'll reassemble in the valley after we take care of this little matter." Justice raised his right hand and touched two fingers to the brim of his hat as he and the Hawkins twins pulled their horses' reins to the left and headed down over the hillside to an area behind the Rebel attackers.

The noise, gunsmoke, and dust rising from the ongoing battle in the valley allowed Ezra and the twins to descend undetected. Nevertheless, they picked their way carefully, staying behind clusters of pine trees on the higher part of the ridge, then moving behind a line of large magnolia trees along the base of the valley. *If this is going to work,* Ezra thought, *we have to maintain the element of surprise.* Ezra and the Hawkins twins stopped long enough to make sure everybody was in position.

"Ready?" Ezra mouthed the words in the chaos. The twins nodded. "Here goes nuthin'," Ezra said. He pulled on the reins of his horse and galloped straight toward the fight with the LaMat blazing, surprising the Confederate troops. Justice took down several officers before the Rebels even realized that they were being attacked from behind. At the same time, the Hawkins twins veered off to either side of Ezra, weaving in between the Rebel positions, firing in every direction.

At the moment Ezra first peeled out from behind the magnolias, it seemed the entire hillside caught fire above the Rebels. Rifle fire poured from the ridge above and behind the Union ramparts, and at the same time rapid-firing, high-powered rifle fire picked off several Confederate privates on the left flank. A spate of bullets could be heard going off in every direction above the Rebels. The gray-coated soldiers looked bewildered as though they weren't sure which direction to shoot or from which direction to take cover.

Recognizing the sudden turn of events, the Union men behind the ramparts boldly stepped up their fire. Several men even crawled out from behind the barricade and took time to aim each shot, resulting in musket balls blasting into Confederate soldiers. Just then a high-pitched searing sound could be heard, and a red flash of fire erupted behind the Rebel lines. Roberto

Hawkins danced his horse around several small howitzers and delivered his first satchel charge. The entire valley seemed to explode in repercussions from the perfectly placed dynamite. A moment later another enormous explosion took place across the valley as Carlos delivered a satchel.

With several key officers down and nobody barking out orders to guide them through the brown grit that filled the air, a large group of confused Confederate soldiers started shooting at one another. When they realized they had killed their own men, the horror sent them into even further panic. A number of Rebel soldiers simply broke ranks and ran for the hills.

Hidden high on the hill behind the Confederates and off to the left, Reginald Bonesteel ripped through bullets as fast as he could reload, spraying the area below with gunfire. Just about the time Bonesteel thought, *We might actually pull this thing off,* he caught sight of a plume of dust rising in the west. *Now what could that be?* he asked himself.

On the ridge above the western shoulder of the box-shaped canyon, Shaun O'Banyon saw the rising dust as well. Peering intently through some field glasses, he alternately turned toward the battle raging below and then back to the dust cloud in the west. Finally, he saw the reason for the dust.

"Awww, no!" he said aloud to himself and the sweet-smelling jasmine shrubs behind which he had set up his lookout. A shudder ran through O'Banyon's body as he watched the cavalry regiment approaching from the west. The riders wore what looked to be Confederate uniforms, or what was left of them, but the distinctive red hatbands, headbands, and red neckerchiefs, visible even from the ridge high above the trail, caused O'Banyon's heart to thump harder. *The Death Raiders.*

O'Banyon quickly sized up the situation. Below him to the east, Ezra Justice and the rest of his squad were exposed. Even though they seemed to be carrying off the ruse, and the Rebs seemed to be in chaos, Ezra and the twins, as well as Nate and Harry White-cloud, were all trapped between the Confederates who had pinned down the Union soldiers and the approaching Death Raiders.

I've got to do something, O'Banyon thought. *I can't allow those devils to get to Ezra, or they will be slaughtered. But what? What can I do to warn them and allow Justice enough time to clear out?*

O'Banyon looked back toward Ezra Justice

130

and his friends. He cut off a small branch from a tree, tied a red handkerchief to it, and began waving the flag frantically, hoping to get someone's attention, but Justice and the other riders were pressing the battle below. Nobody bothered to look up on the ridge in O'Banyon's direction. And the Death Raiders were drawing closer every minute. The cavalry was moving slowly but steadily toward the sound of gunfire. In another minute or so, they'd be right below the ridge where O'Banyon was stationed; and then once past that, they would have Ezra Justice and his men trapped. O'Banyon was resolved to act. He knew it would be foolish to attack the cavalry, but maybe he could slow them down somehow, to intercept them, to detain them, even for a few extra minutes. Long enough for Captain Justice to know that danger was approaching. What? How could he stall them?

Finally, he struck upon a plan — it wasn't the greatest plan, he had to admit, but it was the best he could come up with in the moment. *I'll pretend that I am drunk,* he mused.

O'Banyon crept down along the tree line to some rocks about twenty feet above the trail on which the cavalry was approaching. He pulled his revolver out of the holster and made sure he had a bullet in each chamber. Then he took out the locket Elizabeth had given him and flipped it open. "I'm sorry, Lizzie. I don't like this any more than you do, but I can't stand by and do nothing when good men are likely to die." He kissed Elizabeth's smiling picture and said, "I'll be coming home to you soon. Don't you worry none." He snapped the locket closed, turned it so Elizabeth's picture would face his heart, and slid the locket back into his coat's breast pocket.

The sound of horses' hooves brought him to attention. Hidden behind a rock formation above the trail, he could see the approaching cavalry, but they could not see him. From his vantage point on the far left ridge, Reginald Bonesteel saw O'Banyon perched on the cliff.

"Oh, no," he said aloud. "What's that crazy Irishman going to do now?" Bonesteel was too far away to offer any firepower, but instinctively he began moving along the top of the ridge, keeping O'Banyon within his line of sight.

Shaun O'Banyon heard the first horses about two hundred yards away riding toward him. "What's that the Cap'n likes to say? 'Here goes nuthin'!'" With that, O'Banyon slid down the cliff and staggered out into the road. In his right hand he held his revolver, and in his left hand he clutched his hip flask.

O'Banyon started waving his flask and firing his revolver as he whooped, "The war is over! The war is over, mates. We can all go home!"

Caught off guard, Mordecai Slate raised his arm signaling for his men to halt, just before they trampled O'Banyon.

O'Banyon emptied his gun's chambers, waving his whiskey flask above his head, the liquid splashing out all over him. "It's time to celebrate, men!" he yelled to the horsemen, wobbling back and forth as though inebriated. "The war is over!"

The grizzly men stared at O'Banyon for a moment, then started laughing uproariously at the man they assumed to be drunk.

From his perch high on the ridge, Reginald Bonesteel was dumbstruck somewhere between respect and awe for O'Banyon's courage and utter amazement at the Irishman's foolish ploy.

On the other side of the horseshoe-like ridge, Ezra Justice stopped firing when he heard the gunfire coming from O'Banyon's position. Nobody had to tell him that O'Banyon was in trouble.

For his part Mordecai Slate was not

amused. Straightening his hat, he scowled and huffed, "Would somebody please get this drunk under control!"

Two cavalrymen jumped to the ground and converged on O'Banyon from both sides, grabbing at his arms. But they underestimated the spunky Irishman's strength. O'Banyon easily squirmed out of their grasp, whirled away from them, and continued his outrageous antics. "The war is over, boys! Let's all have a drink!"

O'Banyon eluded another soldier and danced his way back in front of Mordecai Slate. He stopped suddenly, waved the flask up at Slate, and then straightened up as though instantly sober. "My good sir," he addressed Slate in his most charming Irish brogue. "Can I be convincing you fellows to come down off your horses and celebrate with me?"

Mordecai Slate cocked his head and stared at O'Banyon as if he were a lunatic. But O'Banyon carried on undeterred. "Here is the problem," he said. "My friends are over there, and they've gotten themselves into a bit of a mess with some fine Southern gentlemen who are unaware that the war is over. And my friends just need to move off a bit, and we can all be on our way. After all, it is such a lovely day."

Mordecai Slate glared at O'Banyon and said coldly, "Get out of my way, you drunken Yankee."

"Now, my good sir, you seem like a reasonable man. Would you please hear me out?"

"The only thing you're going to hear is a bullet if you don't get out of the way. Move or die."

O'Banyon looked at the flask in his hand, and said, "Oh, my. I didn't think this would be of much help." He threw the flask on the ground and with lightning speed jerked Mordecai Slate off his horse. He let loose with a wicked right-hand punch that caught Slate square in the jaw, sending him reeling into the dirt. Trying to buy as much time as he could for Ezra Justice and the other riders, O'Banyon made no attempt to flee.

Slate's men drew their guns, preparing to fill O'Banyon full of holes. "Don't shoot him!" Slate shouted.

Four of Slate's men pounced on O'Banyon, but the strong fighter sent two of them to the ground, one with a vicious left uppercut to the stomach and the other with a full-strength punch to the nose. Two more outlaw Rebels grabbed O'Banyon from behind while yet another pair attacked him from the front and subdued him.

Slate slowly rose from the ground with death in his eyes. "So you think you're tough," he said as he approached O'Banyon. "Well, let's see."

Mordecai Slate stood in front of O'Banyon and pulled his gloves tightly on his fists. He reared back and landed a wicked blow to O'Banyon's left eye. He followed with a left cross to the eye, opening a cut that spurted blood down O'Banyon's face. Slate continued to beat O'Banyon until he fell as dead weight to the ground. He rolled over in the dirt, looked up at Mordecai Slate, and demurely asked, "Might I assume that a truce is out of the question?"

"Get him up!" Slate growled. Two of the Death Raiders grabbed O'Banyon and pulled him to his feet.

Shaun O'Banyon raised his eyebrows and impishly smiled. O'Banyon hedged, "Tell me now; might any of you wee lads here hail from Ireland?"

"No," Slate responded furiously, "there are no Irish fools here. None but you."

"Well, you don't have to be so rude now, do you?" O'Banyon bantered.

Slate stared at Shaun for a moment. "You've got guts, I'll give you that. What's your name, Yankee," Slate asked almost respectfully, "before I kill you?"

"Sergeant Shaun O'Banyon, sir." O'Banyon replied with more than a slight touch of sarcasm. "Formerly of the famous New York Irish Regiment, and more recently on special assignment under the direct orders of Captain Ezra Justice . . . sir."

"Ezra Justice," Slate sneered. "You can't be under Justice's command. He's dead. I shot him myself."

"Well, now he only has eight lives left," O'Banyon quipped.

"Are you telling me the truth about Justice being alive?"

"If I'm lying, I'm dying," Shaun replied.

Slate laughed and said, "Never truer words spoken." Mordecai Slate jerked his knife from its scabbard and plunged it deep into Shaun O'Banyon's chest.

Slate ripped the knife out of O'Banyon and wiped the blood on his pants. Slate's men released the dying man, and Mordecai and the two Death Raiders remounted their horses.

Shaun O'Banyon seemed to hang between heaven and earth for a few seconds, his body bloody and contorted, but his eyes looking clearly and directly at Mordecai Slate. Without a word O'Banyon slumped to the ground in front of Slate's horse, landing face-first in the dirt already spattered with his own blood. He rolled over, his arms extended straight out from his shoulders, his body forming a human cross, right in front of Mordecai Slate.

High above, on the ridge running behind the canyon, Reginald Bonesteel looked on in helpless horror. Although he hadn't heard a word of the conversation between O'Banyon and Slate, it was obvious to him that the Irishman had hoped to buy some time so Justice and his men could move out of the way of the oncoming marauders. And O'Banyon's ploy had been successful. Ezra, Nate, Harry, and the Hawkins twins had succeeded in creating enough confusion in the ranks of the Confederate contingency that had pinned down the small group of Union soldiers that the Rebels had dispersed and headed beyond the east side of the canyon. Justice and the squad quickly set about helping the survivors tend to the wounded and dying. By sacrificing his own life, O'Banyon had not only saved Justice and the other riders; he'd also saved the lives of the helpless Federal soldiers who had been caught in the irrevocable trap that would have led inexorably to their death.

His penchant for murder momentarily sated, Mordecai Slate raised his arm and growled, "Let's move!" he commanded his men. As Mordecai and his men headed toward Ezra and the others, Justice saw the dust rising from the regiment. Just in time he motioned for his men to hide behind the breastworks. The Death Raiders rode by slowly, staring down at the dead Union and Confederate soldiers. Thanks to O'Banyon's antics, the Death Raiders rode by without spotting Ezra and his men. They stormed up the trail leading away from Justice and the others.

Scrambling across the top of the ridge now, stumbling, falling, getting back on his hands and knees and crawling, Reginald Bonesteel was determined to get to his fallen friend. He tumbled down the hill, almost knocking himself unconscious. Then got up and started again. Finally, he reached O'Banyon.

Bonesteel placed a hand on O'Banyon's neck and could feel that the tough Irishman was still breathing. He leaned over O'Banyon's bloody chest and whispered, "Come on, you despicable toad," he said. "Keep breathing! You can do it, Shaun. Don't die on me, friend. I need you." Bonesteel pulled out his .44-caliber Henry and began shooting rapid fire into the air, intending to draw the attention of his comrades.

Still behind the makeshift breastworks, Ezra Justice and Nathaniel York looked up at each other from the wounded soldier they were bandaging. "Bonesteel," Nate said.

"O'Banyon," Ezra answered.

Satisfied that the soldier was OK, they ran for their horses, hurriedly mounted, and galloped toward the sound of Bonesteel's gunfire. Rounding the bend, just beyond the edge of the far ridge, they saw O'Banyon's wounded body on the ground, with Bonesteel already tearing up strips of cloth and stuffing them inside O'Banyon's coat, trying to stop the bleeding.

Ezra and Nate reined in their horses, dismounted, and ran to their fallen comrade. Ezra knelt in the dirt next to Bonesteel and quickly began examining the knife wound in O'Banyon's chest.

"Nate, get Harry over here, quickly," Justice said, looking up at the somber black man. Nate immediately remounted and took off toward the canyon, where Harry Whitecloud had been tending to the wounded soldiers.

"Hang on, Shaun. You can make it," Ezra said. O'Banyon groaned in pain.

"He's a tough one," Bonesteel said. Bonesteel pulled his canteen off his belt loop, dipped some water on a cloth, and then squeezed it onto O'Banyon's lips. The Irishman stirred slightly, so Bonesteel gently poured the water directly onto his face. O'Banyon's eyelids fluttered but didn't open. Bonesteel applied more water, wiping the fallen soldier's face with a soft cloth. Slowly, almost imperceptibly, O'Banyon's eyelids parted, though his eyes were glazed over and tipping back in their sockets.

Ezra cradled O'Banyon's head in his hands. "Shaun! Shaun, it's Justice and Bonesteel. We're here with you, Shaun. Come on, man. Stay with us."

Harry Whitecloud and Nate York came around the ridge, followed closely by Carlos and Roberto Hawkins, and several of the Union soldiers who had just a few minutes ago been under fire themselves. They dismounted and circled around O'Banyon.

Ezra moved away from O'Banyon's side, allowing Harry to get in close. With his knowledge of Indian medicine and modern medical practices, Whitecloud was the best man capable of tending to O'Banyon's knife wound. Nathaniel York knelt down and silently prayed for their friend.

Harry went to work trying to stop the bleeding. But Slate knew what he was doing with a knife when he stabbed O'Banyon. The big knife had cut arteries that were close to his heart and Whitecloud could not stop the internal bleeding. Perspiration drops covered Harry Whitecloud's forehead as he worked desperately to close up the wound, tying sutures using roughhewn string, but it was clear to all of the men looking on that Harry — and O'Banyon — were fighting a losing battle.

O'Banyon's lips twitched once, then again. His lips parted slowly as Ezra dabbed the wet cloth against the dying man's forehead. "Listen. He's trying to say something," Justice said.

"Li . . . Liz." O'Banyon's receding tongue refused to form the words. "Lizzie," he finally blurted.

"Lizzie. Yes, Elizabeth. She's right here, Shaun." Justice pulled the locket from the soldier's bloody coat and held the picture up in front of O'Banyon's bleary eyes for him to see. "Look, Shaun, here she is. She wants to see you. Hang on!"

O'Banyon's eyes rolled slowly in Ezra's direction as if to say, "I know what you're trying to do, Captain, but it's no use." He raised his left hand and Justice placed the locket in O'Banyon's palm and folded his fingers over the locket.

"Tell, Lizzie . . ."

"We'll tell her, Shaun," Carlos leaned in

toward O'Banyon. "Better yet, you can tell her yourself. Come on; let's get you out of . . ."

"Tell Lizzie that I loved her to the end," O'Banyon said hoarsely. "Tell her that she's been my light and my strength." O'Banyon coughed and blood spurted out of the corner of his mouth.

"Take it easy, Shaun," Justice said. "Don't try to talk right now."

O'Banyon waved his left hand, flinching from the pain in his chest as he did. "Cap'n," he said. He gagged and sputtered more blood but continued speaking. "Tell her to be strong."

"I will, Shaun, I will," Justice promised.

O'Banyon struggled for a breath before continuing. "Captain, please don't bury me out here."

"Shaun, we're not gonna be burying you . . ." Ezra started to say, but O'Banyon waved him off again.

"Cap'n, I'm dying, please take me home."

Ezra's eyebrows raised at O'Banyon's words. "Shaun, I. . . ."

"I beg o' you, Cap'n," O'Banyon gasped, "take me home to Lizzie. Bury me there. My daddy never had a tombstone, never had a proper burial. . . . Don't let that happen to me. . . ."

Ezra Justice looked up and quickly scanned the faces of his men kneeling around their fallen brother. Each man nodded somberly.

"OK, Shaun," Justice said quietly. "We'll do it. I promise you. We'll take you back to Missouri and help Elizabeth bury you on your own land."

"Thank you, Cap'n," O'Banyon whispered.

"Give her this." With his last bit of strength, Shaun O'Banyon, lifted his hand and slowly let the locket slide out of his palm into that of Ezra Justice. "And tell her I will be waiting for her in heaven." O'Banyon's hand dropped to his side. Shaun O'Banyon was dead.

For more than a minute, Ezra Justice knelt there motionless, both knees on the ground, next to his friend, clutching the locket and fighting back the tears that threatened to surge down his face. Reginald Bonesteel took a blanket and placed it over O'Banyon's face, and Big Nate York knelt next to Justice and prayed. "God, please give rest to this good man's soul; have mercy on his dear wife, and help us to fulfill his dying requests. Amen."

Nobody seemed to know what to do next,

so for several minutes, the tough, war-hardened soldiers simply stood or knelt silently. Finally Nathaniel York stood to his feet, raised his arms high in the air, tilted his face toward the sky, and prayed, "O God, into your hands we commit the spirit of our friend and fellow warrior, Shaun O'Banyon. He belongs to you, Lord. Thank you for sharing him with us. Amen."

"Amen," a number of the men said in unison.

Ezra Justice slowly stood up and put one arm around Nate. "Thank you, Nate. You always know the right thing to say, and I appreciate it."

"You just gotta have a little faith, Ezra."

"Yeah, Nate. I know." Justice looked at Whitecloud, "Harry, what do you know about embalming?"

"Mmm, not much, I'm afraid, Captain. The Sioux were never big on embalming because they always believed the spirit of a man might return to his body somehow."

Justice turned to Nathaniel. "What about you, Nate? Do you have any ideas?"

"Well, sir, I read in the Bible where some women prepared Jesus for burial by wrapping his body in cloth, sort of like a mummy, with some sort of spices to keep the body from smelling badly, and a sticky substance to hold the graveclothes together. I think if we can tap into some pine sap, and maybe some berries, and use it to seal strips of cloth as we wrap O'Ban, er, I mean, . . . the body, wrapping the body real tight, we can make it to Vicksburg. Then we might be able to employ the services of an undertaker to prepare the body for burial before we go the rest of the way to Missouri."

"Sounds like a good idea and the best we can do right now," Justice said with a nod. "Let's look around and see what we can come up with."

Roberto Hawkins stepped forward. "We should be able to get good cloth strips off the bodies of some of the soldiers back in the canyon, sir. We'll want to bury them before we move on, anyhow, so they won't be needing their shirts."

"I suppose you're right, Roberto. Go ahead. But let's maintain some dignity for those fallen soldiers, no matter what color of uniform they are wearing."

"Yes, sir. I understand."

"Carlos, give your brother a hand. Reginald, you and Nate stay here and help me move O'Banyon over there into the shade. We'll need to protect his body somehow. I don't want those vultures to get to him before we can get him wrapped up."

A young Union lieutenant approached Justice and saluted. "Captain Justice, sir; I'm Lieutenant Christopher. My men and I would be honored if you would allow us to help. We were on our way to Vicksburg to work with the prisoner exchange when we were ambushed by the contingent of Rebels. We lost seventeen good men in that canyon. We have only eight men who are healthy, but if it hadn't been for you and your men, we'd all be dead. You saved our lives. It is the least we can do to assist you in getting Sergeant O'Banyon to Vicksburg."

"Thank you, Lieutenant," Justice replied. "We could certainly use an extra hand. Let's start by giving those soldiers back there a proper burial. Then we'll get on the road to Vicksburg. Do you think your wounded men can make the journey?"

"Yes, sir, I do. Most of our wounds are superficial. These men are survivors. They can make it."

"OK, let's get busy. It's a long way to Vicksburg." Justice looked at O'Banyon's lifeless form lying on the ground. "Rest assured, Shaun, we'll get you home to Lizzie."

8

Sitting by the open campfire under the stars on the cool mid-April evening, Ezra Justice stared into the flames and took a sip of coffee from the bent tin cup he'd been holding in his hand. He swirled the brackish stuff around in his mouth before swallowing. Even gross coffee tasted good after a long, tough day.

The task of procuring enough pine pitch, herbs, and berries that he and the men had used to wrap Shaun O'Banyon's body had taken several hours, much longer than he'd expected. Then in between each strip of cloth — torn from the clothing of other dead men — they plastered the sticky substance as they turned O'Banyon over and over, wrapping each section of their comrade's body. That too had been much more of an emotional experience than Ezra had anticipated. Carlos Hawkins, nobody's baby, actually broke down in tears as he held up O'Banyon's head so his brother Roberto could stretch a portion of fabric across the lifeless face of the friendly Irishman. Even the stiff and starchy Reginald Bonesteel lost his composure at one point, hurrying off to the bushes to throw up. It wasn't easy to turn a friend and fellow soldier into a mummy, and it caused each of Ezra's men to wretch in his own way.

Ezra brought the cup to his lips again and tipped it forward, oblivious to the fact that he'd already drained most of the coffee. "Blaahhh!" He spat out the coffee grounds that had slipped into his mouth before he realized the cup was empty. He reached over and picked up the pot of coffee, still on the fire, and refilled his cup. "Anyone else?" He lifted the pot toward Big Nate and Harry Whitecloud, sitting on a rock on the other side of the fire.

"I'm done," Nate replied.

"Not me," Whitecloud answered.

"I want to sleep tonight," said Carlos.

"Me, too, if I possibly can," echoed Roberto. "If I drink that stuff, my eyes will be popping out of my head."

"Although I'd much prefer a fine cup of tea, I could use another round, Captain, if you don't mind." Reginald Bonesteel lifted his cup in Ezra's direction and Justice filled the cup with steaming brown liquid.

No more words were spoken as each man returned to his own mental images of the day's events. It had been an eventful day, to say the least.

Actually, the past few weeks have been tumultuous, Ezra thought. *What, with Lee's surrender to Grant at Appomattox, then Lincoln's assassination and funeral in Washington, General Johnston's surrender to General Sherman, the end of the war and the release of all the skeletal figures from the prison camps, and then the bloody battle today with O'Banyon being murdered in cold blood.* A chill caused Ezra to shudder as he recalled again Bonesteel's story of how O'Banyon had willingly sacrificed his life to save the rest of them by offering himself as a scapegoat. *What more can happen in such a short period of time?*

Ezra Justice leaned back and looked up at the stars. He wondered what God thought of all the killing that had been done in his name. Both the Yankees and the Rebels had claimed that God was on their side. Did the fact that the Union had won the war mean that God was on the North's side? A lot of Southerners were good, God-fearing people. Was God punishing them for their support of slavery? Or was Lincoln's assassination evidence that God was really rooting for the Rebels after all? Ezra didn't know, and at this point he didn't much care.

Ezra believed in God, in his own sort of way. But he believed, as his mother had taught him, that God helps those who help themselves. Never mind that Nate later informed Ezra that his mother's oft-quoted principle wasn't even in the Bible, that God could more often be found working wonders for people who could do little or nothing to help themselves. And even people of means and reputation had to humble themselves as little children if they ever wanted to find God. It was all too confusing to Justice. He was just a simple man who tried to do what he felt was right.

Sure, he admired Nate's deep-seated, unflappable faith. Nothing shook Nathaniel York's faith in God — not the demeaning institution of slavery, or the injustices or prejudices of other men and women, or the fear of death itself. Nate believed. And Ezra envied Nate's ability to believe.

"You wanna know your problem?" Nate had often chided Ezra.

"Yeah, tell me."

"You got your faith about a foot too high."

"What are you talking about, Nate?"

"You got plenty of head knowledge about

God, Ezra Justice, but real faith comes from the heart. Your faith is twelve inches too high."

Ezra swished the last bit of coffee in his cup. Maybe Nate was right. Maybe his faith was superficial. But if God was so powerful, why hadn't he protected O'Banyon? Justice glanced over at the mound of blankets covering his fellow soldier, not from the elements but from the sensitive noses of any wild animals that might be lurking nearby, scavengers looking for an easy meal while the rest of the men slept. O'Banyon was one of the good guys walking the Earth. Why did he have to die? It didn't make any sense.

Justice got up and stoked the fire with a stick. He hadn't even noticed that one by one the other men had drifted off to find their bedrolls and some semblance of rest. Only Justice and O'Banyon remained near the fire. Ezra knelt next to O'Banyon's body. "Tomorrow we'll get you started on your way home," Ezra said. "But I guess, in a way, you are already there." Ezra rose, looked down at O'Banyon and said, "Sleep well, my friend."

"Make sure you tie him on there securely," Reginald Bonesteel said to Harry White-cloud as he lashed another piece of rope around O'Banyon's body, tying him down to the makeshift stretcher they had made from two tree limbs with a blanket stretched across them. They had attached the stretcher to a large, strong horse, one the Confederates had left behind in the canyon.

"Don't you think Indians know how to tie knots?" Whitecloud asked Bonesteel.

"Well, 'er, . . . I suppose so," Bonesteel said. "I'm just trying to help."

"I know, Reginald," Whitecloud said with a smile. "It's alright. He's gonna do just fine right here. Don't worry. We'll get him to Vicksburg. Maybe we can get him a real casket in town someplace before we put him on the boat."

"I should certainly hope so." Bonesteel attempted to regain a more sophisticated air. "It's rather tacky, traveling through the countryside, dragging a dead body behind us."

Whitecloud nodded. "He'll be fine, Reginald. Honest Injun."

Behind O'Banyon's body the Union soldiers attached several more stretchers to be dragged by large horses. The men on these stretchers were wounded but still alive. Ezra Justice came by to see Lieutenant Christopher. "Are your wounded going to be OK? It looks as though it is going to be a rough ride back there." Ezra pointed to the make-shift stretchers.

"Better than leaving them behind," Lieutenant Christopher replied. "It may be a bit bumpy, and it won't be a luxurious trip; but once we get the wounded men on the boat at Vicksburg, they will be much more comfortable."

"What's your name, soldier?" Ezra leaned over and asked a man on a stretcher.

"Cartwright, sir. Private Edward Cartwright."

Ezra reached out and clasped Cartwright's hand. "Glad to have you along. That was a close call back in that canyon."

"Yes, sir. Had it not been for you and your men, I would be lyin' back there in the dirt."

"How's the leg?" Ezra nodded toward Cartwright's right leg. His pant leg was completely torn off, and his leg was bandaged from his kneecap to the top of his thigh. "I'm pretty sore, where the bullet hit the bone, but I can still hobble a little on the other leg. If we can get some help before too long, I should be good as new in a couple of months."

Ezra nodded but didn't say anything. He knew the reality was that if he couldn't get Private Cartwright to a doctor soon, gangrene was certain to set in and the soldier's leg would have to be amputated anyhow. "Alright, men. Let's head out," he called to Nate and the others who were already mounted. The Union soldiers fell in behind Lieutenant Christopher, as Ezra mounted his horse and rode to the front of his men who were ahead of the decimated Union platoon. They made for an odd assortment of military men — Ezra Justice and his elite corp of soldiers, dragging the dead body of their beloved O'Banyon, and the battered Union soldiers, dragging their wounded friends behind them. Despite the bleakness of their circumstances, though, the men's spirits were up. They were, after all, heading home.

Located about four miles east of Vicksburg along the Big Black River, Camp Fisk was bustling with activity when Ezra and his unusual group of warriors rode through the fort's front gates. Inside the camp surged a sea of men, some of whom had been stationed at the fort near the end of the war and five thousand others who had shown up recently, having been released by the Confederates from prison camps such as Cahaba and Andersonville.

Ezra checked in with the Union officer in charge of transferring the prisoners, Captain

Edmund Gains, a staff member of Major General Napoleon Dana, Commander of the Union troops in Mississippi. It was Gains's job to assign the many men at Camp Fisk to the various steamers heading north.

"Glad to see you, Justice," Gains greeted Ezra warmly. "We've been a bit worried about getting this prisoner transfer completed without a hitch. I'm sure the presence of you and your men will be a great morale booster. You've made quite a name for yourselves over the past year."

"Thank you, Captain," Justice replied. "The privilege is ours. We're just glad to be of help."

"Good. Let me say that we really want to get as many men moving northward as quickly as possible. It's very important to us that these men arrive safely at Jefferson Barracks, Missouri, or Camp Chase in Ohio. It is equally vital that we make sure the men get on steamships only from the line we have chosen. The federal government is paying for this transfer and has contracted the boats. No men are to travel by any other means than what we have assigned. Do you understand that, Justice?"

"Sure. That makes sense to me," Justice replied. *There will be enough security risks with a transfer this big,* Justice thought. *No use taking a chance on using outside boats that we can't depend on.*

Justice was duly concerned about security issues and possible sabotage efforts. What Justice didn't know, however, was that Gains was seeing dollar signs. The U.S. government had agreed to pay the boat owners a fee for each soldier transported, five dollars per enlisted man and ten dollars for every officer. Consequently, it mattered a great deal to Edmund Gains which boats received the majority of the men being transported.

Gains launched into a spiel about how the transfers were to take place. Ezra listened intently, noting the details of the assignment, asking a few questions, but most of all, sizing up Gains as they spoke. A young-looking man in his mid-twenties, Gains's beard and mustache did little to hide his youthful inexperience. His deep-set eyes seemed to shift in ways that caused Ezra to mistrust him for some reason, even though the officer seemed amiable enough. At the end of the briefing, Ezra shook hands with Captain Gains and rejoined his men out in the camp.

"Looks almost like the prison camps these men just came from," Nathaniel York noted, as he and Ezra looked around.

"It sure does. I'm glad these men won't be here long. After all they have suffered, we need to get them home as soon as possible," Ezra replied.

"How long do you expect we'll be here?" Nate asked.

"Only overnight, I expect," Ezra answered. "There are several steamboats heading north tomorrow morning. One just left New Orleans and should be ready to pick us up at the docks in Vicksburg, right along the Mississippi River. Two others are on their way as well. The plan is to return the men to camps in Missouri and Ohio, and from there to muster them out and discharge them honorably from the army."

"How many men will we take along?"

"I don't really know," Justice replied. "As many as we can."

"And what exactly are we supposed to do, Captain? Just babysit the men as we go for a nice boat ride?" asked Bonesteel.

"I wish it were that simple, Reginald. The Rebels have been mighty successful at sabotaging a number of steamboats, especially those with military cargo, setting fire to some, blowing up others with explosive devices. They've destroyed more than a dozen steamers over the last couple of years.

Part of our job is to make sure the prisoner exchange goes well, but the other part is to keep an eye out for anything that looks suspicious."

"Do you think we still have to worry, even though the war has ended?" Carlos asked.

"Much of the South doesn't even know the war is over yet, Carlos. Secretary of War Stanton has put a squelch on a lot of communication lines since President Lincoln was shot. He doesn't want the South to get renewed hope. Beyond that, a lot of Confederates haven't given up yet. I heard that Forrest's cavalry was still fighting over along the Alabama and Tennessee border."

"Yeah, it may be weeks before things settle down there. And then there may still be occasional independent attacks, I guess," Nate said.

Ezra nodded, "And I sure don't need to tell you what long-standing hatred can do to men and women. Some people become so calloused and accustomed to hurting others, they lose all sense of logic; this war has already dulled our senses to the value of human lives. There's no tellin' how low someone might sink if he thinks he can get revenge for the hurt inflicted on him or his family or even his nation. Hopefully, the prisoner transfer will go smoothly, but we'll have to keep our eyes open. Something about that Captain Gains fellow makes me a little nervous."

9

A single lantern lit the stark back room, the flickering flame casting eerie shadows on the faces of the two figures seated on either side of a small table supporting several bottles of stolen whiskey. "Justice doesn't have a prayer of an idea what's going on," Edmund Gains said and poured another drink.

"Are you sure, Captain?"

"Why, Mr. Coxley, I am absolutely positive of it. I was quite emphatic with him that we want no soldiers being transported by any other steamers but yours. You, Mr. Coxley, are going to be a wealthy man."

"As are you, Captain Gains," said Jacob Coxley, part owner and captain of the *Sultana,* one of three steamboats owned by the "Merchant and People's" line, a loose organization of independently operated boats plying the Mississippi River. Coxley raised his glass, silently toasting their success, and downed the shot of whiskey in one gulp. Gains quickly poured him another drink.

Coxley had not awakened Gains in the middle of the night to pay a social call. Quite the contrary, the swarthy riverboat captain came to press his case. He wanted to receive more of the released prisoners of war being sent north aboard various steamboats. Coxley's boat, the *Sultana,* was originally licensed to carry 376 passengers, but of course, the strains of war had long since set aside those limitations. It was not uncommon during the early months of 1865 for a steamer to carry five hundred to a thousand soldiers when necessary.

The *Sultana,* however, had set out from New Orleans that morning carrying an odd assortment of 250 passengers including twelve nuns from the Sisters of Charity, the Chicago Opera Troupe, the boat's crew, as well as more than seventy horses in the hold below the main decks, along with several mules and donkeys, and a load of hogs going to market. Perhaps the most unusual "passenger" aboard the *Sultana* was a twelve-foot-long alligator that the crew kept as their mascot. "Chops," as the gator was affectionately nicknamed by a one-armed crew member, was housed in a large crate with bars on the top.

Captain Coxley was not content with a partially loaded boat when the opportunity for a far greater number of eager "paying" passengers was so readily available. Moreover, Coxley needed the money — his own financial affairs were floundering — and he was willing to do whatever necessary to increase the profitability of his boat, even if that meant paying off a few officers to get more than his share of the human cargo being doled out by the Union army. Rumors flew around the Vicksburg wharf that Captain Gains or his superior officers were being offered kickbacks between fifty cents to a dollar for every man that could be supplied to the various steamboat captains. Coxley was more than glad to pay the going price. At five dollars per enlisted man and ten dollars per officer, even minus the "pecuniary consideration" for Gains or his bosses, Coxley could still make a good profit, assuming that he could get enough of the released prisoners on board.

Coxley's boat possessed a storied past. Three previous boats had carried the same name, *Sultana,* and all three had perished on the river, two by horrific fires. Powered by steam heated in roaring boilers fed by thousands of pounds of coal, fire was a constant problem aboard the side-wheelers traveling the Mississippi. With the Confederates refining the art of strategically placed explosives, the threat increased even more during the war. But Coxley wasn't the superstitious sort. For all his weaknesses, he was a competent captain who had traversed the Mississippi so many times that few obstacles, storms, or setbacks caused him great concern anymore.

That very morning he'd had a run in with his chief engineer, Nathan Kendricks, concerning a leak in one of the *Sultana's* boilers. Kendricks was a bit eccentric, a fuss-button of a fellow but an excellent engineer. He knew what it took to operate a steamboat safely, and, ordinarily, he refused to compromise, not even for his boss. But these were not ordinary times.

When Kendricks discovered steam escaping from a small crack in one of the *Sultana's* middle boilers, he nearly had a conniption. "We need to dock immediately," he told Coxley.

"Nathan, you know we can't do that," Coxley replied. "We're at least ten hours from Vicksburg, and we have to get there tonight to be ready to take on the soldiers who are coming from Camp Fisk tomorrow."

"We'll never make it," Kendricks said straightforwardly. "That boiler could blow at any minute. We have to repair it, or we will risk the entire boat catching fire."

"Oh, Nathan, calm down," Coxley said. "We'll be fine. I'll take it slow going upriver, but we've got to keep moving. The spring thaw up north is already swelling the river, making it more difficult than usual to navigate. If we don't go today, we might not get there in time. It would be awful if we disappointed those poor soldiers by not showing up tomorrow."

"It would be a lot worse if we showed up on time and that boiler blew 'em to kingdom come!"

"Nathan, take it easy, will you?" Coxley said with a laugh. "You always tend to see the worst in things. I'll make you a deal." Coxley threw his arm around the obsessive engineer's shoulder. "You keep an eye on that boiler until we get to Vicksburg, and then we'll do whatever it takes to fix it. Once the soldiers are on board, the men won't mind a brief delay. Some of them have been in prison camps for several years; a few hours won't make much difference to them. Just get me to Vicksburg, then we'll deal with that boiler."

Kendricks eyed Coxley like a cat watching

a fox. "Aye, aye, sir," he said reluctantly. "But I tell you as sure as I'm living, I refuse to go any further than Vicksburg unless we make the necessary repairs to that boiler. It's just not safe."

"I know; I understand, Nathan," Coxley said, patting the engineer on the back. "We'll do whatever we have to do in Vicksburg. Come with me. Let's have a drink."

True to his word, Captain Coxley traversed the swollen Mississippi at a much slower speed than normal, avoiding the need for any more pressure than necessary on the already overworked boilers. The *Sultana* docked in Vicksburg at about 8:45 p.m. the evening of April 23.

As soon as the boat was tied up safely, Nathan Kendricks went ashore to find the best boilermaker in town, Otis Barton. Meanwhile, Coxley sought out Edmund Gains.

Gains was perplexed at first when Coxley had shown up at his door late at night. "I can't give you any men tomorrow, Captain Coxley," Gains admitted after a few drinks. "I don't have the rolls ready yet. At best I have the names of only three hundred soldiers recorded. We're supposed to keep a list of every soldier who is being transported, and we just shipped out more than thirteen hundred today aboard the *Henry Ames.* And then the *Olive Branch* took another seven hundred men tonight."

"The *Olive Branch?* That's one of our competitors' boats!" Coxley huffed angrily. "Those men should have been on my boat. What kind of game are you playing here, Mr. Gains?"

"Calm down. Don't get your shorts in a bunch," Gains waved his hand in the air. "I didn't know about it either. Somebody pulled rank on me. But don't worry; we'll get you some more men, lots of them. I have several trainloads at Camp Fisk, just waiting to get on a boat going north, any boat. I'll take care of you, Mr. Coxley. And of course, I know you will be glad to take care of me, now won't you?"

Coxley looked at the young Union officer and wanted to kill him. Instead, he replied with a nod and a raised drink. "Of course, Captain Gains. You will be well taken care of for your extra consideration of my concerns."

"I thank you, Captain Coxley. I'm sure you are aware of what a great interest the army has in expediting the departure of these brave fellows to their homes."

"Oh, yes. I've heard. Colonel Stanley met me on the dock and informed me of that fact as soon as I had moored this evening."

"Good. Then I will see to it that first thing tomorrow morning the trains will transfer a goodly number of men to your boat — what was the name again? Oh, yes? The *Sultana*. How could I forget such a regal sounding vessel?"

Coxley put his glass down harder than necessary on the table. "Farewell, Captain Gains. The *Sultana* will be ready to depart tomorrow morning." He stepped out of Gains's dark inner sanctum into the cool night air, grateful for its sobering effect.

Getting the *Sultana* ready for departure was not as simple a matter as Captain Coxley implied. In Nathan Kendricks's mind, the steamboat was far from ready to fight the swift-flowing, flooded Mississippi River. That's why even though it was already nearing 9:30 p.m., the engineer dared to knock on the door of Otis Barton, the best boiler-maker known to anyone on the Vicksburg wharf.

"What do ya want?" Barton groused without a word of introduction when he opened the door to his living quarters, located behind his metalworking shop. Barefooted, and bare-chested except for the straps to his bib overalls, Barton had been interrupted at night far too many times to think that anyone wanted him for any other reason than to work on a boiler. Consequently, he dispensed few pleasantries with his potential customers.

"Good evening, Mr. Barton. I'm Nathan Kendricks, chief engineer aboard the steamship *Sultana*. We set out from New Orleans this morning, and we're docked here in Vicksburg. We have a boiler that's giving out, and we don't dare go any farther until we get it repaired."

"So you had to get me out of bed?"

"I'm sorry, but we are scheduled to leave first thing in the morning with a full load of passengers, livestock, and former prisoners. I'm sure you understand the pressures these days to keep the steamers moving. And my boss, Captain Jacob Coxley, will, no doubt, insist that we continue on upriver, even if we cannot repair the boiler. That, as you know, would be extremely dangerous. Sir, I beg your help. I have cash or gold, whichever you prefer."

"Fools," Barton spat out. "These steamboat captains are all losing their minds over money. What good is the money if your boat is on the bottom of the river or floating in pieces out to the Gulf of Mexico?"

"I agree," said Nathan. "Does that mean

you'll help me?"

Barton glared at Kendricks and scowled. He knew he couldn't leave a fellow boiler man in the lurch. But he didn't want to give the impression that he was happy about it either. "Will you make it worth my while if I leave my wife and children tonight to come help you with your boiler?"

"Guaranteed."

"Alright. Stay right there till I put on some work clothes."

Kendricks stood outside Barton's door-way, anxiously pacing back and forth while he waited for the boilermaker. About three minutes later the door opened, and Barton appeared again wearing the same bib over-alls with the addition of an undershirt and shoes. Without a word Barton headed straight to the wharf, causing Kendricks to have to hurry to keep pace with him. They boarded the *Sultana*, and Kendricks directed the boilermaker to the problem area, still hot from the day's journey.

Barton put on a pair of heavy gloves to avoid burning his hands and then ran his fingers over the entire boiler. In the middle section, he stopped abruptly, his hands on a two-foot-wide bulge in the boiler's wall. Barton glared again at Kendricks. "Where'd you say you embarked from?"

"We left New Orleans early this morning," the engineer replied.

"And you didn't notice *this?*" Barton pointed to the protrusion in the metal. "Why didn't you do something with it before you left N'awlins?"

"We weren't leaking then."

About that time, Captain Coxley came around the corner to the middle boiler, and Kendricks introduced Barton. Coxley quickly focused on the bulge. "Can you fix it?" Coxley asked.

"Looks to me like you're gonna have to replace at least two of these large safety sheets of metal," Barton said. "That's the only way to do the job right."

"Can't you just do something that will see us through until we get to St. Louis, Mr. Barton?" Coxley implored. "I'll make it worth your while."

Barton shook his head. "Naaw, if you don't want me to do the job the way I see fit, I don't want nuttin' to do with this mess. You got a real problem, here, Captain." He nodded to Kendricks, "And you know exactly what I'm talking about."

"How long do you think it would take to fix it right, Mr. Barton?" Kendricks asked.

"A couple of days, maybe more."

"Out of the question!" Coxley boomed.

"We must find a way to be on the river tomorrow morning."

"Suit yourself," Barton said flatly. "You boys have a nice night." He picked up his tools and walked off the steamer with Kendricks dogging him all the way to the street, begging him to come back.

"Please," Kendricks begged. "Just do the best you can under the circumstances."

"I don't want nothing to do with that steamer, Kendricks. And you should know better even to ask. Besides that bulge, those boilers look to me as though they are all burned out. How long have you been running with an insufficient supply of water in those boilers?"

"Look, I know the boiler needs to be repaired more thoroughly, but if you can just help us to get to St. Louis. That's the captain's hometown. He has connections there, and he can get the work done much more efficiently."

"Do you mean to say much less expensively?"

"Yes, that too, but I know he will pay you well if you can pull us out of this jam. If you don't, his entire business may go down."

"And if I do, his entire boat may go down."

"You can do it, Mr. Barton. You're the

best. You can do something to keep that boiler working till we get upriver. For the sake of a fellow river rat like me, for the sake of those poor fellows who lived those long months in those prisons, please help us get that load to St. Louis."

Barton's expression softened. "And you're sure the captain will rectify the problem once you get home?"

"I'm certain of it. Our lives are at stake on board that boat, as well as the passengers. Coxley's a good captain. He doesn't want to have a problem during a trip. But you know how this war has cost all of us. He's been strapped for cash, trying to make a go of it and keep the business afloat till things get better. There's not been much excess money to use for routine repairs."

"Fixin' that boiler ain't exactly routine repairs."

"I know, Mr. Barton. That's why we need your help. Please, sir."

"Oh, alright. But only on the condition that you pull that boiler outta there before you come back to Vicksburg again."

"You have my word on it."

"Enough babblin', Kendricks. Let's go."

Jacob Coxley nearly ran down the loading ramp and hugged Otis Barton when he saw him walking back toward the *Sultana's* deck, carrying his tools. Nathan Kendricks followed closely behind, almost as if he were afraid Barton might change his mind. And once Barton began working on the boiler, he almost did renege, especially when he realized what Captain Coxley wanted him to do.

"We don't have time to replace the two entire sheets of metal," lamented Coxley. "Let's confine your work to that area where the bulge is the worst. If you can simply patch that area, I assure you we will have the remainder of the work done immediately upon our arrival in St. Louis."

"Let me get this right. You want me to patch that twenty-six-inch-by-eleven-inch section right there," Barton said, pointing to the largest portion of the bulge.

"Yes, that's right."

"Alright. But first we need to shut down the boilers completely so we can force that part of the boiler wall back into position before we put a patch over it."

"No, no, no!" Coxley cried. "We won't have time to do that. Just put a patch over it. I promise you, we will make the repairs according to your fullest recommendations upon our completion of this trip."

Barton looked hard at Kendricks. "And

you promise, as well."

"Absolutely, Mr. Barton. As I said earlier, we're also on this boat. We'll not take undue risks with our own lives."

"I will do as you ask, Captain, but I must warn you, in all my twenty-eight years of experience with boilers, I've not seen a situation with which I feel less comfortable. I hope you men are in a right relationship with God."

"Why is that?" Kendricks asked with a laugh.

"Because you might be meeting him sooner than you think."

"You just patch the boiler, Mr. Barton," Coxley said dismissively. "We'll worry about meeting God when the time comes."

Barton went to work patching the boiler at the place where the protrusion seemed the most pronounced and the metal the weakest. Even fitting the patch directly over the bulge without replacing the sheets of metal was a meticulous task; Barton worked throughout the night and into the next day to get the job done. A perfectionist in his craft, he was far from satisfied with the work, but it was the best he could do. As he wearily walked off the boat, he had a bulge of dollar bills in his pants pocket and a lump in his throat.

10

Ezra Justice felt a nervous excitement as he shaved that morning. He glanced at a calendar; it was April 24, 1865. In many ways this was going to be a great day. Hundreds of soldiers were going to begin their journeys home. Some of those boys hadn't seen their wives or children in more than three years. Ezra finished shaving, threw some water on his face, and shook Carlos Hawkins, who was sleeping on the floor. "Your turn, Carlos," Ezra said with a laugh to the smooth-faced Carlos.

"Ha! Maybe when he grows up, he'll be able to grow a beard," Bonesteel quipped.

"Hey, watch it, there paleface," Harry Whitecloud jumped in. "Some of us have hair on our heads so we don't need any on our faces."

"That's right," Roberto crowed. "You guys who can't grow hair on your heads have to let it come out your nose and ears!"

Ezra smiled at the lighthearted banter between his men. The boys were obviously in a good mood this morning. Making matters even better, while they had waited yesterday for Captain Gains to assemble his list of men to be transported, Big Nate and Bonesteel had wrangled some solid pine planks from which they were able to make a strong coffin for O'Banyon's body. Something about placing their friend in the makeshift casket relieved the sense of uneasiness they'd had in dragging their comrade the many miles to Vicksburg.

Captain Edmund Gains arrived at Camp Fisk early on the morning of April 24 to help manage the prisoner exchange. Gains had already decided that rather than assigning a mere four hundred men to Captain Coxley, it would be good to conclude the matter by shipping all the remaining men at Camp Fisk aboard the *Sultana.*

"We have about thirteen to fourteen hundred men remaining at the camp," Gains had informed Captain Jacob Coxley before leaving for Camp Fisk. "They are all yours," he added with a feigned grin. "Do you think you can handle that many?"

For his part, Captain Coxley was thrilled to learn of Gains's new plan. After all, the *Henry Ames,* the steamboat that had taken thirteen hundred men from Camp Fisk just a day or so earlier, was no better suited to handle such a large number of men than was the *Sultana.* "It may be a bit crowded," Coxley replied, "but I'm sure we'll manage just fine. And sir, thank you, and my compliments to your friends."

"Glad to be of service, Captain Coxley. Colonel Stanley will be paying you when he arrives on the *Sultana.*" Gains nodded toward Coxley, and Coxley fully understood the implications of the officer's comment.

Ezra Justice and his men were waiting at the railroad tracks when Gains arrived at Camp Fisk. Gains energetically set about directing the operation of loading the prisoners onto the trains next to Camp Fisk to make the short trip to Vicksburg four miles away. Grouped according to their native states, the men shuffled onto the boxcars. Many of the men shouted praises to God as they hobbled onto the crowded train. "Hallelujah!" one man shouted.

"Glory, hallelujah!" another man corrected him.

Some men wept openly at the prospect of finally going home, while others shouted the battle cries of their home states.

Captain Gains was doing a good deal of shouting as well. He wanted to get as many men into Vicksburg and aboard the *Sultana* as quickly as possible. "Let's get more men over here in this car," he called again and again, waving his arms frantically trying to direct the sea of humanity moving toward the train.

"That's a lot of men getting on board those train cars, Nate," Ezra said as the two men sat on their horses observing the loading process.

"It sure is," Nate replied. "Too many, if you ask me. Looks a lot like a slave train."

Ezra nodded. "It's a good thing they aren't going too far, but I sure hate to see some of those weak fellows squeezed into such tight quarters."

As the morning wore on and the disheveled as well as the disabled former prisoners made their way onto the train, Gains became increasingly impatient. "Can't we hurry it up back there, Private?" he cajoled one of the eighteen young men whom he had assigned to travel with the prisoners to St. Louis.

"The men are moving as rapidly as they can, Captain," the private replied. "We've already lost a number of men from exhaustion. They don't have a great reservoir of energy, I'm afraid. It doesn't take much to tire them out."

"Alright. Well, any man who falls down or can't make it onto this train can wait for the next," Gains instructed. "I want these men on their way."

"Yes, sir," the private responded.

"Captain Gains, the train is full," another private called from the step of a caboose crammed with men who looked as though they'd been packed into the car with a crow bar.

"Good," Gains replied. "I have another two hundred men from Vermont that need to get on this train yet. Let's make some room."

"Sir, in all respect," the young man protested, "I don't think the train can safely carry another two hundred men. The cars are swaying badly already."

"It's a relatively flat ride between here and town, soldier," Gains replied. "Load the two hundred from Vermont."

About ten in the morning, another steamer, the *Lady Gay,* arrived at Vicksburg. The boat had a passenger capacity larger than the *Sultana* and could easily have taken hundreds of the prisoners from Camp Fisk, relieving some of the burden off the sister boat. Reuben Hatch telegraphed Edmund Gains at the camp with a request to that effect.

Gains sent back a terse wire stating: "All the men can be put on one boat — the *Sultana.*"

Around noon the *Lady Gay* pulled out of Vicksburg and continued its journey up the Mississippi. The steamer was not carrying a single former prisoner of war. A few minutes later, the first trainload of men from Camp Fisk arrived in Vicksburg.

Back at the camp a second trainload of prisoners was already being loaded. While Gains focused on loading the Union prisoners into the train cars, Ezra Justice and his men kept a sharp lookout for anything that might disrupt the freeing of the soldiers. When the second train was nearly full, there still remained an enormous number of frail men at the camp.

"Are you sure all these men are going to be able to travel aboard one boat?" Justice inquired of Gains during a lull in the loading process.

"No question about it, Captain. Don't give it a thought."

"Alright," Justice replied somewhat reluctantly. "My men and I are going to ride on in to town to keep an eye on the loading process there. If anything comes up here, send a message right away, and we'll get back here as fast as we can."

"No problem, Captain Justice," Gains replied. "Everything is going precisely as planned."

The second trainload of prisoners arrived in Vicksburg with Colonel Lyle Stanley in command. Colonel Stanley had collected Captain Coxley's money from the paymaster for transporting the soldiers, so as the prisoners boarded the *Sultana*, Stanley sought out Coxley aboard the steamer. Stanley impatiently pushed his way through the crowd to Captain Coxley's stateroom.

He knocked on the door. "Coxley!"

Captain Coxley opened the door and invited Stanley to enter.

"Close the door," Coxley said nervously.

Colonel Stanley didn't move from the doorway as he reached into his satchel and pulled out a package. He handed the package to Coxley. "We're expecting fourteen hundred passengers, give or take a few. Here's your fifty-four hundred dollars, Captain Coxley, minus, of course, my fourteen hundred and Captain Gains's seven hundred."

"It's been a very profitable day for both of us," Coxley said.

Shortly after the second trainload of prisoners began boarding the *Sultana,* Ezra Justice and his men reached the wharf by horse-back. Justice and Nathaniel York showed the men's federal passage forms to the quarter-master who had lost track of how many soldiers were getting onto the boat. The Hawkins twins led the squads' horses up the gangplank and down into the boat's hold, already crowded with horses, mules, pigs, and other livestock.

As Ezra and Nate approached the ramp leading to the main deck of the boat, once again, the enormous number of men being led onto the *Sultana* caused concern to stir in Ezra. Line after line of soldiers filed aboard the vessel built to accommodate less than four hundred. Once on board the men continued their rejoicing. Justice, however, wasn't so enthusiastic. Ezra shook his head. "I don't know, Nate. This doesn't look good. There's hardly going to be enough room on this boat for these men to stand up, let alone eat, sit down, or sleep."

"I know what you mean, Captain," Nate said with concern. "And the line of men is still coming."

"If this boat should have a problem while all these men are on board, we could have a serious situation here," said Ezra. "Half of them can barely walk; many of them are frail and emaciated and would drown in a few minutes if anything happened to the boat and they had to swim for their lives — especially with the river running so swiftly — and most of them would be consumed alive if we ever had a fire on board. This boat is an accident waiting to happen."

Ezra felt compelled to do something. "Hold up there, soldiers," he called to the men behind him. "Hang on a minute till we see what's going on around here. This boat is already overloaded, and there are hundreds of other men behind you waiting to get on. Let me see if we can secure passage aboard another boat. It will be much safer for you."

Just then a uniformed officer wearing large yellow stripes on his shoulders stormed up to Justice. "What in the world are you doing there, soldier? Who do you think you are?" He pushed his hot, red face and sweaty brow right in front of Justice's nose. "What is your name, soldier?"

"I'm Captain Ezra Justice, sir, and I'm just trying to make sure we treat these men right. They have served their country nobly and have suffered for it, and it's a shame the way they're being packed onto this boat. It's worse than some of the slave boats. There are too many men on board for their own good."

"Well, I'm Colonel Stanley, and I'll tell *you* what is good for the men." The colonel motioned to the privates down on the dock. "Keep the line moving, men!" The line of men surged forward again. Stanley turned back to Justice and growled, "This is my jurisdiction, Justice, so stay on board and shut up, or get off the boat. I don't really care one way or the other. I know you and your boys have some sort of hotshot clearance from Sherman, but that doesn't mean a thing to me other than I have to put up with you. If I need your help, I'll ask for it. But until then, don't go giving orders around here."

"Yes, sir." Justice offered a halfhearted salute. He and Big Nate watched Stanley whirl around and rush off in a huff.

"I do not like that man," Nate said. "How did you keep from decking him, Ezra?"

"He outranks us, Nathaniel. You gotta respect the rank, even when you can't respect the man."

"You're a better man than I am, Ezra."

"No, I'm not, Nate, but nobody wins if we sink to his level."

On the other side of the boat, Harry Whitecloud and Reginald Bonesteel were encountering a different sort of delay. They had lugged O'Banyon's coffin up the gangplank and were about to go aboard the *Sultana* when one of the steamboat's junior officers shouted, "Halt! Stop right there. No dead bodies are allowed aboard this boat."

Whitecloud didn't say a word. He simply put the casket down on the deck, pulled his sawed-off shotgun out from his side holster and aimed it at the crewman.

"As I was saying, sir," the crewman stammered, "just bring that box right down here." He motioned toward the back of the boat. "We'll make some room next to the other large boxes we are carrying."

Whitecloud replaced the shotgun in its holster and picked up his end of the coffin again. He and Bonesteel stepped on board, carrying O'Banyon with them.

"Quite tactful, Mr. Whitecloud," Bonesteel deadpanned. "Impressive. Well done."

Harry Whitecloud came close to smiling but didn't. "Not impressive, Bonesteel. Rather convincing, wouldn't you say?"

Reginald Bonesteel raised an eyebrow and laughed out loud. "There might be hope for you yet, Injun!"

Not even the *Sultana*'s captain knew the true number of passengers on board the steamboat that day. When Ezra Justice met Captain Jacob Coxley shortly after midday, Ezra asked the captain straightforwardly, "Captain Coxley, how many passengers does your boat usually carry?"

Coxley was characteristically upbeat. "Well, sir, in peacetime, we usually run about three or four hundred passengers; but lately in these past few months of the war, we've been carrying far more."

"How many people are on board today?" Ezra probed.

Coxley was almost boastful in his answer. "Right now we have about one thousand people on board, counting men, women, a few children, even a few babies. And we are expecting about four hundred more soldiers before we start upriver."

"Is there no danger in carrying that many passengers?" Justice asked.

"Oh, my, no. We've carried that many people a number of times before."

"Will there be enough room for every-body?"

"Truthfully, it will be a bit tight if pas-sengers congregate on the deck areas or in the aisles; but because many of the soldiers are not carrying gear, they won't take up quite as much room as would other military passengers."

About three that afternoon, the *Pauline Carroll,* a steamboat from a competing line, docked at Vicksburg on its way upriver. "Hey, look at that boat," Carlos Hawkins called to his brother as he leaned over the *Sultana's* hurricane deck, an upper deck holding a group of small cabins usually used for officers. "It hardly has anyone on it. Why doesn't the army take some of the men off this boat and put them on that one?"

"Because the government has already contracted with this line," Roberto replied. "At least that's what Captain Gains told Captain Justice. I guess it comes down to money."

"But that boat is practically empty!" Carlos pointed out.

"I don't think that matters," Roberto replied more correctly than he knew. A few hours later, while men continued to chock onto the already clogged decks of the *Sultana,* the *Pauline Carroll* backed away from the wharf at Vicksburg and headed upriver with only seventeen passengers on board.

It was late that afternoon when the third train packed with prisoners pulled into the station at Vicksburg. Back at Camp Fisk, Edmund Gains sighed in relief. Finally, he had cleared the camp of all thirteen hundred or more parolees. Little did Gains know or care, but because he had not taken the time to count the number of men boarding the trains and ultimately boarding the *Sultana,* the actual number of prisoners joining the more than one hundred paying passengers, eighty-five crewmembers, and twenty-one military guards already aboard the steamboat was not in fact fourteen hundred but closer to twenty-two hundred!

Ezra Justice and Nathaniel York continued to circulate among the men on board the boat, watching for anything that might look suspiciously like an explosive. The boat was so packed with soldiers, it was hard to search any concealed space since nearly any open spot was soon occupied. Men were everywhere, trying to find something to hold onto, a place to sit down, or, in the case of the sickly, a place to lie down. On the boiler deck, the deck that held the more affluent passengers' staterooms, the ship's bar, and the main dining cabin, men filled in every open spot, with many leaning their backs against the warm boilers themselves.

Just below the hurricane deck, Justice and York met Anna Harvey, an attractive young mother carrying a baby in her arms. "Good afternoon, ma'am," Ezra said, tipping his hat slightly toward the woman. "Afternoon, ma'am," said Nathaniel.

"Good day, gentlemen," Anna replied cheerily, but then her tone turned more somber. "Have you officers noticed that deck up there, above us?" she asked as she pointed toward the hurricane deck. "It looks to me as though it is beginning to sag in the middle since all the former prisoners have started loading onto the boat. Do you see what I mean?"

"I believe I do, ma'am," Ezra said, staring at the bowing floorboards above them. "I think I better have a word with the captain. Thank you for pointing out the problem."

"Thank you, kind sir. My husband, William, and I booked passage aboard this steamer because we thought it would be safer than traveling with our baby by train. Now I'm not so certain."

"Nor am I, ma'am," Ezra replied. "If I were you, I would consider boarding another steamer."

"I'll talk to my husband about that," Anna said as she headed toward her stateroom.

When Justice found Coxley and drew his attention to the sagging deck, Coxley appeared unconcerned. "Oh, yes, it does that sometimes. It's nothing to worry about. But to prevent any accidents, I'll order that no more men be placed on the upper deck.

Thank you, Captain Justice, for your concern."

Safety wasn't the only concern on the *Sultana.* Many of the men aboard the boat had just been released from Andersonville and Cahaba and hadn't eaten a good meal in months. Hundreds of them who had entered the prison camps as strong, strapping men were now skeletal figures weighing between eighty and ninety pounds. There was the real danger of them dying of malnutrition and disease before the steamer ever reached Missouri. Although meals on board were limited to the first-class paying passengers, the ironic danger existed of someone being too compassionate and trying to give the frail, starving soldiers too much food too soon, causing their bodies to go into convulsions.

Nevertheless, compassion ruled the day. At about six o'clock in the evening, Roberto Hawkins sat down on a box and pulled some corn bread out of his knapsack to eat. Just as he was about to take a bite, he caught a glimpse of an emaciated, elderly looking man huddled over in the corner of the deck. Roberto froze in midair. He got up from the box, climbed over several soldiers sitting on the floor of the deck, and knelt down next to the older man. "How ya doin', old-timer?" Roberto asked.

"I'm going home," the man replied hoarsely.

"Yeah, I know," Roberto said. "But you better eat something or you ain't gonna make it. You need to keep up your strength. Your family's probably been waitin' on you a long time. You don't want to die on them now."

"Don't have nuthin'," the man said as he rocked back and forth sleepily.

"I know," Roberto continued, "but I do. Here, my friend." He placed the bread in the old man's hand. "It isn't much, but it will fill one of those spots in your belly."

The elderly Union soldier looked up at Roberto and whispered, "Thank you!" He picked at the bread, pinching off one morsel at a time, eating it slowly and looking up at Roberto's face as if he was worried that Roberto might disappear.

Carlos Hawkins had been watching his brother giving his food to the old soldier. When Roberto came over to him, Carlos said, "That was a good thing you just did there, brother. That dear man wouldn't even take his eyes off you. He was watching you as though you were an angel."

"Well, that's the first time I've ever been accused of that!" Roberto tried to make light of his act of kindness. "Truth is, Carlos, we're surrounded by a lot of hurting soldiers on this boat. If we can do anything at all to ease their suffering, I want to try to do it."

"I'm with ya, brother," Carlos said. "I have a few things in my knapsack that some of the guys might be able to digest. Let's see if we can distribute them without causing a riot." The Hawkins twins moved carefully about the deck, sharing their food with some of the starving men, doling out tiny portions to as many of the sickly as possible, searching for every crumb until both their knapsacks were completely empty. Neither Roberto nor Carlos ate a bite, yet strangely they never felt more full.

11

The *Sultana* finally pushed back from the wharf in Vicksburg at about 9:00 p.m. on April 24. Nobody knew for sure the exact number of released prisoners that had made it on board. Edmund Gains knew that he was seven hundred dollars richer and Captain Jacob Coxley only knew that his boat was covered down with humanity every direction he turned. It was almost impossible to walk on any of the *Sultana's* decks without bumping into people or having to turn sideways to get through the crowd. Coxley had decided to recount the number once he got to St. Louis.

Except for the civilian passengers who had paid hard-earned money for passage aboard the boat and were now as cramped as the soldiers, the passengers' spirits remained high. Men talked of the homes they'd left behind and to which they were now returning. Some spoke of wives or girlfriends they couldn't wait to see. Others wondered what their children looked like since they hadn't seen them for several years. Most talked about the simple things: how much they anticipated a good, home-cooked meal, taking a bath, and sleeping in a bed. One young soldier spoke for many when he told Reginald Bonesteel, "All I know is that I am mighty fortunate to have survived the horrors of this war, and the hell of the death camps, and now to be heading home. I can't wait to sit down to a good meal with my family. Every day will be a day for which I give thanks."

As the boat churned into the night, moving slowly northward up the Mississippi River, the air grew cooler. It had rained heavily earlier in the evening, and the temperature dropped dramatically following the downpour. To avoid the chill, many men huddled together on the open-air decks; others simply tried to sleep on the cold decks without a pillow or a blanket. They were used to the bedding at Cahaba; they could handle the cold, wet decks of the *Sultana* for a day or two.

Nathaniel York and Reginald Bonesteel sat atop Shaun O'Banyon's coffin, partially so they could make sure that nothing happened to it and partially because that was the only place left for them to sit. Several Union soldiers sat on the floor, leaning up against the boxes and O'Banyon's coffin. With little else to do, late-night conversation flowed freely.

"What's the deal with the guy in the box?" one of the soldiers asked. "He must be pretty important for you to lug his body all the way to Missouri."

Nathaniel York laughed. "No, he was not important in the eyes of the world. Just to us. His name was Shaun O'Banyon, and he was a real character, wouldn't you say, Reginald?"

"He was a character alright," Bonesteel said with a grin. "He was always chiding me with something about how beautiful the hills of his native Ireland were and how the Irish deserved to be free from Great Britain. He sure knew how to get under my skin at times. But I genuinely enjoyed having him around."

"How'd he die?" one of the skeletal figures listening in on the conversation asked.

"I still can hardly believe that," Bonesteel said. Taking a deep breath and exhaling slowly, he leaned his head back against a box above the coffin before speaking. "He willingly put himself in a position to be killed in cold blood, just so he could save us. Captain Justice and our guys were trapped between a Rebel cavalry unit and a part of a Rebel infantry regiment. That's when O'Banyon became a sacrifice for us. By willingly offering his life to be killed by the enemy, he bought our freedom by giving us time to get out of the jam."

Several of the Union soldiers listening to Bonesteel telling the story nodded in understanding. Bonesteel went on, "One of his dying requests was that we take him home to his wife, Lizzie, for burial."

"So that's why Captain Justice feels obligated to carry his coffin to Missouri?"

"Yes, Captain Justice loved O'Banyon like a son. We all did, really. I even liked him a little myself."

"My, what kind of commander loves his men like that?" one of the prisoners said, shaking his head in amazement.

"I don't know," Bonesteel admitted, "but that's just the sort of man Ezra Justice is. Nate, there, has known him a lot longer than I have. How would you describe him, Nate?" Bonesteel looked over at Nathaniel York, who was nodding affirmatively.

"Ezra Justice is a good man. He's a meek, gentle man; but don't let that calm demeanor fool you. He's a tough guy, a strong, fearless leader who is willing to lay his life on the line every day." Nate spoke slowly, as though he were looking at a picture of Justice in his mind. "He expects the best from himself and from the men he works with. He seems to have an internal compass in his heart, pointing him to the right things. Not that he never makes a mistake; but when he does, he's quick to admit it and vows never to make that same mistake again. And Ezra Justice takes loyalty seriously," Nate said. "If you're a man of integrity and good moral character, there's nothing he won't do for you."

"How long have you served with him?" one of the soldiers asked Nate.

"I've known him almost my entire life," Nate replied. "We grew up together on a plantation that his parents owned. I was part of their property, but Ezra never saw me that way. He treated me like an equal. It didn't matter that I was black and he was white; as far as he was concerned, we were brothers. It cost him dearly with his family, too."

"Why? Did they mistreat darkies?"

"No, not that I know of. But they couldn't understand how the son of a Southern plantation owner could be opposed to slavery. To them it was just a fact of life. It was a part of business, a cultural thing. But to Ezra slavery was an abomination. When the war started, most of Ezra's family and relatives sided with the Confederacy, of course, but not Ezra. He left the plantation and went off and joined the Union Army. His family was appalled, angry, and embarrassed. But Ezra did what he felt was right in his own heart."

"How'd you get hooked up with Ezra Justice in this war?" one man wanted to know.

"Early in the war the Yankees swept through Nashville and other parts of Tennessee; and suddenly, for the first time in my life, I was free. I guess I could have gone anywhere; but when I thought of Ezra and all he'd given up for me, I said, 'I've got to get into this fight and try to help other men get free.' So I joined the Colored Regiment headquartered not far from the plantation. That's where Ezra found me last year."

As Nate was telling his story, a heartrending wail pierced the air. The men's attention turned to the source of the sound, a man in a tattered uniform, lying on the deck. He looked to be in his mid-forties, although it was difficult to tell the soldier's age because his body was so gaunt and his skin so sallow. "Oh, God, help me!" the man cried out, obviously in pain.

Nate and several of the men, including Bonesteel and Harry Whitecloud, gathered around the dying man. A throng of men crowded in behind them.

"What can we do, soldier?" Bonesteel asked.

Harry Whitecloud shook his head so Bonesteel could see, as if to say, "There's nothing much we can do to save this man."

"I'm dying . . ." the man said weakly, "and I've never been afraid of anything in all my life, but I'm scared now."

Nathaniel York pressed closer to the man and put his hand on the man's shoulder. "It's alright, my friend. We're here with you."

"No. No, it's not alright," he gasped. "I've done horrible things. I've been a thief. I've robbed people; I've cheated on my wife; I've even murdered a few people. Now I'm dying, and I know it's too late to make anything good of my life."

"It's never too late to start doing the right thing," Nate said kindly.

"It is for me. I'm about to meet God," the soldier said, wheezing, "and there's no reason why he'd let me into heaven. I deserve to go to hell."

"So do the rest of us, friend. Besides, you don't get into heaven by being a good person or doing good deeds. You get into heaven by trusting in Jesus. Did you ever go to church in your life?"

"Yeah, a couple of times."

"And did you ever hear that God loved you so much that he sent Jesus to die on the cross to pay the price for your sins, and mine, and the sins of all of us?" Nate looked around as several of the men nodded their heads in agreement.

"My kids told me something like that," the man lying on the deck whispered.

"Do you remember that during the crucifixion of Jesus, there were two bad men on the crosses next to him?"

"Yeah, I do."

"One guy cursed God and died. The other guy — the thief on the cross — cried out to Jesus. He'd been a bad man, too; his life had been wasted, and now it was over, but he acknowledged Jesus as God's Son, and Jesus said, 'Today you will be with me in paradise.' One man died and went to heaven, and one man died and went to destruction. Which man are you most like, my friend?"

"I want to go to heaven, but there's no time for me to go to church."

"You don't have to go to church to meet God. You can meet him right here. All the thief on the cross had time to do was to acknowledge Jesus as the way to God, and he went into heaven. If you'll trust in Jesus, today you can be with him in heaven, too."

The dying man reached out his pale, fragile white hand; and with as much strength as he could muster, he gripped Nathaniel York's big black hand. "I'm trusting Jesus," he said with a nod. He gasped for breath and continued talking, his eyes on Nate but looking far away, as though he were talking to someone else. "Jesus, you are my Lord and Savior. Please forgive me of my sins." He squeezed Nate's hand one more time, and his hand slipped to the deck.

Nathaniel York bowed his head as large tears formed in the corners of his eyes and dripped down his face. He felt bad that there was nothing they could do to save the soldier's life, but in his heart Nathaniel knew the man's spirit was now in heaven, even though his lifeless body lay on the deck of the *Sultana*.

Nathaniel York could not have imagined, however, how many more men and women on the boat would die before this trip was over.

"More coal, men! I need more coal, now." The junior officer in charge of firing the

Sultana's boilers, and thus creating the power to negotiate the mighty Mississippi, emphatically cracked a whip, letting the crewmen know that he meant business. The men responded well, shoveling the coal into the roaring blaze as fast as they could scoop it out of the coal bin.

Captain Coxley had been steering cautiously, avoiding sudden turns and dramatic increases or decreases in speed, and the steamboat was making good progress up the river. But whether because of the exorbitant weight from the massive number of passengers, or the swirling, flood-staged waters of the river itself, the boat's boilers were having to fire harder to keep the *Sultana* plowing through the water at a normal pace, somewhere between eight to ten miles per hour.

"More coal!" the fireman called again. "Come on, men. We must keep that fire hot."

Engineer Nathan Kendricks made frequent trips to the boiler deck, nervously checking the patch that Otis Barton had applied to the boiler in Vicksburg. "Keep an eye on this area of the boiler," he told a crewman, "and let me know if you see anything unusual."

"Unusual, sir?"

"Yes, you know, any signs of stress or anything like that," Kendricks replied. He dared not be too specific, but Kendricks had good reason to be concerned. Complicating matters still further, any quick movements by the men on the top decks caused a rocking of the boat that threatened to capsize the steamer or possibly cause an explosion in the boilers. "You've got to keep those men still upstairs," the engineer implored Captain Coxley. The captain sent a message to one of Edmund Gains's officers to pass the word among the soldiers not to move around any more than necessary.

By the morning of April 25, the steamboat arrived at Helena, Arkansas, where the boat docked temporarily to take on supplies. Morton Jamison, a photographer taking pictures of the swollen Mississippi River, was so shocked when he saw the *Sultana* pull into the dock carrying such a large load of men, he decided it would make a fascinating photograph. Jamison set up his camera on the west bank of the river, facing in the direction of the steamer. Some of the men looking over the siderails on board the *Sultana* noticed the photographer preparing to shoot the photo, so they began waving. In their excitement to have their image preserved for posterity, other men began crowding over to the side of the boat. The *Sultana* dipped low on its side and started to tip over. Cups and plates slid off the dining room table; weaker men tumbled over on the decks, and the steamer's smokestacks creaked and tilted dangerously.

"Get back! Get back!" a crewman screamed. "Move back before we capsize!" Enough men quickly jumped back toward the other side of the boat to keep it from capsizing but not before the photographer captured a historic photo showing the densely packed boat at the dock. The rapid motion in the opposite direction set the *Sultana* heaving again, with more men and material being tossed around like toys. For nearly a full minute, the large steamboat rocked back and forth in the water, from one side to the other, finally coming back to center as the men were able to balance out the load on the top decks.

"Whew, that was a close call," Roberto Hawkins said to Lieutenant Christopher, the Union platoon leader from the boxed canyon skirmish.

"I'll say," the lieutenant replied. "It would be a shame, after all you and the rest of Captain Justice's men did to save our lives back in that canyon, for us to die on a rocking boat!"

"Ha, I was more afraid just now," Roberto said with a laugh, "than I was with those Rebels shootin' at us."

The loud honk of a foghorn interrupted their conversation, as the *Sultana* began to move. Lieutenant Christopher grinned. "Well, it feels like we're pulling out, so our next stop should be Memphis, and after that, St. Louis. Pretty soon, you'll be back on dry ground again."

"And not a moment too soon for my liking," Roberto replied.

With long plumes of smoke belching from the two giant smokestacks that rose on each side in the rear section of the steamer, the *Sultana* eased back out into the swift-flowing Mississippi. The men in the boiler room went to work again, heaving the coal into the fiery furnace, heating the water that created the steam that drove the huge paddle wheels on each side of the boat, pushing it against the powerful current.

The trip upriver lapsed into the mundane, with the soldiers and other passengers resting, relaxing, or idly passing the time as best they could in the cramped conditions. Ezra Justice tried to relax, too, but something within him caused him to remain restless. He decided to check around the boat, just to make certain that everything was OK.

"I'm going to take a little walk," he said to Nate.

"I'll come with you, Captain."

"OK, fine. Things seem to be going well, but I just have an uneasy feeling, Nate."

"I know what you mean. I can't put my finger on it, but this entire affair reeks of money under the table and graft. It turns my stomach that those guys back in Vicksburg would put their desire for profits above the safety of the weary soldiers who have suffered so much during these past few years of war. To think that these good men who were practically starved to death, deprived of clean water, eaten up by all sorts of bugs and vermin, and who endured the indignities, insults, and abuses from the Confederates would now be treated like this by the Union army — packed on this boat like animals going to a slaughter house — well, I don't know, Ezra. It just ain't right."

Ezra and Nate slowly made their way around the main deck, nodding or saying hello to the physically drained but excited former prisoners of war. Nothing, not even the crowded conditions aboard the *Sultana,* could stifle their joy in knowing that every mile up the river, every minute, each moment, they were getting closer to home. Many others waved enthusiastically to Ezra and Nate as they walked by.

The two friends covered each of the upper decks, then moved to the hold below the main deck, to where the animals were kept during the trip. The large, open room was crammed full of livestock, including a full load of pigs, mules, donkeys, and about seventy horses.

"Wheweee! Smells like an indoor farm down here, doesn't it?" Nate howled.

"Even worse," Ezra said, "there's hardly any food for the animals. Some of them may not even make it to St. Louis."

They walked past some large crates and were about to head back upstairs when they were surprised by a loud slapping sound. Both Ezra and Nate jumped back and reached for their guns at the same time.

"Hey, calm down, fellows!" one of the crewmen working in the hold called to them. "No need for alarm. It's just Chops over there in the big crate."

"Chops?" Ezra asked as he lowered his LaMat.

"Yeah, right over there. The alligator in the crate with the bars on the topside." Ezra, Nate, and the crewman walked in the direction of the crate while the crewman explained. "That's Chops, our boat's mascot. One of the fellows brought him back from the swamps of Louisiana about six months ago, and he's been with us ever since. We don't have much entertainment aboard this boat, so the fellows enjoy aggravating ol' Chops here." Ezra and Nate peered inside the crate's bars as the crewman banged on the top of the crate. Chops went wild, thrashing about in the crate, chomping at the steel bars.

"Friendly fellow, huh?" Nate said with a laugh.

"Not really. We have a one-armed crewman who tormented him once too often," the crewman offered, nodding his head and pursing his lips.

"Do you ever let him out of the crate?" asked Nate.

"Not very often. When we do, we have to tie up his jaws and keep a strong rope on him because if he got loose, his tail would wipe out half the boat before we got him back in his box."

Almost as if concurring with the crewman's assessment, Chops thrashed against the wall of his crate with such force the crate tipped a few inches off the deck and slammed back to the floor.

"I see your alligator is well fed," Ezra said sarcastically, as the crewman threw some chickens to Chops. "Where's the feed for the other animals down here?"

"I don't know," the crewman stammered. "The captain told me we didn't have room for any more feed."

"Yeah," Nate said, "he's not getting paid per animal."

"When we get to Memphis, I want more feed put on this boat," Ezra said.

"You'll have to talk to the captain about that," the crewman answered nervously.

"Trust me," Ezra said. "I will."

As Ezra and Nate walked back toward the stairwell, Nate looked at Ezra and said, "Whatever happened to the idea of sailors having talking parrots?"

Justice didn't respond. His mind was focused on something else. "Nate, do you notice anything unusual about this boat?" Ezra asked as they climbed the stairs to the hurricane deck.

"Other than the fact that people are crammed on here with hardly enough room to sit down and we've got an alligator in the hold? Could there possibly be anything more unusual than that?"

"Yeah, beyond that. Have you noticed that there are not nearly enough lifeboats on board? I've seen only one lifeboat and the boat's yawl, for all these hundreds of men, women, and children. If something ever happened where we needed to get people off this boat in a hurry, they wouldn't stand a chance."

"How about life preservers?" Nate asked. "Any of those around?"

"I think some of the passengers may have life preservers in their cabins, but other than that, I haven't seen any at all. Let's take a look and see if we can find some."

Ezra and Nate opened every hatch or compartment door that they came to and found only three boxes containing a total of seventy-six cork-filled life preservers — not even enough for the crew members — and some of them were mildewed, broken, or had other obvious problems that would keep them from being of much help to a drowning person.

Ezra looked at the shabby life preservers and glanced around at the throng of people on board the *Sultana.* "I've got a bad feeling about all this," Ezra said.

12

The *Sultana* moored at the dock in Memphis around 6:30 p. m. on April 26, 1865. Ezra and his men peered intently toward the dock, watching, standing at the ready, should any funny business break out. But the docking was uneventful. Ezra and the squad watched cautiously from the upper tier as members of the Chicago Opera Troupe hurried down the boat's gangplank and up the cobblestone riverbank at Memphis. "I'll bet those people couldn't wait to get off this boat," Harry Whitecloud chuckled as he watched the troupe heading toward their engagement at Atheneum Hall.

Once the few disembarking passengers and their luggage were put ashore, Captain Coxley announced, "We will be docked here for several hours, so if you wish to go into Memphis for a short time, feel free to do so. Please be back on board by 9:30 this evening, as we will be shoving off for St.

Louis shortly after that time." A number of soldiers, even those who could barely walk or were otherwise disabled, took the Captain up on his offer and got off the boat for a while, happily going into town as free men. Some of the soldiers who had money headed straight for the first saloon they could find on Beale Street.

While the boat was docked at Memphis, Ezra Justice cornered Captain Coxley in the pilothouse. "Why is there not more food for the soldiers and feed for the animals aboard this boat?" Justice wanted to know.

"Go talk to Colonel Stanley," Coxley stated sarcastically. "He's your commanding officer."

"I hope you can live with this, Captain," Ezra said as he walked out of the pilothouse.

Many of the soldiers that had disembarked returned to the boat several hours later, stone-cold drunk. One young man stumbled up the gangplank, wobbling awkwardly, nearly falling into the water. Harry Whitecloud saw an accident getting ready to happen, so he bounded down the stairs and worked his way through the long line of men snaking their way back onto the steamship. Meanwhile the young man was making little progress. He'd take one step forward, get jostled by another soldier, and he'd slip two

or three steps backward. Teetering dangerously over the railing, the young soldier
nearly toppled into the water again, just as
Harry Whitecloud reached him and latched
onto him with a powerful grip.

"What kind of firewater have you been
drinking, son?" Harry asked as he pulled
the young man back from the rail.

"Whiskey, sir! Tennessee whiskey."

Harry looked at the young man's boyish
face. "And how old are you?"

"Fifteen, sir. Turned fifteen last month, I
think."

"What's your name, son, and how long
have you been in the army?"

"Matthew Robinson, of the Indiana Volunteer Cavalry. I enlisted when I was thirteen.
I was captured by Forrest's cavalry somewhere in northern Alabama, and the Rebs
sent me to Cahaba. That's where I spent
the last eighteen months. I was there when
the camp flooded and we had to stand in
water up to our waists for several days with
the rats and the water moccasins. I thought
sure I was gonna die right there in that
camp, but I made it through. So when a
couple of fellows from Indiana asked me to
go celebrate our freedom, I was thrilled to
accept the invitation. I'm just glad to be
alive!"

"Well, if you keep drinking that stuff, you might not make it much longer."

"Yes, sir. Thank you for your help."

"Come on, Matthew Robinson." Harry put a strong arm around the young man's shoulders and helped him up the gangplank. "Let's get you back on board, and maybe you can sleep off a bit of that whiskey." Harry maneuvered Matthew onto the deck and found a place where he could lie down without having to fear being trampled if he fell asleep.

By 10:00 p.m., most of the passengers who had disembarked in Memphis had reboarded the *Sultana.* An hour later, Captain Coxley sounded the foghorns and backed the steamboat away from the dock. He wasn't going far, though, just across the river to Hopefield, Arkansas, where the crew loaded on another thousand bushels of coal. With its decks brightly lit, the steamer finally eased away from the coaling station and started upriver again.

Around midnight Nathan Kendricks walked down to the boiler deck one more time, making his final rounds before ending his work shift and turning over responsibility for the boat's power to his assistant. Nathan checked the four boilers, each one eighteen feet in length and noted that they were filled with boiling water and steam. He monitored the gauges and was happy to see that all four boilers were producing approximately 135 pounds per square inch of pressure. He moved to the furnace that kept the boilers hot. The huge furnace stretched almost entirely across the lower deck beneath the boilers; and the shirtless crew, smeared with coal dust and dripping with perspiration, worked constantly to keep the fire red-hot. Kendricks paused long enough to joke with some of the men shoveling coal into the flames. "If it's this hot here, I sure wouldn't want to go to hell!"

"Hell is probably cooler than this furnace room," one of the sweaty men responded.

Almost reluctantly, Kendricks approached the boiler with the patch on the side. "How's the metal holding?" he asked Randall Pallston, one of the crewmen. "Any problems?"

"No, sir. We're looking good."

"Let me know if you notice anything," Kendricks said. "That boiler puts out about 135 pounds per square inch of pressure. When a cubic foot of water is heated under pressure, it has about twice the amount of power as a pound of gunpowder."

"Yes, sir. I understand," Randall said,

chuckling to himself, placating the engineer's passion for dispensing interesting but useless facts about his precious boilers.

Just behind him and above his head, out of Randall's sight, the pressure on the patch bubbled and pushed outward, like a ticking time bomb that could explode at any second.

Shortly after one in the morning on April 27, with the *Sultana* churning through the water at about eight miles per hour, Ezra Justice and his men gathered outside the pilothouse, the small room rising above the hurricane deck, where the captain steered the boat. "I don't think there's much more we can do at this point," Ezra said, "so we might as well try to get some sleep. We still have a long night ahead of us, so let's take one-hour shifts of guard duty. The passengers are settling in, and this chilly drizzle is sending a lot of men on the decks looking for cover, so I don't think we'll have any trouble. Just make sure that nobody does anything stupid, like trying to light a fire to keep warm."

The men laughed. "Anyone want to volunteer for the first hour of guard duty?" Ezra asked.

"I'm wide awake," Bonesteel said, "thanks

to several cups of fine tea I was able to procure from one of the lovely female passengers in the dining room downstairs. I'll be glad to take the first shift. You men can rest well, knowing that everything is under control with Reginald Bonesteel on the watch."

"Oh, that will make me sleep better," Carlos teased.

Roberto Hawkins yawned deeply. "Ohhh, I'm so tired that once I fall asleep, if I can get to sleep in this rain, it will take a bomb to wake me up."

"I could use some shut-eye myself," Harry said.

"I vote for Brother Bonesteel to stay awake all night," Nate quipped.

"OK, Reginald. You've got the first shift. If anything looks suspicious, wake up the rest of us," Ezra instructed.

"Will do, Captain," Bonesteel replied. "I'll let you know at the first sign of any trouble."

Now that his boat was safely on the river again, Captain Coxley retired for the evening, turning the wheel over to George Kayton, his seasoned pilot. On the way to his stateroom, Coxley met Joseph Elliot, who was searching for a few feet of space on which to sleep somewhere on the crowded decks.

"Good evening, Captain," Elliot said to Coxley as he turned sideways to allow the captain to pass by.

"Good evening," Coxley responded. "I'm sorry about the lack of space. I fear that we overestimated our capacity. I dare say, this is the largest group we've ever transported up the river, especially under the spring conditions."

"You do have quite a crowd on board, sir."

"Well, we will be disembarking before you know it."

Inside the pilothouse George Kayton was straining his eyes into the dark night trying to keep the *Sultana* in the middle of the river. Without a system of levies in place, the spring thaw and rains swelled the river far beyond flood stages, causing the Mississippi to spread to more than four miles wide at points above Memphis.

Ezra Justice picked up his bedroll and started toward the deck to find a spot to lie down. Before he did, he pushed open the door of the pilothouse and called inside, "Are you doing OK in there?"

"I'm fine," Kayton replied. "I've run this river so many times, I could almost do it blindfolded. After a few years or so, you steer by memory rather than sight. Good thing, too, especially on a night like this. It's mighty dark out there. Those rain clouds have us socked in, and there's not a star in sight. I haven't seen the moon all night."

"Well, I'm glad to hear you have all that experience," Ezra said with a wave.

"Have a good night, Captain Justice."

Ezra stepped over several sleeping soldiers as he made his way to where Harry Whitecloud, the Hawkins twins, and Nathaniel York had found some space on the deck to spread out their bedrolls. Justice plopped down on the hard deck next to Nate and pulled a covering up over his shoulders.

"Are you still awake, Nate?" Ezra said quietly.

"Yes, Captain, I am," Nate replied in a whisper.

"Nate, would you mind praying for us?"

"Sure I will, Ezra. Is there a specific reason?"

"I don't know, Nate. My heart is heavy, and I don't know why."

"You know, of course, that you don't need me to talk to God for you. You can pray for yourself."

"Yes, I'm sure that's true, Nate. But you know me. I'm not too good at putting my prayers into words. You're much better at that sort of thing than I am. Yet I gotta tell ya, I feel strongly that we may be in danger, and we ought to pray for protection."

"I couldn't agree more, Ezra. Let's pray." Nate looked up toward the sky and, with his eyes wide open, began to pray, "Heavenly Father, we don't know exactly why you have placed us on board this boat, but we know we are not here by accident. You have put us in position to be instrumental in the lives of these men and women passengers and crew. Give us wisdom concerning how we can best serve you. And protect us from any evil that might come upon us during this trip. We know that the enemy would try to destroy us, but your plan is for us is to have a good life, a future, and a hope. Thank you, Lord. We are trusting in you. Amen."

"Thanks, Nate," said Ezra. "I needed that. Good night." And with that, Ezra rolled over, and in a few minutes was fast asleep.

13

William Rowberry, the *Sultana's* chief mate, had replaced Captain Coxley standing next to George Kayton in the pilothouse as the pilot carefully steered the boat through a series of small islands about seven miles north of Memphis.

"The boat is running rather smoothly tonight, is she not?" Rowberry asked.

"Yes, everything seems to be functioning well," Kayton replied.

Rowberry pulled out his pocket watch and looked at the time. "It's 1:59 now. What time do you think we'll make St. Louis?"

Kayton never answered the question. Just as he opened his mouth to speak, he and Rowberry, the boat's steering wheel and control panel were blown completely out of the pilothouse as three of the *Sultana's* four mighty boilers erupted like a volcano. The explosion ripped instantly through the decks directly above the boilers, flinging fire, live coals, and splintered timber into the night. Hot ashes and flaming coals rained across the *Sultana,* starting fires everywhere they landed. An entire center section of the steamer was obliterated instantly, while whole chunks of the upper decks, including most of the pilothouse, were blown completely off the boat. What remained of the pilothouse crumbled and dropped, as did the deck in front of it where Ezra Justice and his men had been asleep. The upper decks of the *Sultana,* already sagging under the heavy load of passengers, splintered and dropped, the wreckage combined with a mass of human bodies, many of which were now in pieces, or at best lacerated or burning. In less than a second, the hurricane deck's floor tilted and crashed right into the middle of the deck below, with the boat's timber superstructure toppling in every direction, the wreckage imprisoning hundreds of men.

Ezra Justice woke up to a violent jolt and the rumbling, rolling thunder that sounded like a thousand tornadoes. "It's the end of the world!" he heard a voice screaming. At first Ezra thought he was dreaming, but then he heard a multitude of men screaming, and amidst the cacophony he heard the doleful voice again. "It's the end of the world!"

Ezra jumped to his feet and tried to get his bearings. The heat was intense as fire raged all around him. He saw Nate, already lifting a beam off a trapped soldier. But the twins, Harry Whitecloud, and Reginald Bonesteel were nowhere to be seen. Ezra could only hope that they were still alive.

It seemed as though the entire perimeter of the boat had collapsed inwardly, with everything sliding toward the center as though being sucked down a giant funnel. At the bottom of the funnel, all around the circumference, a huge bonfire roared, and within the large opening of the funnel was cold, swirling water, already black with human bodies piled atop one another, many of whom were sinking and taking other men to the bottom of the river with them. Above and around the periphery of the funnel, everywhere Ezra looked flames were feeding on the pile of rubble that only moments before had been the steamer's decks and superstructure.

Awful wails arose all around him as men burned alive under the fallen timbers. Worse yet, there were the screams of the men scalded by the boiling water that had sprayed large sections of the *Sultana* when the boilers erupted. The superheated water had literally peeled men's skin from their faces, arms, or other portions of their bodies that had been exposed to the night. Those who had not died instantly were now groping in darkness; some were totally blind, others blinded by their pain. Grotesque sights and agonizing shrieks and groans of the injured and dying pummeled Ezra's senses. Added to that, the awful stench of burning human flesh reeked all around him. Ezra gagged and nearly threw up from the smell.

Chaos and confusion reigned as sleeping soldiers, as well as women and children sleeping in the cabins below, awoke to hell on the river. Frail men, who had barely survived the Confederate prison camps, now clung to tilted pieces of decking, dangling over the roaring blaze. Others were desperately trying to climb back up the steeply slanted boards. In the moment that Ezra looked up and saw the men, three or four more lost their grip and dropped helplessly into raging fires below.

"Are you OK, Ezra?" Nate called from across the burning deck.

"Yeah, I'm fine. How about you?"

"I'm doin' OK. Have you seen the other guys?"

"No, not yet. I'm hoping they slid down to one of the lower decks when this one gave way."

"I pray so," Nate said. "When that deck blew, we were all bouncing around like rubber balls."

"Right now, Nate, let's see what we can do to help some of these folks around us."

"Sure thing. Where to start is the question," Nate said.

"Anywhere. Everywhere," replied Ezra.

Nate crossed the deck to where Ezra was working to pull a man out from under a pile of rubble. When they got about half the stack off him, the man was able to squirm out of the mess. He crawled to his knees and brushed fragments of debris from his hair and clothing. The freed soldier rasped to Nate, "You saved my life."

"Are you OK?" Nate asked.

"Yeah, thanks to you."

"Good. Then go help somebody else."

Nate and Ezra went to work trying to free another man trapped under large pieces of pipe and wood. They began heaving beams off the man, extricating him just as the burning portion of decking above them collapsed and crashed where the man's head had been a moment previously. Ezra and

Nate helped the man to his feet. As they did, Nate caught a glimpse of the water off the side of the deck. "Lord o'mighty, Ezra. Look!" Nate pointed toward the water. All around the edges of the *Sultana,* as far as Nate and Ezra could see, was an oval ring comprised of bodies, many of whom did not appear to be moving.

Just then they heard the sound of wood pounding against wood. It seemed as though the noise was coming from the hatchway to the hold below the main deck. The hatch had jammed and a one-armed man was trying to pull the heavy door open by himself. Ezra and Nate ran to him, and the three of them yanked on the door together. It wouldn't budge. They could hear the cries of the men on the other side of the hatchway, but there was no way they could get the door to open. "Here, try this!" a familiar voice called. Roberto Hawkins handed Ezra a thick metal bar to use as a lever. "Put it in that opening right there and lift, as the other men pull."

Ezra pushed the makeshift crowbar in between the deck and door and pressed down with all his might as the three other men gave one mighty heave. The door flew open, and out came a rush of coughing and choking men followed by steam and thick smoke.

"Good to see you, Roberto." Ezra threw his arm around Roberto's shoulder. "Thanks for your help. Where's Carlos? Is he OK?"

"Yeah, he's on the other side of the boat. I saw him, and he waved back to let me know he was alright."

"Any sign of Bonesteel or Whitecloud?"

"No, sir. I haven't seen them."

"Keep an eye out for them. They could be in trouble somewhere."

"Yes, sir. There are a lot of hurtin' men upstairs. Maybe we ought to check there." Ezra, Nate, and Roberto moved toward what was left of the stairwell leading to the second tier. They climbed up the outside of the staircase and then swung up onto the deck. As they rounded the edge of what was once a cabin above the boilers, they saw where pieces of sheet metal, pipes, and pieces of machinery had driven through the upper deck like cannon shrapnel, killing and maiming dozens of sleeping soldiers and other passengers where they had been lying.

"These guys never had a chance," Roberto said sadly, stepping over a mass of men in tattered blue uniforms.

Ezra started to take a step over several

dead men when he stopped cold. There, kneeling on the deck, his arms drooping at his side, his eyes wide open and staring back at Ezra was Colonel Stanley, the officer that Ezra had confronted about the overloading of the *Sultana* back in Vicksburg. Stanley had been impaled by a ragged-edged, four-inch pipe, eighteen inches of which was sticking out the front of his chest with about six feet of pipe coming out his back, extending through the floor. The awkward position of the pipe kept Stanley kneeling surreally upright with his head tilted back on the pipe.

Nate came alongside Ezra and laid a hand on his shoulder. "I guess Colonel Stanley didn't know what was best for the men after all," he said quietly.

Ezra didn't say a word. He simply nodded his head. "Let's move on," he said after a few seconds.

At first, Harry Whitecloud thought that the weather had merely turned nasty, that perhaps the awful boom he'd heard was a thunderclap above them and that the flashing light meant that the boat had been hit by lightning. Harry had been sleeping soundly when the boilers exploded, the powerful blast lifting him off the decking where he'd been lying in front of the pilot-house and pitching him backward. Had the top of the pilothouse still been there, Harry would have slammed into it like a bug on a storefront window. But most of the pilot-house had blown farther back, and Harry felt himself hurtling through the air, landing on a pile of men behind the smokestacks.

Harry started to apologize as he pushed his long black hair back on his head. "Did I hurt you . . . are you . . . ?" Harry stopped short. The men on whom Harry had landed were dead.

Harry scrambled to his feet. He looked up and saw a ferocious fire raging behind the smokestacks, with the stacks themselves belching forth fire rather than the usual dirty, coal-black smoke. Harry and the hundreds of men who were squeezed on the decks below him moved closer to the *Sultana*'s stern, since the fire was sweeping in the opposite direction, enveloping the entire front of the boat in an inferno that seemed to rise on both sides of the steamer.

At least five hundred men or more sought refuge on the stern of the boat while the wind and the moving boat itself drove the flames toward the bow. Harry heard a loud, grating, cracking sound and watched in horror as the enormous, burning wheelhouse fell away from the *Sultana.* Now spinning slowly out of control, the boat began to turn with the current of the river, sending the flames, ashes, and debris in Harry's direction.

The men on the deck below saw the raging fire and surged toward the remaining safe area on the tip of the boat's decks. Chased by the flames, dozens of men leaped from the second and third tiers into the dark Mississippi. Dozens more jumped on top of them. At least a hundred men who could not swim or were too weak to swim were pushed and shoved into the water, whether they wanted to be or not. Injured men — some with multiple broken bones — and others who had been badly scalded by the boiling water cried for help. Many crawled along the decks, trying to flee the fire. Some of those crawling were trampled by the stampede of men trying to elude the fires. Some simply gave up and, in their agony, crawled to the edge of the boat and rolled themselves into the water to drown. In the mad rush and hysteria, Harry felt completely helpless.

Although he tried to save a few, Harry's efforts seemed futile. Backed to the edge of the boat by the roaring flames, the men had given up hope. They tumbled into the dark, swirling abyss.

Reginald Bonesteel had been making his rounds on watch, patrolling the hurricane deck, moving slowly and nonchalantly from the steamer's bow toward the stern when the explosion occurred. Bonesteel felt himself lurching forward, then sliding face-first across the floor of the deck. Almost simultaneously, a mountain of men and mangled, dismembered bodies rained down on top of him, their blood spattering on Bonesteel's face and uniform. Severely injured passengers and wreckage from the boiler deck below surrounded him. Trapped under the weight of men and debris pinning him to the floor, Bonesteel could barely breathe as he struggled to free himself. Gasping for air, Bonesteel desperately pushed against the man on top of him, trying to create an air pocket.

It was no use. Bonesteel's world was going black. Just as he was about to lapse into unconsciousness, Bonesteel heard a creaking, then a guttural grinding sound, as the front portion of the hurricane deck he was lying on gave way, falling out from under him, slamming to the deck below. Bonesteel's body slapped off the deck as it hit the boiler deck below, and the crunch on top of him felt as though he'd been run over by a cannon. The fallen portion of deck formed a steeply inclined bridge from one deck to the other, causing the pile of men and debris to slide forward. The downward motion also sent men and debris bouncing off the deck and allowed Bonesteel enough room to scramble on his hands and knees, moving below the pile toward a bright light he saw ahead. Pulling on a piece of pipe stuck through the flooring, Bonesteel pulled himself out of the pile, only to discover that the bright light he'd seen was an inferno in front of him.

Swooooosh! A gale of fire flared in his face. Bonesteel glanced around searching for a safe escape and quickly backed away from the fire toward an open section of the boat, a spot that used to be a cabin, he guessed. The sickening scene and the awful sounds aboard the burning *Sultana* bombarded Bonesteel's senses. Roaring, crackling flames, exploding ammunition, the hoarse, screaming cries for help by both men and women, the cries of terrified children.

Several women — members of a group known as the Christian Commission — were kneeling next to the railing, praying for help, apparently oblivious to the rapidly encroaching flames. Ever the gentleman,

Reginald Bonesteel approached the women tactfully and said, "I appreciate your prayers, ladies, and I'm certain we are in desperate need of them. However, if you don't move back hastily from that fire, you will soon be speaking with the Lord face-to-face." The women gathered their soiled and wet garments around them and re-treated. Bonesteel looked around the boiler deck to see who else he could help. He didn't have to look far.

14

Reginald Bonesteel hadn't seen Ezra Justice or any of the squad members since the explosion, but in his heart Bonesteel knew that if the men were alive they'd be doing exactly what he was doing — trying to help as many of the struggling passengers as possible.

Within twenty minutes of the blast in the *Sultana*'s boiler room, nearly the entire steamboat was ablaze. More and more passengers were facing the grim reality that they could either stay on board and be consumed by fire or risk taking the plunge into the cold dark whirlpools of the Mississippi. Bonesteel made his way down to the lower deck where numerous men and even a few women were already standing on the debris at the edge of the boat, working up the courage for their leap of faith. Many of the men's clothing had already been seared off them by the blast, the blazes, or the boiling water; those whose clothes were intact were stripping off their garments, getting ready to jump into the cold river with as little weighing them down as possible. The women, for the most part, retained some bodily coverings, whether their nightclothes, or wrapping themselves in sheets or blankets, trying desperately to maintain some modicum of modesty even under the horrendous conditions. But at least one woman was completely naked, leaning off the edge of the boat, waiting for an opportunity to dive into the water where she wouldn't land on some piece of wreckage or, worse yet, a pile of human beings.

Many of the men were praying — some begging God for help, others asking for forgiveness; many were entreating God to save them in this world or the one to come — some in loud passionate voices, some in panicked tones and phrases; others making their requests known to God in strangely formal, graceful, almost poetic prayers.

Still others were cursing everybody from God to their parents. Presidents, politicians, and generals seemed to be prime targets for verbal tirades — especially Abraham Lincoln, Jefferson Davis, Robert E. Lee, William Sherman, or Ulysses S. Grant.

Bonesteel pulled some wreckage off a frail

soldier and helped him to the area where many were jumping off the boat. *Such an odd scene,* he thought. On one area of the deck, a group of women and children dressed in nightclothes were weeping profusely. That was hard enough for the stoic Brit to handle. But then he saw a group of battle-hardened soldiers, men who had undoubtedly stood heroically in warfare, facing the worst musket and cannon fire without flinching, men who had survived unspeakable conditions in the death pens pawned off as prison camps. These same men now stood near the edge of the flaming *Sultana* wringing their hands, flailing their arms madly, screaming with such guttural cries of agony and despair that even Reginald Bonesteel's confidence was shaken.

Bonesteel grimaced as he heard the screams of men hitting the water whose bodies had already endured severe burns. He looked to the other side of the boat where about twenty or thirty men at a time were leaping off the side, often landing on other men already floundering in the river. Bonesteel gulped hard as he watched dozens of heads bobbing like corks in the water, then disappearing. He waited for the men to resurface; many never did.

"Mr. Bonesteel!" he heard a familiar voice calling. "Mr. Bonesteel. Please, sir. Will you help me?"

Bonesteel peered through the smoke and haze until his eyes fastened on a man lying on the deck, dressed in a soiled undershirt and a pair of torn-up Union soldier's pants, his leg wrapped in bandages.

"Cartwright?" Bonesteel called. "Is that you, Cartwright?"

"Yes, sir. Private Edward Cartwright. You and Captain Justice saved me from certain death in that boxed canyon, remember?"

"Of course I remember, Private. How are you? Were you injured further in the blast?"

"No, I had a tarp over my head when the boilers blew scalding water over the deck. The dirty tarp probably kept me from being cooked alive. But Mr. Bonesteel, I do need your help."

"What can I do for you?" Bonesteel asked, kneeling down next to Cartwright and looking at his bandaged leg.

"Please, sir. I beg of you, please throw me into the water."

"What? Absolutely not! You wouldn't stand a chance with your leg all shot up like that. The river is running swift and cold and would be a challenge for a man with two good legs and arms."

"Reginald, look at me," Cartwright implored. "My leg is broken in several places, I have at least one bullet in the bone, I can't walk, and the fire is getting closer and hotter every minute. At least in the river I might have a chance to survive. If I stay here, I'm going to be nothing but ashes for sure."

Bonesteel grappled with Cartwright's logic and the moral dilemma it created for him. He knew in one sense that the courageous private was correct — his only chance to survive was to get off that boat — yet at the same time, by helping him to jump into the swirling river, incapacitated as he was, Bonesteel felt he would be virtually helping the man to commit suicide.

"I don't know if I can do that . . ." Bonesteel began.

"Reginald! Please. Help me. I'm a dead man if you won't!"

"Wait a minute. I have an idea." Bonesteel found a stateroom door hanging from its hinges. He grabbed the door and felt a surge of adrenaline as he literally ripped the door out of the doorway. He carried the door over to where Cartwright was lying on the deck. "Here. Let me help you onto this. Slide up here," he said, as he reached out a hand and pulled Cartwright onto the door. "I'll drag you over to the edge, and try to ease you off. The door should keep you afloat. Hang on tight, though, because with so many men in the river, somebody is liable to try to knock you off the door."

Bonesteel dragged the door and Private Cartwright to an area of the deck where the boat's railing had been destroyed. "Are you ready, Private?"

Cartwright clung to the door like a child to its mother. "Yes, sir. I think so."

"OK, here we go."

"Mr. Bonesteel?"

"Yes, Private Cartwright?"

"Thank you, sir."

Bonesteel shook his head. "Don't thank me; just hold on. May God be with you, Private Cartwright."

"And with you, Mr. Bonesteel. If I don't make it, I'll be waiting to catch up with you in heaven."

"That's a deal, Mr. Cartwright. And may God have mercy on both of our souls if I am doing the wrong thing by pushing you off." With that, Bonesteel shoved the door partially over the edge of the boat, holding onto it as long as he could before letting go, waiting for an opportunity to avert as many men as possible in the river already black with bodies. When Bonesteel saw a brief opening in the water, he released his grip.

The door carrying Private Cartwright slid off the boat, hit the muddy water, and disappeared. Bonesteel watched and waited, ignoring the flames behind him. Finally, after about ten seconds, the door reemerged, with Private Cartwright still clinging to it for dear life. Bonesteel strained his eyes to see into the darkness, catching a glimpse of the door as it floated away from the *Sultana.*

Whether out of feelings of futility or hopefulness, Bonesteel wasn't sure, but he thought, *If that door can help keep Cartwright alive, maybe some of this wreckage can help keep some other men afloat.* Working tenaciously, he started grabbing anything he saw that might float and tossing it overboard to the men in the water. With Samson-like strength he pulled doors off cabins, even tearing the wood sheeting off the sides of cabins where he could.

Bonesteel was bent over, trying to tear up some matting on the deck when he heard, "Hey, brother, could you use a hand?" Bonesteel looked up and saw Carlos Hawkins standing over him. Carlos was filthy dirty with blood and dirt smeared on his face and half his shirt ripped off, but he was smiling.

"Well, aren't you a sight for sore eyes?" Bonesteel deadpanned. "Fancy meeting you in such a place as this."

"Good to see you, too, Reginald. What are you doing there?" Carlos pointed to the mat.

"I'm trying to toss some life preservers to those men in the water," Bonesteel replied. "These mats and doors might serve as crude life rafts. There sure isn't much else for these men to hang on to."

"Good idea. Let me help you." Carlos and Bonesteel pulled the matting off the floor and tossed it into the water. Together, they grasped a heavy stateroom door, yanked it off the hinges, and carried it to the edge of the boat. The moment the door hit the water, a desperate, hysterical soldier pulled himself partially onto the door. No sooner had that soldier grabbed hold, five more men struggled to gain access to the make-shift raft. Bonesteel and Carlos watched helplessly from the deck as the men in the water fought fiercely with one another for position on the door, wasting what little strength they had left.

"No!" Carlos called into the din. "Help one another; work together! Don't kill one another!" Carlos couldn't tell whether the men heard him or not. One by one they knocked each other off the door, until all six heads disappeared below the dark water, and the door floated downstream with no one aboard.

Bonesteel and Carlos stood on the deck and dropped their chins to their chests in frustration. Even in these dire circumstances, selfishness had reared its ugly head, pulling six more men to their deaths.

A group of crewmen and soldiers were grappling with the *Sultana's* lone lifeboat, attempting to lower it into the water, while maintaining their positions, ready to fight off anyone who tried to get into the boat before them. The boat was designed to hold about seventy-five people, but the moment it hit the water, men started clamoring into the small craft. Ten, twenty, fifty men . . . soon there were a hundred people and more crowding into the boat.

A middle-aged woman, barefoot and wearing only a long nightshirt, stood shivering on the side of the *Sultana,* begging someone to help her get into the lifeboat, but the men ignored her plaintive cries. "Get out of the way, lady," one man roughly shoved her aside. His insolence may have saved her life.

A moment or two later, the lifeboat, now packed with more than one hundred fifty anxious passengers, began to take on water. A few moments later the overcrowded lifeboat plunged beneath the water, taking its passengers on a dark, cold journey to the bottom of the Mississippi.

His heart pounding at the sight, Bonesteel stood staring at the spot where the lifeboat had disappeared, hoping against hope that it might reemerge. It didn't.

"Come on, Reginald," Carlos said. "There's another small boat on the stern. We might be able to get some passengers into it." Bonesteel and Carlos ran toward the boat's stern where the *Sultana*'s yawl was stored below the lower deck. The small sailboat-type craft was not used so much to shuttle passengers since the *Sultana* normally docked to let passengers on or off. But the crew members sometimes used the yawl to procure supplies or simply to get to a town on shore when the *Sultana* was in the middle of the river. It couldn't carry many people, but it was certainly a viable means of saving some.

But when Bonesteel and Carlos got to the stern, they looked down over the edge and saw the yawl already being launched — commandeered by five crewmen — and carrying not a single soldier or paying passenger. Two men in the yawl were pushing the boat away from the *Sultana* while the three others were using boards or pipes to swat away any passengers trying to get into the small craft with them.

"Can you believe those guys?" exclaimed Carlos. "That boat can't handle a lot of people, but they could save some if they cared to. Surely it can fit more than five people on board safely."

"Of course it could," Bonesteel agreed. "But those crewmen don't care about anyone else but themselves. If I had my Henry with me right now, I might seriously consider shooting every last one of them."

"Harry! Over here! Help me." The voice belonged to Roberto Hawkins who was frantically working to extricate a young man trapped below the deck, pinned under some heavy boiler grating that had formed a triangular prison above him.

Harry Whitecloud came around the rubble and ran over to where Roberto was kneeling over the boy, who was hanging onto the grates, dangling above the fire that was edging ever higher, up the wall of wreckage below him. As Harry got closer, he recognized the young man as Matthew Robinson, the fifteen-year-old boy soldier Harry had helped aboard the *Sultana* the day before.

"Good to see you, Injun. I'm glad you're OK."

"Yeah, you too," Harry answered. But there was no time for a reunion.

"Grab onto his hands," Harry instructed. "Hurry, we don't have much time. That fire is moving too fast."

Roberto held onto Matthew's hands, while Harry worked to wedge one pipe against the other, hoping to pop one of the bars loose above Matthew's head. The heat was so intense that the men couldn't touch the bars with their bare hands.

"I'm burning!" Matthew screamed, as the flames enveloped his legs, eating their way quickly up his clothing.

"Pull him higher!" Harry said to Roberto. Together the men stood up and pulled Matthew as high as the grating would allow, the young soldier's anguished face nearly pressed against the hot grates as his outstretched arms and hands extended through the pipes, clinging to Harry. Roberto scrambled around the grates, trying to find something that would loosen the jam above the boy. He crashed heavy beams against the flooring around the grates, to no avail.

"Oh, God! You said you'd never give us any more than we can handle. I can't take any more," Matthew cried. The fire roared around him, and the young man let out a bloodcurdling squall. Matthew Robinson's grip fell limp. Harry and Roberto felt it at the same time and looked at each other knowingly. There was nothing else they could do but let go and watch Matthew Robinson's flaming body fall into the hellacious fire pit below.

"Come out of there, you ugly thing!" Squire Terrill, the crewman who had shown Ezra Justice and Nathaniel York the huge alligator hidden in the boat's hold, was pounding on the side of the crate trying to get the gator out of the large box. Although flames and smoke and about ten inches of water filled the hold, Terrill wasn't really concerned about the animals, least of all the gator. He simply wanted the crate to serve as something he could use to float out of the *Sultana.* Many of the horses and other animals were dead already; others had escaped somehow in the confusion following the explosion and were roaming the hold unfettered. Still others were already in the river.

While men searched the boat for anything they thought would float — doors, windows, shutters, large pieces of debris, carcasses of dead horses, pigs, and donkeys, or bales of hay — the fire continued to ravage the *Sultana,* rapidly diminishing the prospects of anything that might serve as a life raft. That's when Terrill thought of Chops and his large crate. The fire had evidently spooked the gator because he wouldn't come out of the crate, although he thrashed about angrily. "Come on, Chops!" Terrill roared at the gator. "Get out of there." He flung the door of the crate wide open and banged violently on the sides of the box with a board. Chops refused to budge.

Terrill found a Union soldier's rifle with a bayonet still attached floating in the rising water in the boat's hold. He picked up the rifle and began poking inside the crate. Of all the men aboard the *Sultana,* Terrill was one who should have had a healthy respect for the lightning speed of the angry alligator. But he foolishly underestimated the gator's quickness. Exasperated and growing more frantic by the moment in the smoke, flames, and rising water, Terrill lunged toward Chops with the bayonet end of the gun, catching the gator's tough skinned back with the blade. Before Terrill had the chance to pull the gun back out of the cage, Chops' huge teeth snapped down on Terrill's arm, jerking him into the crate. In a flash, the gator released Terrill's arm, and latched onto his waist, tossing the sailor around in the crate like a rag doll. Terrill had nowhere to hide. When Chops was through with the crewman, the alligator slid out of the crate and into the water, his nose and beady eyes the only part of his large body visible. Terrill didn't move.

Up on deck Ezra Justice and Nathaniel York were trying desperately to save another large box, the coffin carrying their friend, Shaun O'Banyon. Amazingly, when the boiler exploded, the coffin remained on board, slamming up against the wall of the main deck, pinched beneath some debris and heavy beams. In their valiant efforts to save as many injured soldiers as possible, Ezra and Nate had forgotten about O'Banyon's coffin. But when soldiers began scavenging for anything that would float, Ezra recalled the large pine box that Bonesteel had lined with pine pitch to help seal out the air and moisture. Justice knew that if he didn't get to the coffin before somebody else did, Shaun O'Banyon might receive the same sort of ignominious burial his father had been given. And Justice had promised O'Banyon that he would not allow that to happen. So while helping as many passengers as they could, Ezra and Nate made their way back to where they had last seen O'Banyon's coffin.

"There it is!" Nate said, pointing to a pile of burning rubble. Ezra and Nate began digging around the coffin with their hands. They struggled to pull the decking and beams off the pine box as the fire and smoke swirled around them. Finally, they were able to get a hold on the coffin and drag it from the flames.

"Now what do we do with it?" Nate asked as he sat down on top of the coffin and wiped the sweat and grime off his face.

Ezra looked around at the flaming frame of the *Sultana.* The steamer was drifting with the current, picking up speed as it went, fanning the flames into even more fury. It was obvious that time was running out for the boat. "The fire is going to take this thing down before much longer," Ezra said. "I guess we'd better get off before that happens. Are you ready for a swim, Nate?"

"As ready as I'll ever be, Cap'n," Nate replied. "What about the other guys? Do you have any idea where they might be?"

"No, not really. Why don't you take a quick survey of the boat and see if you can find them. I'll stay here and guard O'Banyon's coffin. If you see the men, tell them we gotta make a jump for it as soon as possible. They need to do the same. We can't be too far from Memphis, especially as fast as we're drifting downriver, so if we get separated and they make it to shore, tell them to meet us on the riverbanks there."

"Got it, Captain. I'll be back as soon as I can," Nate said as he started back toward the main part of the burning boat. Nate stopped abruptly and turned around. "And Ezra, if I'm not back in fifteen or twenty minutes, you and O'Banyon go for it without me."

Justice nodded his head but said, "You just get back here, Nate."

Nate was no sooner out of sight when four men stumbled toward Ezra out of the smoke. "Let's get that box in the water," one of the biggest men called out.

"Sorry, this is a coffin; and it's staying with me," Justice answered.

"Are you crazy? We need to get off this boat now," another man railed.

"Then you will have to find something else to hang onto because this coffin's not going into the water until I say so," Ezra said.

"If you won't give us the box, we'll just take it from you," the big man said as he swung hard toward Ezra's face. The other three men jumped on Justice, attempting to knock him to the deck. That was a mistake.

Justice blocked the first man's punch with

his right forearm; and while his arm was still in the air, he whirled around and caught his attacker with a hard kick to the stomach. The attacker crumpled over, flopped to the floor with a thump, and didn't move. Ezra rotated just in time to catch the second attacker with a body chop to the shoulder area. The man stumbled backwards and tumbled over O'Banyon's coffin. The third man dove at Ezra's midsection, but Justice saw him coming just in time. He locked his hands above his head and brought them down like a hammer, pounding the man's head into the deck.

The fourth man stared at Justice and simply backed away. "Gather up your buddies and find something to float on," Justice said.

As Ezra was catching his breath, he looked across the deck and saw Anna and William Harvey, the attractive couple dressed in their bedclothes, with the mother carrying their young baby in her arms. William Harvey had found a life preserver somewhere and was fastening it over his wife's head. They looked as though they were getting ready to jump overboard.

"No! Wait!" Ezra called to the couple. "Stay with us, and you can hold onto the box." He pointed to O'Banyon's coffin.

"I'm not going to have my wife floating on top of a dead man, sir," William Harvey said.

"The river is cold and fast," Justice replied. "Even if you are an excellent swimmer, it won't be easy to stay afloat unless you have something to hold on to."

"First of all, I *am* an excellent swimmer and my wife has a life-preserver," Harvey said. "That's all we need."

"Don't you understand?" Justice said. "A few minutes in that water and hypothermia will paralyze your arms and legs. You won't be able to move. You've got to have something stronger than you to hang on to. My friends and I are going to push the coffin off in a few minutes. We'll help you to keep the baby out of the water. Don't try to go it alone, please."

"Listen to him, William," Anna Harvey implored. "The man is making sense when nothing else on this hideous night does. What do we have to lose by waiting a few minutes?"

"Nothing besides our dignity, Anna," William Harvey huffed.

"Dignity? William, are you out of your mind? Look at us? We're practically naked out here in the freezing cold in front of all these men, and we're about to be burned alive! What dignity are you worried about?"

"Just jump when I do, dear," the woman's husband said, as he reached to take their child out of her arms. Anna Harvey looked at her husband for a long moment before releasing their child into his grip.

"I hope you know what you are doing, William," she said.

"Jump now!" Harvey called as he leaped off the boat's deck, still gripping their child in front of him. When Anna Harvey saw her baby going overboard in the arms of her husband, she hesitated no longer. She followed behind her family, plunging into the ice-cold river.

Justice watched the woman dip below the water and then pop back up, thanks to the flimsy life preserver. She immediately began looking around frantically for her husband. William Harvey was flailing away in the murky Mississippi. Anna Harvey saw her husband struggling and grabbed a piece of a log floating by and clung to it, hoping that she could get to her husband and they could rely on the log to keep them afloat. She watched in stark terror as her husband's arms splashed less and less, then saw his head go under the water and bob back up once . . . twice . . . the third time William Harvey went under; he and the baby disappeared beneath the water. Anna Harvey screamed, "My baby! My husband and baby are gone!" But in the middle of the muddy, swirling river, with nearly a thousand other men and women fending off the cold and trying to stay alive, there was nothing anyone could do.

"Captain Justice says to meet in Memphis if we get separated," Nate said to Bonesteel, Harry Whitecloud, and the Hawkins twins who were still in the area near where Matthew Robinson had died. "There's not much more we can do on board the boat, so we're going to drop O'Banyon's coffin into the water and try to get it to shore. There are a lot of people already in the water, so when you go in, make sure you have something to hang on to. Many of the men can't swim or don't have the energy to swim in the cold water, so be careful that you don't allow anyone to pile on top of you."

"A number of men are still alive on board, Nate. They are burnt badly or may have broken bones. They won't be able to swim. Are we just going to leave them?" Harry Whitecloud asked.

"The only way we can help them is to get to Memphis. We can get some military boats to start searching the river and, hopefully, send some skiffs over to the *Sultana* to rescue any remaining passengers. But it won't do us or them any good to stay here any longer. It's still several hours before sunup. We've got to get help."

"That makes sense," Harry said. "It's just that I hate to leave an injured person behind."

"I understand," Nate replied. "But right now, Captain Justice is convinced that the best way we can help them is by getting off this boat and then coming back for them."

"Let's try to stick together as much as possible," Carlos said to the other men. "Where's the captain and O'Banyon's coffin?"

"Down on the lower deck. He's waiting there for us."

"Alright, let's go skinny dipping," Roberto joked weakly. "Oooh, that's gonna be cold swimming tonight."

Roberto was right. The men stripped off their shirts and shoes, stashed their weapons in a watertight leather pouch lashed to the coffin, and carefully lowered O'Banyon's pine box into the Mississippi. When they dove in next to the floating box, the sudden chill nearly took their breath away. Even some strong men could not have survived swimming from mid-river to shore, and many of the sickly, emaciated, former prisoners of war stood little chance on the wide, swollen river. What little heat they could generate in their bodies quickly dissipated in the ice-cold water. Many good, determined soldiers simply passed out due to hypothermia; they quietly slipped beneath the surface, never to be seen again.

Ezra Justice and his men were not immune to the cold. "I've never been so cold in all my life!" Carlos yelled to Justice from the other side of O'Banyon's coffin. "Oh, God, please help us," Nate prayed.

"Keep praying, Nate," Justice shouted. "But keep swimming, too."

15

If the sights and sounds aboard the blazing *Sultana* were heartrending, those in the river, though not as visible or prolonged, were equally wrenching. Muffled screams, moans, and anguished cries for help from those struggling to survive as well as those close to drowning in the dark could be heard rising just above the water. It was difficult enough for Ezra Justice and his men to push away from the *Sultana,* knowing that there were still living creatures aboard the floating inferno. Seeing the dead and hearing the dying in the river was even worse.

Between swimming, trying to help others who were struggling in the river, and holding onto O'Banyon's coffin as they nudged it along toward what they thought was the shoreline, Ezra and his men looked back at the steamer with a mixture of distress and fascination as it drifted downriver along with them. Every so often, they could see the dark shadow of a human being standing against the red glow. Then the shadow would be gone.

Burning debris still littered the river, casting strange, eerie images on the water as Justice and his men spotted other floating objects. A dead horse drifted by with two naked men sprawled atop the animal. Ezra couldn't tell if the men were dead or alive. Men grasping all sorts of objects — anything to keep their heads above water — slipped by. Ezra felt something bump against him in the dark water. He reached down to feel what it was and pulled up the lifeless form of a little girl about ten years of age. He struggled in the water, trying to secure her to O'Banyon's coffin but she slipped from his grasp. Finally, reluctantly, Ezra let go of the body. As familiar as he was with death, the little girl's senseless demise nearly overwhelmed him, and the muddy river water mixed with his own tears.

Just above Memphis, the Mississippi River split around several large islands and a number of smaller ones. Most of the small islands were mere patches of land projecting up out of the water, some hosting vegetation while others were simply barren sandbars. All became sanctuaries for any men or women lucky enough to have landed on them in the darkness.

As Ezra and the men pushed farther away from the *Sultana,* they heard a strange sound. "What is that noise?" Roberto called.

"It sounds like singing," Harry said.

Sure enough amidst the screams of men and women calling out for help, praying, or cursing came the unmistakable sound of voices singing. As Ezra and the men passed by a tiny island, they could faintly make out the figures of four naked men perched in trees, singing "Amazing Grace" at the top of their lungs.

"That is the strangest quartet I've ever seen or heard," quipped Nate, as he watched the unusual singers.

"I guess those words have special meaning to them now," said Ezra.

"Keep singing, boys!" Carlos called out to the quartet as he floated by. "We'll be back to get you as soon as we can."

"Thank you! God bless you," someone called back into the darkness.

Ezra and the men held on to O'Banyon's coffin while swimming sideways against the current, attempting to guide the box closer to shore. Bonesteel's seals of pine pitch helped keep the coffin afloat when, at times, all six men had to hold on to it in the swift current, especially when they had to struggle through one of the river's many dangerous whirlpools. At times one or two of the men could lie on top of the coffin, trying to rest for the next burst of energy they would need to expend.

During one of those drifting periods, Nate and the Hawkins twins were on one side while Ezra, Harry, and Bonesteel were on the other side. Nate looked over to his side and saw a head with two beady eyes staring at him. The sight would have scared the socks off him, if he'd been wearing any. "Whoa! What is that?" he shouted.

The beady-eyed creature came closer to Nate in the darkness. "Watch it now!" Big Nate called out. "Look out!" He waited until the creature got within two feet of him, and then Nate lashed out with a flurry of punches to the animal's face. Flailing about in the water like a madman, Nate heard the Hawkins twins laughing at him.

"Nate! Nate," Carlos called. "Take it easy, brother. It's a mule. A dead one at that!" The other guys howled in laughter.

"My, my," Harry Whitecloud hooted, "you sure beat the daylights out of that dead mule."

"Aw, keep quiet," Nate replied. "If you'd seen that gator like Ezra and I did, you'd be a little more concerned."

"Ah-ha!" Bonesteel joined in. "So that's it. Now you're seeing alligators. I'm beginning to worry about you, Nate. Maybe you should start drinking English tea instead of that muddy water you call coffee."

"There was a gator on board that boat," Nate protested. "Wasn't there, Ezra? Tell them."

"Yep. Sure was, Nate," Ezra replied.

The men floated farther downstream, holding on to O'Banyon's coffin; they were illuminated by the glow from the burning *Sultana.* At a turn in the river, the group encountered a number of other survivors on various floatation devices, everything from broken chairs to mattresses to driftwood. About ten men had congregated on a large piece of the *Sultana's* roofing, looking like the top of a small house drifting downstream with men hanging off every portion of the eaves. On the side closest to Ezra Justice, a young woman clung to a chimney pipe. As O'Banyon's coffin floated nearby the roofing, Ezra was surprised to hear somebody call his name.

"Captain Justice," a weak voice called out. "Captain Justice, over here. On the roof."

Justice peered into the semidarkness trying to see who was calling his name. "Who's there?" he called.

"It's me, sir. Lieutenant Christopher, from the canyon, back near Vicksburg. Remember, you saved my life."

"Yeah, I remember. How are you holding up, Lieutenant?"

"Better than some, but my arms and legs will barely move I am so cold."

"Are you injured?"

"I was near the glass on one of the upper cabins, and it sliced me up rather badly, but I can't feel the pain anymore."

"Can we do anything to . . ." Ezra began to ask, when a violent thrashing wave whipped against him, nearly knocking him loose of O'Banyon's coffin. "What was that?" Roberto shouted. Ezra raised up in the water just far enough to see the beady eyes moving in Christopher's direction. He knew the answer to Roberto's question.

"Watch out! It's a gator, and he's coming your way!"

"A what?" Lieutenant Christopher thought that he had heard Justice wrong. His mind could not fathom an alligator in the cold Mississippi River.

"It's an alligator!" Justice shouted. "Pull yourself up onto the roof. Hurry!"

"You've got to be . . . aarraghh! Help!" The gator grabbed Christopher's legs and whipped him into the air, his body twisted like a pretzel, before Chops slapped him down hard on the water. Lieutenant Christopher shrieked in pain and horror, and then he disappeared below the surface as did the beady eyes.

A moment later the gator resurfaced, his powerful tail thrashing against the floating rooftop, ripping men from the roof, knocking them into the water. The gator's powerful jaws clamped down on one man after another, pulling him under the water until each man stopped squirming.

"He's gonna kill them all!" Harry Whitecloud called.

The alligator was circling around the rooftop, the beady eyes headed toward the woman who was shrieking hysterically, trying to pull her bare legs out of the water, but the cold had long-since robbed her of any feeling in her lower extremities. Try as she might, she could only pull her head and shoulders onto the rooftop.

"I'm going to get her," Ezra called to Nate. Justice began swimming in the woman's direction. He reached the rooftop just as the gator's tail whipped against the pipe that the woman was clinging to so tenaciously. The pipe snapped like a toothpick, sailing into the air and splashing somewhere in the river. The woman rolled all the way across the roof in the same direction, sliding off the eaves and into the water. Her arms slapped the water frantically as she tried to hold her head above the current.

The gator slipped below the water line, moving toward his prey.

Justice saw the gator's eyes just before it dove. Ezra had to decide whether to go for the woman or attempt to fend off the gator. He chose the woman, reaching her just as her head began to dip below the surface. Ezra arched his arm around the woman's head, cradling her chin on his forearm, as he turned her over on her back and began pulling her toward O'Banyon's coffin. The woman's eyes were open, looking up into Ezra's face as he kicked hard and swam with one arm. Reginald Bonesteel and Harry Whitecloud saw them coming and swam out to meet them, leaving the coffin to the Hawkins twins and Nate. Bonesteel and Whitecloud reached Ezra and the woman and helped Ezra pull her back to O'Banyon's coffin.

"Let's get her on top of the box," Ezra said. While Nate and the twins steadied the coffin, Ezra climbed on top of it. Bonesteel and Whitecloud struggled to hand the woman up to him, her wet bedclothes clinging to her body. Still conscious and shivering from the cold but otherwise unable to move, the woman lay on her back and stared up at Ezra Justice, who was kneeling on one knee above her on the coffin's lid.

"Thank you," she mouthed the words, but nothing came out.

Justice looked at the woman's pretty face and recognized her immediately. He was looking into the eyes of Anna Harvey. But now was not a time for getting reacquainted. Ezra glanced at the water and saw the beady eyes moving toward the twins. "Watch out, Carlos! There he is! Look out, Roberto!" Justice was standing on the coffin now, pointing toward the water, tracking the eyes getting closer by the second. Carlos was looking around, scanning the surface but unable to spot the gator. Roberto held on to O'Banyon's coffin with one hand and had pulled his knife with the other. The eyes kept coming.

From his position on the box, Ezra could see the glassy eyes getting closer, just a few feet away from Carlos. Ezra pulled his knife, waited until the gator was right below him, and then he leaped off the coffin. He landed on top of the gator's rough-scaled back, the force of his landing pushing the strong alligator deeper into the water but barely slowing him down. Ezra hurriedly turned himself around in the opposite direction and straddled the gator like he was riding a wild bull. Justice threw his arms around the gator's enormous jaws and squeezed. Unable to open his mouth, Chops attempted to throw Justice off his back by rolling over in the water. Ezra's head splashed below the surface; but he continued to hang on, his knees digging into the side of the huge alligator, his strong arms sealing the gator's jaws shut. Chops rolled the opposite direction, causing Ezra to come out of the water just long enough to catch a breath before rolling into the water again. Justice kneed the gator even harder; Chops thrashed his tail viciously in the water, slapping water in every direction, trying to rid himself of his rider.

The gator surfaced again, bringing Ezra up with him. Ezra let go of the alligator's jaws with his knife hand and plunged the blade with all his might into the alligator's eye. Ezra jerked the knife out, wrapping his arms around the alligator's jaws again. The alligator lurched furiously in the water, then dove below the surface, tossing Justice off backward. Ezra had no sooner hit the water when he reached up and grabbed the gator's dangerous tail that was lashing back and forth above him. Still clutching his knife, Ezra reared back and slammed the blade into the alligator's soft underbelly, directly into its heart. The gator thrashed its tail violently once more, then slowly rolled over dead and floated away in the strong current.

Exhausted from the fight, Ezra had no strength left to swim. As he started to go under, he felt the strong hands of Nathaniel York and Harry Whitecloud pulling him toward O'Banyon's coffin. The men grasped Ezra's arms and pulled him up over the top of the wooden case, his back and head lying awkwardly on top of Anna Harvey's feet, his own legs hanging over the side of the box.

"Are you OK, Ezra?" Harry asked. "Did he get you anywhere? Anything broken or bleeding?"

"Tell me you're OK," Nate implored.

Ezra opened his eyes and said, "Well, except for the pain in my back from the way you guys have me lying on this poor woman's feet, I feel pretty good."

"Thank you, Lord!" Nathaniel York laughed as he and Harry helped Ezra to sit up on the edge of the coffin.

Ezra turned to Harry Whitecloud and said, "I want to thank you and Nate for hauling me back. I was about to visit Davy Jones's locker."

"Believe me, Captain," Harry Whitecloud said. "That gator wouldn't have been satisfied until we were all visiting Davy Jones's locker."

As the river straightened out and the current increased, Ezra and the men looked up to see two shocking sights. The gutted but still blazing *Sultana* swept around the turn, moving closer to them. The second and much more welcome sight was that of an approaching small boat with a lantern hanging off the front of it, weaving back and forth across the river. As the boat drew near to the group huddled around O'Banyon's coffin, Ezra could see a middle-aged man pulling on the oars; the man wore a Confederate soldier's uniform.

"Are you people OK?" the man called.

"Yeah, we're doing alright," Ezra called back. "How far are we from shore? I see some lights up ahead."

"You're a mile or two above Memphis," the soldier replied. "And the shore is about a mile and a half across from here. With that steamer still burning, I don't dare get too close with this small boat. So I'm just trying to save as many as I can out of the water. Do you want me to take you to shore?"

Ezra looked at Anna. "How about you, ma'am?"

"No, I'll stay with you."

"No, we can make it," Ezra called to the man in the boat. "A lot of people out here on this river are in far worse shape than we are. Maybe you can help them."

"I'll try, but I could use some help. Can you spare a man to help me pull some of these people out of the water?"

"Why don't you go, Nate?" Ezra said.

"If you want me to, Ezra." Nate turned and waved at the man in the approaching rowboat. "I'll go!" he shouted to the Confederate soldier as the small boat pulled up next to O'Banyon's coffin.

"You're a black man," the soldier in the boat said, the surprise evident in his voice.

"And you are a Confederate soldier," Nate answered.

"You're right about that. But Yankees and Rebels both drown pretty much the same way. Besides, the war is over. Black, white, Yankees, or Rebels, we're all in this thing together, so it's time we started acting like it. What's your name, son?"

"Nathaniel York, sir."

The Confederate reached out his hand

and grasped Nate's big hand. "Colonel Justin Berry, an honor to meet you. Well, come on, Nathaniel York. We have work to do."

Big Nate climbed into the rowboat and took the oars from the old soldier's hands. "Let me do this, and you watch for people in the water." Nate turned back toward his friends, "Ezra, I'll meet you all in Memphis. You men be careful."

Nate and Colonel Berry rowed off in the direction of the *Sultana,* pulling men out of the river as they went. When they had taken on all they dared, they rowed the men to shore, and then turned around and went back for more.

It took another hour for Ezra Justice and his men to maneuver O'Banyon's coffin out of the strong current and into still water along the shoreline. When they finally pulled the box out of the water and onto the muddy shore, the first hint of dawn was breaking. The men carefully lowered Anna Harvey to the ground and laid her back so the morning sun could warm her chilled body. Exhausted, the men collapsed on the ground but only for a few minutes. Harry Whitecloud stood up and said, "I'll get a fire started."

"I've never in my life been so glad to have

my feet on solid ground!" Roberto said.

"I must say, many times through the past few hours, I wondered if we'd ever see another morning," Reginald Bonesteel admitted.

After a few minutes of rest, Ezra pulled himself up and looked around. Daybreak had brought a sense of relief, but it also revealed the true devastation of the *Sultana's* disastrous explosion. Everywhere Justice looked he saw the shoreline littered with dead bodies. It looked as though a major battle had taken place along the riverbanks, leaving unburied soldiers lying in various positions in the mud. Dark splotches in the muddy Mississippi indicated still more victims were floating down the river. Up the shoreline, Justice spotted a man, woman, and child, all lying face down in the murky, still water.

Looking out farther, Ezra noticed one of the small islands where soldiers were hanging in trees, clutching bushes, or lying along the banks, trying desperately to keep their heads above water while hoping to be rescued. In the distance church bells rang; and steamboats sounded their horns and bells, alerting Memphis to the tragedy and the immediate need for rescue workers. Small boats, cutters, and several military gunboats left the wharf in search of survivors. Crewmen aboard the steamer *Bostonia II,* traveling downriver, saw the *Sultana* burning and sent out a yawl to help rescue people out of the cold water. Other boats traveling upriver began to be inundated with dead bodies floating past Memphis.

Sitting on the shore, Ezra saw the *Sultana* round a bend, still circling slowly, still burning. The boat drew closer, then caught in an eddy at the head of an island where it stuck and continued to rotate surreally in the water. Now that the boat was closer, Ezra could see a number of men huddled on the hull of the boat. Debris burned all around them. "Look there!" he said to his men. "There are still people alive on that boat. We've got to do something."

"Do you want to try to float the coffin back out there?" Roberto asked.

"I have a better idea," Carlos called. "Over there, look. There are some trees that have been knocked down. If we can lash them together somehow, we can make a raft. Give me your belts, men."

Bonesteel and Whitecloud were already pulling out some rough logs nearly twelve feet long. They spaced them about six feet apart and with the belts and some wire they found along the shore, they lashed the logs together and laid several smaller trees across them. The raft was shaky and uncomfortable, but as they shoved it into the water, it stayed afloat.

Using rough boards as paddles, Ezra and Bonesteel navigated the raft toward the *Sultana,* pulling up to within ten to fifteen feet of the burning boat. While Bonesteel kept the raft wedged close, Ezra swam over to the side and scaled the wall up to the main deck, pulling himself over the railing and onto the floor. The macabre sight that greeted Ezra's senses nearly overwhelmed him. Dead bodies, charred bones, and body parts were strewn in every direction Ezra looked. The awful smell of burnt flesh seemed to surround the boat. The fire had burned a huge hole through the center of the deck, and the flames were now leaping out of the hull like a blaze in a fireplace.

The hull itself was covered with beams and flooring from the upper decks and all sorts of burning debris and was intensely hot. Justice made his way over to the tip of the boat, the only area that had not yet been consumed by fire and where twenty-five men had squeezed into a space normally occupied by six men. Many of the men had burns over large portions of their bodies, especially their hands and faces, from trying to fight the flames. They had backed up inch by inch, and now there was nowhere left to go. Several men were seriously injured with broken bones and could hardly move.

"We've come to get you off this boat, but we can take only six men at a run," Ezra said, pointing to the raft below. "Let's go. Quickly now, but be careful getting into the raft. It is not the most stable craft you've ever been on."

"Neither is this one," an elderly soldier said with a grin and an undaunted spirit.

"OK, get six more ready to go. We'll be right back," Ezra instructed.

The first six passengers sat tenuously on the log raft as Ezra and Bonesteel rowed them to shore. Harry Whitecloud swam out to meet them and helped pull the men off the raft into the waiting arms of the Hawkins brothers, who helped them to the ground next to O'Banyon's coffin. As soon as they unloaded, Justice and Bonesteel immediately returned to the *Sultana* again.

By now the remaining men had wrapped wet blankets around themselves in an effort to fend off the unbearable heat. The fire was licking at the deck in front of them. There was no time to spare. "Give me the wounded and injured men next," Justice instructed. "In case you must jump before we get back, don't panic. It's daylight now, and if you are in the river, somebody is sure to find you."

Justice and Bonesteel took the injured to shore, made another run, and then one more. As the last seven men were climbing down the sides of the *Sultana,* the flames erupted on the hull in the exact spot where they had been hunkered down just moments previously; a roaring fire engulfed the entire bow.

"Row, Bonesteel, row!" Justice shouted. The two strong men poured every remaining bit of energy into pulling the makeshift raft away from the boat. They had paddled about twenty feet away from the fiery wreckage when the *Sultana* heaved as though making one last gasp for breath and then plunged below the surface of the river, dropping about twenty-six feet and landing on the Mississippi riverbed. An enormous cloud of steam rose off the river where the boat had disappeared. The strong suction caused by the sinking steamer and the huge wake that followed nearly capsized Justice and Bonesteel's fragile raft, but the two soldiers kept rowing hard, and miraculously the raft remained afloat. After a few frightening seconds, the river went back to normal flood stage, and unless a person knew what horrible events had recently transpired, all evidence of the *Sultana's* existence was gone.

The evidence of the steamer's demise, however, was strewn up and down the Mississippi's banks on both the Tennessee and the Arkansas sides of the river. Wreckage and bodies were everywhere, it seemed. By the time Ezra and Reginald Bonesteel had paddled the last of the *Sultana's* survivors to shore, Harry Whitecloud had started a bonfire to keep the men warm and also to serve as a beacon for rescuers. Harry and the Hawkins twins had already collected half a dozen other survivors and had them resting as comfortably as possible along the riverbank.

A farmer came by driving a horse-drawn open wagon and offered to take some of the injured men to a hospital in Memphis. Ezra and Harry Whitecloud carefully lifted Anna Harvey into the back of the wagon with the others. Anna had lost her precious child and husband and was suffering from exposure and hypothermia but otherwise it seemed that she might survive.

Her eyes brightened when Ezra leaned over the side and said, "We'll try to come to the hospital to check on you later today."

"I'd be most grateful," she said. "I have no family in this part of the country. William and our baby were all I had. Now that they are gone, I don't know what I'm going to do."

"Don't concern yourself about that right now," Ezra said, gently patting her shoulder. "You just rest and get better. We'll see you later."

He watched the woman with admiration as the wagon pulled away. Even in these awful circumstances, the brightness in her eyes reflected a quiet strength within her heart, a quality that Justice recognized and appreciated.

16

By eight in the morning, the Memphis riverfront was in chaos. More dead and mutilated bodies washed ashore every few minutes along the Mississippi's banks. Even callous and crusty riverfront workers — men who had been on the wharf for years and had seen and heard it all — couldn't keep from getting choked up at the horrendous sights. Rescue crews pulled in human beings like fishermen might land a large catch of trout. Wounded, injured, scalded men and women were pulled into any craft that could ply the Mississippi; the survivors were then hauled to the riverfront where horse-drawn ambulance wagons transported the victims to local Memphis hospitals.

The people of Memphis and the small communities along the river responded immediately to the tragedy, ignoring normal business matters or other responsibilities for a time and throwing themselves into the rescue efforts. Many residents along the Tennessee and Arkansas riverbanks opened their homes, taking in dozens of injured and dying passengers and trying to make them comfortable lying in their living rooms, on their porches, anywhere they could find space.

All day long, search and rescue efforts continued on the river. But even battle-tested soldiers had difficulty grappling with the gruesome task. The sailors aboard the U.S.S. *Vindicator*, a steamer manned by mostly older soldiers, had to stop mid-river to clear driftwood that had gotten lodged in its paddle wheels after floating downstream from the *Sultana*. To their horror, the soldiers discovered the boat's paddle wheels clogged with dead bodies instead.

The farmer returned several times to the location along the riverbank where Ezra and his men were caring for the survivors they had found. Once the survivors were all transferred to town or to hospitals, the farmer made one last trip to pick up Ezra's men and the coffin of Shaun O'Banyon.

"Easy, now," Roberto said to Carlos, Harry, and Reginald as they hoisted the coffin on board the wagon. "This fellow has already had a rough ride. We don't want to lose him now." Ezra sat up front with the farmer, and the other men sat in the back and steadied the coffin as the rickety wagon bounced over the pock-marked dirt road.

"Where are you goin'?" the farmer asked after a few minutes.

"That's a good question," Ezra said with a laugh. "We're just glad to be going any-where — and especially traveling on a safe form of transportation."

"How 'bout I drop you at Beale Street?" the farmer suggested. "That seems to be where a lot of activity is focused right now."

"Good, that's where we want to be. We need to find our friend who was helping to transport survivors off the river, and we'll need to get some fresh clothes. I'd also like to wire General Sherman with a report."

"Sherman?"

"Yeah, he's our boss."

"He's probably busy today. You know they just caught Lincoln's assassin yesterday. Some actor fellow. He calls himself John Wilkes Booth."

"No, I hadn't heard that," Ezra replied.

"We've been rather occupied," Bonesteel said.

"For the next few days, everything you're going to read in the papers around here is going to be rather depressing," the farmer said. "I heard this morning that a number of people have already purchased advertising space in the local newspaper, offering rewards and asking if anyone has seen their loved ones lost on the *Sultana.* It's going to be a tough time for a lot of people."

The farmer pulled the wagon in to the wharf area on the edge of Beale Street. The wharf was a frenzy of ambulances and wagons loaded with the wounded, injured, or dying passengers from the *Sultana.* In addition, dozens of survivors were being unloaded by the rescue boats. Their faces and bodies black with smoke, many of the men were burned, bruised, or scalded. Standing waist deep in water, helping to carry men to shore was Nathaniel York.

"My brothers!" he called, when he saw Ezra and the men getting off the farmer's wagon. "I'm so glad that you finally got here. It's been a busy morning here, as you can see."

"Why am I not surprised to find you here?" Ezra asked with a smile, as he slapped Nate on the back. "I should have known that you'd be wherever the hurting people were. How did you make out with the rescue efforts?"

"Colonel Berry and I succeeded in pulling forty-five men from the river, as well as two women and three small children. That's not counting the dead, of course. But we managed to save fifty people. Most of them are in hospitals here in Memphis, but a few simply got up and walked away under their own power. I wasn't going to argue with them."

"Have you seen anybody we know, Nate?" asked Ezra.

"Well, Mrs. Harvey is in Gayoso Hospital. She seems to be responding well, but she took some severe blows out there."

"Any others?"

"No, sir. I'm sorry, Ezra. I haven't seen anyone even remotely familiar."

Along the shore the women of the Sanitary Commission, a ladies aide society, waited patiently. As the men walked or were carried to solid ground, the women gently washed each person's face. They helped remove any remnants of dirty, wet clothing still worn by the survivors and gave out red flannel shirts and underwear to wear instead. Many of the men had lost their clothes in the fire; others had stripped them off before plunging into the river. The compassionate women on the wharf were not embarrassed by the men's nakedness and worked with uninhibited yet modest discretion, assisting each man into a waiting ambulance, wagon, or carriage, sending him off as rapidly as possible, with a "God bless you, sir" to the nearest hospital. Women survivors were treated the same way, except instead of the red shirts and shorts, the women were wrapped in blankets.

Ezra and his men found a hotel on Adams Avenue. The clerk behind the counter stared at their wet, shredded clothing, their faces smeared with soot, oil, and blood, and their singed hair. "I'm sorry, gentlemen. It is not our policy to let out our rooms to men who do not have any baggage, and who look . . . er, shall we say, shabby?"

Reginald Bonesteel pulled his Henry .44 out of the leather weapons sack. "I've been looking forward to shooting this baby, just to make sure the water didn't get to it and that everything is still working properly." He raised the Henry toward the clerk behind the counter.

"Yes, I see," the clerk said hastily. "I'm sure we have a lovely room on the back side of the hotel where you men will be quite comfortable."

"It could be on the back side of the moon, and I wouldn't care right now," Nathaniel York said.

"As long as it has a tub and some water and a place to lie down," Carlos added.

"Yes, sir. All of our rooms have sinks and water pitchers. And soap, too!" The clerk paused as though making sure that Ezra and the men understood. "And we can bring you all the warm water you will need."

"We'll need plenty," Roberto Hawkins said. "I want to take a nice long bath."

After cleaning up and resting for an hour or so, the men went to get clean clothes at a general store in town. Ezra then went to a telegraph office to send a wire to General Sherman alerting him of his whereabouts and the tragic accident aboard the *Sultana*. Meanwhile the Hawkins twins unloaded O'Banyon's coffin. Reginald Bonesteel and Harry Whitecloud went to see an undertaker to make arrangements to leave the case in his care overnight.

After all the perfunctory details were taken care of, Ezra and the group decided to go to the homes and hospitals to see if they could help identify any deceased passengers and to encourage any survivors. They started at Soldier's Home, a small facility that was overwhelmed with more than 250 severely injured passengers. Gayoso and other hospitals were equally crowded with injured and burned men and women sitting or lying in the halls, on the floor, anywhere space could be found to make them as comfortable as possible until the medical personnel could get to them.

Visiting in the hospitals, it quickly became obvious to Ezra and the men that the nightmare was not yet over for many of the people being treated in the medical centers. As Justice and his men walked down the corridors, grim sights abounded. The agonizing cries of the men and women who had been burned or scalded were heartrending.

"Can a couple of you guys give me a hand with this man?" a doctor called out from where he was kneeling on the floor over a burn victim.

Ezra and Harry stooped down to help the doctor lift the man onto a table. His skin was beet red and had the texture of an onion peel. If the men even grazed his skin with their hands or clothing, the man's burnt skin fell off onto the table. Ezra and Harry moved the man to a ward with dozens of other men who were severely scalded. The room itself seemed to wail in misery, as the agonizing groans, moans, and outbursts from the patients echoed off the bare walls.

"How much pain can a person endure?" Harry Whitecloud asked as he passed a burn victim.

"If it's any consolation, in most of these cases, their suffering will be short-lived," a physician told Ezra Justice. "Many of these men — probably about one out of every two — will be relieved by death in just a few hours. We're doing all that we can to make them as comfortable as possible until they die."

"That's the best you can do?" Harry Whitecloud sounded irritated.

"We were not prepared to receive such a large number of burn patients. We've wired for help, more medical supplies, and morphine. Doing skin grafts will be possible in a few weeks, perhaps, for some who survive, but many of these people have had such traumas to their bodies, they are barely functioning. We're doing everything we can for them."

"I understand," Harry said. "I didn't mean to imply that you were shirking your duties. It's just so heartrending to hear their cries and not to be able to help them."

"You can pray for them," the doctor said. "Pray for their souls. That is the most important thing you can do right now. Their bodies may die, but their souls will live forever."

"May we pray for these men right now, doc?" Nathaniel York asked.

"Absolutely. I wish you would."

Nate looked at Ezra.

Ezra shook his head affirmatively.

The men split up two by two and circulated throughout the room, offering brief prayers and a few words of encouragement over each person in the ward. Many of the patients were delirious in pain, others were incoherent, but some understood every word.

"God bless you," one horribly burned man said, wheezing as he reached up to Ezra. "Thank you for coming. I know God has heard your prayers, even if not all of us could."

"Take it easy, my friend," Ezra said, looking down at the man on the gurney. "The end of this life is the beginning of eternal life. You believe that, don't you? If God helps you to get better here, good. If you go to meet him there, that will be even better."

"I know that's right," the man answered hoarsely. "I'm trusting in Jesus, and I'm not afraid, either way."

"That's the spirit," Justice replied, as he gently touched the man's shoulder.

As the men left the ward and walked down the corridor, they heard a raspy voice call out, "Bonesteel."

Reginald Bonesteel looked around and saw a man lying on a bed, his legs covered by a sheet. "Private Cartwright," he said in amazement. "My good man . . . I am so glad to see you!"

Bonesteel, Ezra, and the rest of the squad gathered around Cartwright's bed. The man had a few gashes on his face and hands but otherwise looked to be in fairly good shape. He looked up at Ezra and the men as he shook hands with Bonesteel. "This man saved my life," he said. "He found a door, put me on it, and shoved me overboard . . . even though he had quite a few misgivings about the matter, I do believe. Isn't that right, Mr. Bonesteel?"

"Quite a few," Bonesteel said with a smile. "Truthfully I didn't think you would make it."

"You asked God to be with me, and he was," Cartwright said.

"Glory be!" Roberto gushed.

"If Mr. Bonesteel hadn't helped me, I most likely would have burned to death on the *Sultana.* But thanks to him, I'm alive. The doc said I might even be able to go home in a few weeks."

"That's wonderful, Private," Bonesteel said.

"And how's the leg?" Ezra asked, recalling the nasty wound Cartwright had received. He nodded toward the sheets covering Cartwright's legs.

"Well, I'll have to learn to walk again," Cartwright said. "A surgeon had to amputate the wounded leg," he said, as he pulled back the sheet, revealing his one bruised leg, and the absence of the other. "But he saved my life by doing so. I have a lot to be thankful for."

"Yes, we all have a lot to be thankful for," Ezra said.

Tears welled up in Cartwright's eyes. "If it wasn't for you men, I'd have been dead twice within the past few days. I know God sent you as my guardian angels. Thank you."

Ezra nodded. "You're going to make it just fine, Private. Incidentally, what is your first name?"

"Edward, sir. Private Edward Cartwright."

"Alright, Edward Cartwright, you get home and have a happy life." Ezra and the men shook hands with Private Cartwright and went on their way. They spent most of that day in the hospital, encouraging the wounded, helping the doctors and nurses move patients, and carrying out the corpses of those who didn't make it.

As a matter of discretion, they avoided going into the women's ward unless a doctor or nurse needed their assistance. Many of the women patients, especially those who had been burned, were in various stages of undress, so the men respected their privacy as much as possible.

Near the end of the day, however, as Ezra and the men were preparing to leave the hospital, they walked by the doorway to the women's ward. A nurse called after them. "Excuse me! You there," she said, pointing toward Ezra Justice. "One of our patients would like to see you before you go."

"Me?" Ezra pointed at his chest.

"That's what she said. She says that you saved her life, and she would like to thank you."

"Oh, really?"

"Yes, sir. Right this way. She's behind that curtain over there, the one that separates the ward. Please follow me."

Ezra shrugged his shoulders and said, "I'll meet you men out front. Nate, come with me."

"Excuse me?"

"Just come, Nate."

"Yes, sir. Sorry, sir," he said with a twinkle in his eye. "I didn't catch your drift at first." Ezra and Nate followed the nurse into the women's ward, carefully averting their eyes from anything that might seem improper for them to see. The nurse smiled at the men's chivalry. She led them to a beautiful, petite woman, covered up to her shoulders by a sheet, everything else but her head and hands covered by long-sleeved, high-necked beige pajamas. The attractive woman was sitting up at about a forty-five degree angle, an open Bible lying on her lap.

Ezra and Nate recognized Anna Harvey immediately. "Hello, gentlemen," Anna said demurely. "I am so glad to see you." She nodded at Nate and looked at Ezra, their eyes connecting.

Ezra quickly broke the gaze. "And we're glad to see you, ma'am," he said. "You were quite a trooper out there last night."

"And you, good sir, saved my life. From the bottom of my heart, I thank you so much." She looked first at Ezra then at Nate. "Thank you both. I didn't really want to jump into that water in the first place, but William — my husband, um . . ." she paused and wiped a tear from her eyes. "I'm sorry. William, my late husband, was insistent, that we should jump. I suppose he was right in one sense because I am here. But he and our baby . . ." Large tears flowed down Anna Harvey's face. "William and our precious baby did not. . . ."

"We know, ma'am," Ezra said quietly. "We're so sorry. You have our deepest condolences at the loss of your husband and child."

"Thank you, gentlemen. I was just reading in the Scripture where Jesus told some women, 'If you believe in me, you shall live, even if you die.' I believe that . . . but I'm going to miss my family so much. I still can't believe they are gone. I keep looking at the hallway, half expecting William and our baby to come through the door at any moment. But I know they won't be coming. . . ."

Anna Harvey dabbed at her eyes with a clean, white handkerchief. "The women of the Sanitary Commission," she said, nodding toward the handkerchief. "Have you ever seen such compassion and kindness? They brought me this handkerchief, and these lovely, soft pajamas." She swept her delicate hand from her neck down across the sheet covering her body. "They were so kind and caring to do so. My clothes were in tatters."

"Yes, ma'am. We know," Ezra said, his face flushed a bit as he stood awkwardly looking at Anna.

Nate broke the silence. "But you seem to be doing quite well, now, ma'am. Are you injured?"

Anna smiled up at Nate. "Nothing serious. Just a broken heart." Her eyes dropped to the Bible. "But I know God will see me through. And I'm sure that I am not the only wife and mother who is going to be dealing with loss this week. So many families were looking forward to seeing their loved ones who have been away for such a long time. It just doesn't seem fair, does it?" She looked up at Ezra. "After all their suffering in those prisons and finally getting to safety, congratulating themselves on surviving, and looking forward to starting life afresh . . . then that awful calamity on board the boat. It makes me shudder to think that so many noble heroes will not be going home after all."

"Yes, ma'am," Ezra said quietly.

Anna Harvey shook her head and smiled. "I apologize for going on so, but there are so many questions running through my mind right now. Why did this happen? What does it all mean? Where am I supposed to go now? What am I to do? Perhaps you have some of those same questions."

"Yes, ma'am, we do. But we have one more mission to fulfill, so we know where we will be heading tomorrow," said Nate.

"Oh?"

"Yes, ma'am," Ezra said. "We're taking one of our comrades home to be buried."

"He died as a result of last night?"

"No, a few days ago," Ezra replied. "He

saved our lives. So it is only fitting that God used us to help save yours. I don't know what it all means just yet, but I do believe that nothing happens without God's awareness. He must have a plan for us. There's some bigger reason why we are still alive today when so many others around us are gone."

"You are a perceptive man, sir," Anna said, looking again deeply into Ezra's eyes. She shook her head slightly, as though coming back from some profound thought. "I'm sorry, gentlemen. We've never been properly introduced. My name is Anna Harvey." She reached out her hand to Nate.

"I'm Nathaniel York, ma'am. So glad to know you."

Anna reached toward Ezra, taking his rough hand in hers and holding it softly. "And you, sir?"

"I'm Captain Ezra Justice, ma'am. We actually met on the deck of the *Sultana* before the accident, but I can't blame you for not remembering."

"Oh, I didn't forget, Captain." Anna smiled and looked down at the sheet, before looking back up at Ezra. "I owe my life to you, Ezra Justice. I will never forget you, not for a single day. And I shall thank God for you and pray for you each day for the rest of my life."

"Er . . . ah, thank you, ma'am." Ezra reluctantly slid his hand out from Anna's. "I believe it is time for us to be going, isn't it, Nate?"

"Huh? Oh, yes, sir, Captain Justice. It has been a pleasure, ma'am." Then with that same twinkle in his eye that Ezra had seen before, Nate said, "And I do hope that our paths cross again under much more pleasurable circumstances."

"Thank you, Mr. York," Anna replied. Her eyes brightened. "I appreciate that, and I hope you are a prophet." She smiled openly, her face radiant.

"Good-bye, ma'am."

"Please call me Anna, if I may call you Ezra."

"It would be my pleasure," Ezra said.

"And it's not good-bye, Ezra," she said with a smile. "See you later. May God be with you and keep you safe. And may we meet again."

"I hope we do, Anna," as Ezra nudged Nate toward the door. They stopped in the doorway to wave one more time to Anna Harvey, who waved to them from her bed.

"I think she likes ya, Ezra," Nate said as the two men bumped into each other going through the doorway.

"We saved the woman's life, Nate. What would you expect?"

"Oh, I don't know," Nate replied, whimsically raising his eyebrows and smiling broadly. "I just think she likes you."

"Aw keep quiet." Ezra said. "Let's go. The other guys are probably going stir crazy out front." But as they walked away, Ezra thought, *Anna Harvey. She was rather pretty. And she did seem to like me.*

17

"Yes, sir; these are some of the finest animals I've ever had here at the stables," said James Tucker, the owner of a livery stable on the edge of Memphis. Ezra and his men were shopping for new horses since theirs had been trapped in the hold of the *Sultana.* "It really grieves me that I lost my horse in that boat," said Carlos Hawkins, as he patted a brown stallion.

"I know what you mean," Ezra replied. "I was pretty attached to mine, too."

"Ahhh, I have the perfect horse for you, Captain," Mr. Tucker said. "He's big and strong. That white horse right over there."

"He looks like a fine animal," Ezra agreed. "How old is he?"

"Just on the south side of four years old," Tucker replied. "He'd make a great horse for you for a long time to come."

Ezra saddled the horse and took it for a ride. By the time he came back, he was sold.

"I'll take him," he said.

"Don't you want to know how much he's selling for?" Tucker asked.

"I'm sure you're an honest man, Mr. Tucker. Besides the army is paying for him."

All of Justice's men carefully picked out new horses, as sort of a perk granted by the Union army. The Hawkins twins selected dark brown stallions; Harry Whitecloud found a beautiful brown and white palomino; Reginald Bonesteel found a large, sleek stallion; and Nathaniel York chose a light-brown beauty.

As the men loaded their belongings and horses and of course, Shaun O'Banyon's coffin, on board the *St. Patrick,* another steamer that would take them the remainder of the trip to St. Louis, they felt eerily uncomfortable. Many of the soldiers who survived the nightmare on the *Sultana* were understandably nervous about getting back on board another steamboat, supposedly taking them to safety.

The search and rescue efforts continued on the river, but it was generally accepted that at least eighteen hundred people had perished due to the explosion on the *Sultana.* Rumor had it that the death toll was even higher. Nobody knew for sure, and because there were no accurate rolls that listed the names of men who had boarded the *Sultana* in Vicksburg, the true death toll would never be known. Of the nearly 2,500 soldiers, civilians, and crewmen on board, only 783 survived. Only 18 of those were civilians or members of the *Sultana's* crew. Less than 150 men had survived the *Sultana* unscathed and were ready and able to complete their trip along with Ezra Justice and his men to St. Louis.

"I have to be straight with ya, Ezra. I'm not all that happy about getting on another steamboat," Nate said, as the boat pulled away from the dock in Memphis.

"Nate, the *Sultana* was a catastrophe waiting to happen. Besides that, we have to get O'Banyon home."

"I wonder how many people perished on the *Sultana*," Nate said.

"Too many," Ezra said quietly.

Nate and Ezra stood on the deck of the steamer silently gazing out across the still-flooded lowlands as the boat turned upstream in the muddy Mississippi. Each man seemed lost in his own thoughts. There was no need for words.

A short distance up the river, Ezra and Nate suddenly stood to attention. There, rising from the depths of the muddy water, and now partially visible because the water level had receded a bit, were the remains of one of the *Sultana's* large smokestacks. Like a gravestone on the water, the stack marked the spot and kept a vigil over the sunken vessel and the dead men, women, and children that lay with her.

Ezra just bowed his head as the *St. Patrick* steamed by the wreckage.

Nate finally broke the silence. "Captain Coxley and Colonel Stanley must be burning in hell right now."

"No doubt."

Sadly, outside of Memphis and the surrounding communities, few people in the United States even knew that the country had just suffered the worst maritime tragedy in the history of the nation. They were consumed with reestablishing life at the end of the war and caught up in the awful circumstances surrounding President Lincoln's assassination and the capture of John Wilkes Booth. The fact that more soldiers had died in Tennessee and Arkansas was not news to the rest of the continent.

Roberto, Carlos, Reginald, and Harry joined Ezra and Nate on the deck. The spring sunshine warmed their faces, and a slight breeze ruffled their hair as the boat traveled northward. "What do you fellows think you will do after we deliver O'Banyon to his wife?" Ezra asked.

"I'd like to finish my education," Harry said. "I want to become a doctor and then go back out west and work with the Sioux again. They have an idea that the white man has some great medicine men, but they just don't trust the white man's methods."

"What about you, Reginald? Will you go back to West Point?"

"I think not, my good Captain Ezra," Bonesteel said with a laugh. "I've had about all the stuffy military routine that I can handle. These past twelve months have been some of the toughest of my life, but I have to be honest with you. Working with you men has been the most fulfilling time of my life. Actually, I think I'm starting to like you Americans," Bonesteel said with a laugh. "There's something about wide open spaces and freedom that is intoxicating to me. I'm up for a new adventure, and I hear that there are fortunes just waiting to be made out west. That seems to be a likely direction for me."

"How long do you think it will be before the army musters us out?" Carlos asked.

"I'm not sure," Ezra replied. "Probably a matter of weeks or a month or two at the most, I suppose."

"What about you, Ezra? What are your plans?" Roberto asked.

"Right now the first order of business for me — for all of us, really — is to get Shaun's body back to his wife and to bury him on his own land. We made that promise to him and once the soldiers get off this boat safely, that's where we're heading."

It was bittersweet saying good-bye to the men who had started out on the journey from Vicksburg with Ezra Justice and his men. A few of the men who had family members waiting for them at the docks embraced their loved ones in tearful reunions. The other men stoically tried to wave good-bye, but more than a few broke down in tears as they hugged fellow survivors, men with whom they had served and fought, with whom they had endured the horrors of Cahaba or Andersonville prison camps, and with whom they had beaten the odds by getting off the blazing *Sultana.*

While Ezra and Harry took care of the paperwork regarding the former prisoners, Reginald Bonesteel secured a horse and wagon. He and Nate and the Hawkins twins carried Shaun O'Banyon's coffin off the *St. Patrick* and loaded it in the buggy for the final portion of the trip.

"Do you think anyone has notified Mrs. O'Banyon that her husband has died?" Carlos asked, as the men mounted their horses.

"I don't see how they could have," Ezra replied. "He's been with us the entire time, and nobody even knows that Shaun was killed. I didn't mention it in my wire to General Sherman. Telling him about the *Sultana* was enough."

"So she doesn't even know that her husband is dead?" Roberto asked.

"I'm afraid not," Ezra answered.

Justice and his riders headed northwest from St. Louis, west of the Mississippi River into Missouri. They cut southwest to Jefferson City, about 135 miles away, and less than halfway between the river and Kansas City. Wherever they could, they loaded onto a train, although it was not always possible, especially as they neared their destination — Clinton, Missouri. A small, dusty, midwestern town, partly organized by Daniel Boone's son, Daniel M. Boone, Clinton was named for DeWitt Clinton, governor of New York and a strong proponent of the Erie Canal. About 150 miles southwest of Jefferson City, Clinton in 1865 could not be reached by train, so Ezra and his men covered much of the last portion of the trip by horseback. They were tired and dirty by the time they reached the outskirts of the town.

"How are we going to find O'Banyon's farm?" Carlos asked, as the men rode into the Clinton town square, pulling behind them the wagon carrying their friend's coffin.

"I'm hoping that somebody in town knows where he lived. Let's spread out and see what information we can discover. Nate, you and Bonesteel go to the general store; Roberto, you and Carlos go over to the livery stable; and Harry and I will check out the saloon," Ezra replied. The men headed off in their respective directions to ask around town for information regarding the whereabouts of the O'Banyon farm.

Riding into town, Ezra noticed a man dressed in a Confederate soldier's long coat saddling his horse. Around his neck was a red bandanna; another red handkerchief circled his wrist, and a red hatband with a long tail stretched down his back. Ezra recognized the tell-tale outfit immediately — the Death Raiders.

Harry Whitecloud saw the man, too, and instantly reached for his gun.

"Easy, Harry," Ezra said quietly, staying his hand.

"Why is a Death Raider in this town?"

Harry hissed angrily.

"I don't know. But let's find out what we're dealing with. Up ahead there's a saloon. Someone in there might have the information we need."

At the general store Nate and Reginald saw two more members of the Death Raiders loading supplies into a wagon. "Looks like we've got some trouble in this town," Nate said under his breath to Reginald.

"Yes. I'm glad I spent my time on the *St. Patrick* cleaning Mr. Henry," Bonesteel replied. "I wonder how many of them there are . . . and if the big man is here."

"Big man? Do you mean Mordecai Slate?"

"Yes, the big man who murdered O'Banyon. I'd love to see him face-to-face."

"Wouldn't we all, Reginald? Wouldn't we all?"

Ezra and Harry tied off their horses at a water trough and stepped up to "The Redheaded Lady," one of the first saloons in Clinton, opened by Leonard B. Watson back in 1837. The double-log cabin structure, formerly known as "Pollard's Tavern," stood on the northeast corner of the square and was the hot spot in town.

Justice pushed open the swinging doors, and he and Whitecloud stepped inside. They paused for a moment as their eyes adjusted to the light and carefully sized up the men in the room. A few men were seated at tables in the small establishment, and several men stood near the bar but no Death Raiders. Ezra and Harry sidled up to the bar. The bartender was washing some glasses, and when he saw the newcomers, he glanced around the room nervously. "What will it be?" he called without taking his hands out of the sink behind the bar.

"How about some information?" Ezra asked.

The bartender again looked around furtively. "We don't dispense information here. Whiskey, wine, or beer. That's all. What will it be?"

Ezra ignored the bartender's comment and continued, "We're looking for the farm that belongs to Shaun O'Banyon and his wife, Elizabeth."

"What do you want to know for?" the bartender probed.

Just then the two men who had been at the general store loudly entered the saloon and stepped up to the bar. "Whiskey," one of them said.

"Make it a double," the other man added. "And put it on Mordecai Slate's tab."

Ezra's head snapped up at hearing Slate's

name. He glared at the two men and felt the hairs on the back of his neck begin to bristle.

"Hurry up, barkeep," the first man called.

The bartender quickly placed a shot glass on the bar and filled it up past the line. He filled the second glass and started to pull the bottle away when the first man grabbed his arm, causing whiskey to pour all over the bar. "Leave the bottle," the roughneck said. "Better yet, get us two more bottles. And charge them to Mordecai Slate. That's *Mister* Mordecai Slate to you."

Harry Whitecloud's blood was beginning to boil.

"I'm drinking to the South. May she rise again soon!" The man drinking doubles was shouting. "Who will join me?" he roared, holding his glass high in the air.

A hush fell over the entire barroom. Several men sitting at tables close to the door got up and slipped out. Others simply sat staring straight ahead.

"I said, 'Who will join me in toasting the great Confederacy and Jefferson P. Davis, or whatever his name is.' " The belligerent double-drinker sauntered over to Harry Whitecloud, who was standing with his face toward the bartender, without saying a word. "What about you, Injun?" He shoved

Harry's arm.

Harry said flatly, "I'm not drinking."

His friend moved over next to him. "I never heard of an Injun who didn't like firewater. Hey bartender, give me a glass. I'm gonna pour the Injun a drink."

"I said I'm not drinking," Harry said icily, looking straight ahead.

Suddenly he turned to look directly at the two. "Especially with men who have raped and murdered all across the North and South."

Slate's men turned, their faces contorted with rage. "Injun, you're dead!" The Death Raiders went for their iron, but the men had no idea who they were drawing down on. Before the first man's gun cleared leather, Ezra's gun flashed, the bullet catching the loudmouth in the chest. Harry grabbed the gun wrist of the other man and thrust his knife into his throat. The first man stood staring at Ezra for a long moment while the blood trickled from his vest, then he fell over dead. The second man dropped his gun as his hands sprang instinctively to his throat. Harry's knife had neatly sliced the jugular vein. In less than five seconds, the gunslingers were both on the floor, dead.

Another of Slate's men heard the commotion from outside, burst through The Redheaded Lady's swinging doors, and was met by Ezra Justice's fist, smashing a brutal blow to his face. The man dropped like a rock. Justice picked up the man and shoved him into a chair right in front of his two bloody comrades lying on the floor.

Ezra looked at the thug and realized that he was just a boy, not much more than sixteen years old. Ezra grabbed a chair and placed it directly in front of him. "He's just a kid, Captain!" Harry called. Ezra straddled the chair and stared the boy right in the eyes. The boy's eyes were wide and unblinking. He glanced back and forth between Ezra and the dead bodies lying on the floor.

Ezra looked at the boy. "I want some information," he demanded, "and I want it now."

The boy glanced at the two members of the Death Raiders, then at Ezra, then back at the two dead men, without moving his head.

"What?"

"I said, I want some information."

Jittery, the boy looked all around the room as though hoping for some help.

"Talk!" Ezra demanded.

"What do you want to know?"

"Where's your boss?" Ezra growled.

"Mordecai Slate?"

"That's right."

"He's over in the courthouse, the dark-brick building across the way."

"What's he doing there?"

"I don't know. He runs this town. He can do anything he wants. He can have anything he wants — whiskey, money, women — which I think he is partaking in right now," the boy said with a nervous laugh.

Ezra glanced around at the other men in the room, most of whom had backed up against the walls, with a few left seated at tables. "Is that right?"

The men nodded affirmatively.

"And you men let him get away with that?" Harry addressed the men against the wall.

"They don't have any choice," the bartender offered.

"That's right," the boy said. "Slate will kill them in a moment, and they know it. And that's exactly what he's gonna do to you as soon as he finds out what you have done."

"Where is the sheriff?" Harry asked the bartender.

"Slate and his men killed the sheriff and one of his deputies as soon as the sheriff tried to interfere."

"How many men does Slate have?"

311

"Don't tell him!" squealed the boy.

In a flash Ezra snapped his .44 from his holster and pressed the gun right between the boy's eyes. "Then you tell me, or you will never see another sunrise."

"Twenty, maybe twenty-five or thirty on some days," the boy stammered. His cockiness had turned back into fear.

"Where are they?" Ezra demanded.

"A lot of the men are out roving about, seeing what they can find. Every day a few men come or go, some bringing back loot they've plundered from the countryside, others going out to find more. They bring it back and dump it at the courthouse, and Slate distributes it from there."

"Why here? Why is Slate and your gang in Clinton?"

"Clinton, Splinton, it doesn't matter to him. It's just another place to plunder, as far as Slate is concerned. When he has had his fill, we'll move on to the next place."

"Do you remember the man who stopped you along the road in the canyon outside Vicksburg about three weeks ago?" Ezra asked.

"Oh, yeah . . . that drunken Irishman."

"Why did Mordecai Slate kill him?"

"Because that guy jerked him off his horse and knocked him to the ground. I think

Slate may have let him go if he hadn't done that."

"Alright, kid." Ezra pulled the gun away from the boy's eyes. "I'm going to give you a chance. Get on your horse and get out of town. Go home, wherever home is. If I see you in this town again, you're going to be as dead as those two men on the floor. Do you understand what I'm saying?"

"Yeah, I understand."

"And don't make any stops on your way out of town. None. Not at the courthouse, not at the hotel, nowhere. Get on your horse and go. Now."

"Yes, sir. I'm on my way." The boy ran outside the saloon and leaped onto his horse. He spun the horse around and drove his spurs into the animal's side. The horse reared a bit and took off, heading off out of town at a dead run.

Meanwhile, inside the saloon, Ezra kept his .44 in his hand as he searched the faces of the men against the wall. "I'm looking for Shaun O'Banyon's farm. Does anybody here know where it is?"

The men looked at one another, but nobody said a word. Ezra leaned over the man whom Harry had killed with his knife. He turned the man over on his back so he was lying with his neck toward the men in the saloon, the knife still stuck in his throat. Ezra stood up, looked at the men, then leaned over the dead man again and pulled the knife out of his neck. He walked over to a big man sitting at a table nearby and wiped the blood from Harry's knife on the front of the man's shirt, right near his heart.

"I'm looking for Shaun O'Banyon's farm," he said. "Do you think you might be able to tell me where I can find it?"

"About five miles out of town," the big man said so quietly he could barely be heard.

"What's that? I didn't hear you," Ezra said. "Speak up."

"About five miles out of town, out near the old, abandoned mine. Beyond the river and up against the side of the mountain." The big man spoke loudly enough for everyone in the room to hear. "That's O'Banyon's property. That's where the O'Banyon lady lives. But I wouldn't get too close if I were you. She doesn't like company, and she'll tell you so with a shotgun."

18

Elizabeth O'Banyon began her day just as she had every other day since her husband Shaun had gone off to war. She stepped out on the front porch, let the sun drench her finely chiseled facial features, and stretched her arms above her head. Looking out at the tree line beyond their home, nestled in the foothills of the Ozark Mountains, she never ceased to be enthralled by the natural scenery all around her. And she never considered the truth that others readily accepted — that Elizabeth O'Banyon's own natural attributes greatly added to the exquisite beauty of the area.

Her bare feet reached the edge of the porch, and her toes curled over the step as she looked out at the panoramic scene in front of her. "Perhaps today," she said, as she had every day for the past several years. "Perhaps today my Shaun will come back to me."

She smiled as she felt the spring breeze gently caress her skin. It was as though God was saying to her, "Your Shaun is safe."

Elizabeth busied herself with the farm chores. A woman of charm and grace, Elizabeth was nonetheless a hard worker and not afraid to get dirty — especially since Shaun was not there to do the never-ending work around the property. Elizabeth tumbled into bed every night nearly exhausted but happy. She wanted to keep the property looking good so when Shaun came home, it would seem almost as if he'd never left the farm.

The farmhouse was not large, but it was a true reflection of Elizabeth — petite and earthy, with a bit of a flare, a white frame house with a large front porch with a white banister. Elizabeth recalled dreamily how, before the war, sometimes she and Shaun would sit on the porch at night and watch the moon and stars above them as they talked about their future together.

"Sometimes I worry, Shaun, what I would do if anything ever happened to you."

"Oh, don't trouble your pretty head with such nonsense," Shaun would say. "Nothing's gonna happen to me." Nevertheless, Elizabeth's words did cause Shaun to become more concerned for Elizabeth's welfare if he were not at home during a flare-up with the local Indian tribes.

Although the town of Clinton had been founded more than twenty-five years earlier, the settlers in that part of Missouri still encountered sporadic problems with the Pawnee Indians, the largest remaining tribe in the area. For the most part, the O'Banyons were on good terms with the Pawnee, but every so often some settler would kill or maim a member of the tribe, and then it wasn't safe for anyone around Clinton. Even Shaun and Elizabeth had to be prepared to protect themselves when some of the young Pawnee bucks would go on a killing rampage.

In 1861, as the war drew closer, Shaun took special precautions to safeguard his young wife, as well as himself. Behind their house was a flat-faced mountain, and within the moutain was an abandoned gold mine, once thought to be a rich treasure trove but long since given up as worthless. To Shaun O'Banyon, however, it was worth more than gold. Inside the mine were tunnels and air passages and a natural underground water supply. Shaun found a small heavy iron door that he installed on the opening of the mine and some small but heavy iron frames that he installed as gun ports. Once inside the mine the iron door could be locked from within, and the cave was virtually an impenetrable fortress. Considering that someday Lizzie O'Banyon may have to use the mine to protect herself from the Pawnees, Shaun began storing ammunition and several guns in the caves, as well as lanterns and oil, dried food, vegetables that Elizabeth canned in the fall, two cots, and even a small stove on which she could cook. "I think we could survive in the mine for two or three weeks if we ever had to, Lizzie," Shaun once said.

"Well, I pray that we never have to," she replied, "but it's nice to know that we could. In the meantime it's a good place to store all my canning and some of the salt-cured meat. Of course, if you would get rid of some of that ammunition, Shaun O'Banyon, I'd have more room in there for things that really matter — like food!"

"Now, Lizzie, one day you may thank me for loading in all that ammunition. In the meantime it's better to have it and not need it than to need it and not have it."

"You and your Irish logic," she snipped, then smiled when Shaun wasn't looking. Elizabeth O'Banyon appreciated her husband's concern for her and for setting her up to survive even if he wasn't there should their home come under attack.

Before Shaun went off to war, he made Elizabeth promise that she would maintain the fortress in readiness at all times. "This war probably won't last too long, but you never know about these kinds of things," he told her. "Please, Lizzie; if you want me to sleep at night and not to toss and turn worrying about you, please keep the mine stocked and the lanterns filled with oil. You may never have to use them, but if you do, I'll feel better knowing that you are safe inside the cave."

"Oh, alright," Elizabeth said. "I do enjoy canning, and the mine is the perfect place to keep things cool and dry. So I guess it won't be too much more work to keep everything else stocked up, too."

Now, more than three years later, Elizabeth still regularly refilled the lanterns in the mine and restocked the food supply. She kept the guns clean, too, and she knew how to use them.

Rumors had been swirling around Clinton for the past few weeks that the war was drawing to a close, that it seemed almost certain the Union army was going to cut off the last of the Rebel forces and the nation would get back to work, trying to heal the wounds that had been inflicted in recent years. Then there was all that awful stuff about President Lincoln being shot that sent everyone into a tizzy. Finally the news came that the war was over. But then that bunch of unsavory-looking fellows moved into Clinton.

Lizzie had seen them one day when she had gone into town for supplies. It seemed that about twenty-five or thirty of them had virtually taken over the town. Rude, arrogant roughnecks who claimed to be former Confederate soldiers, they certainly did not reflect the honor practiced by General Robert E. Lee. Quite the contrary, in Elizabeth O'Banyon's opinion. Even their name was despicable — the Death Raiders, they called themselves.

It didn't take long for the reputation regarding their propensity for pillaging, raping, and other violence to spread throughout the countryside. Fear created some unlikely allies, as weak men allowed evil to have full sway because they were unwilling to challenge Mordecai Slate and his men. Clinton's sheriff, Karl McCain, and his deputy had bravely confronted Slate, telling him to control his men. Slate simply laughed, and without warning, drew his gun and shot the sheriff and his deputy in cold blood. With no law to constrain them and nobody willing to resist them, the vicious members of the Death Raiders simply gave in to their passions and perversions.

"Hey, little lady, what's your name?" one of the creeps had accosted Elizabeth as she carried a sack of feed from the general store to her wagon. "Shouldn't you have a big man to carry that feed for you?"

"Maybe she needs you to go home with her today, to help her unload all those supplies in that wagon," said one of the other unkempt men wearing a red headband around his hat.

Elizabeth ignored both of the men and continued to load the wagon.

"How 'bout that, missy?" the first man asked. "How'd you like me to come home with you tonight?"

Elizabeth had endured enough of their insolence. "Yes, come right along," she retorted. "My husband would love to meet you."

"If you got a husband, how come he ain't loadin' the wagon, missy? Makes me think that you are all alone out there on that farm . . . so if you're all alone, you must be lonely, and I'm just the man to fill that loneliness." The two men burst into lascivious laughter.

Elizabeth reached into her wagon, pulled her 16-gauge shotgun out from under the seat. She pointed the shotgun right at the big-mouth's head. "You show your face at my farm," Elizabeth said, her Irish temper flaring, "and I will blast it off."

Elizabeth climbed onto the wagon seat and laid the still-cocked shotgun across her lap. She picked up the reins and urged her horses forward. She sat erect and kept her gaze straight ahead as she drove off. Yet for all her bombast the encounter with Slate's men had made her uncomfortable and had caused her to feel more than a little vulnerable.

That had been several days ago, but today had dawned bright and beautiful, a fabulous fresh spring morning. Elizabeth decided that she would get some of the chores done early, and then later in the afternoon she would put some new shoes on a few of the horses.

The clanging of the hammer against the iron forge echoed off the mountainside behind the O'Banyon home. It was the sound one might expect to hear from the blows by a burly blacksmith straightening a piece of hot iron, but the blacksmith in this case was a petite young woman. By mid-afternoon, Elizabeth was so busy hot-shoeing her horses that she didn't even notice the band of thugs riding up the horseshoe-shaped trail in front of her home. Had it not been for the O'Banyons' dog, Setter, a copper-colored mutt that Shaun had always given more dignity than he deserved by implying he was an Irish setter, Elizabeth may have been taken completely unaware. But as Elizabeth bent over the fire, heating the horseshoes, Setter began barking incessantly.

"Setter, what in the world is wrong with you?" Elizabeth asked, standing up straight, her blacksmith's apron hanging over her shoulders. She wiped her fingers across her face, leaving a charcoal smear, as she flicked off the perspiration above her eyebrows that was dripping down her cheeks, dotting the nape of her neck. That's when Elizabeth saw the trouble approaching.

Six armed horsemen wearing variations of Confederate Army uniforms, some decked out with red bandannas, and all wearing red headbands, approached the O'Banyon home. Even before Elizabeth could see their faces, she heard the man in the middle barking out orders to the others. "Adams, Barnes, collect the stock and kill a steer for supper; Carson, you and Mitchell, take the house, find the money, and look for any silver or anything else worth carrying away." It was clear to Elizabeth that these men had not come for a social call.

When the men spied the pretty woman, they took on a different tone. "Well, well, what do we have here?"

"Nothing like a pretty woman in a blacksmith's apron to warm me up," one of the ruffians hooted.

Elizabeth slowly reached over and grabbed the long-handled iron poker with a clamp that held a hot horseshoe in the fire. She eyed the men cautiously, especially the one in the middle. Obviously the leader, he seemed disinterested in her for himself; but it was also apparent from the banter Elizabeth could hear that he would not be opposed to his men having their way with her. It sounded as though he was offering her as some sort of reward to his men. Elizabeth angrily poked the horseshoe further in the fire.

The horsemen rode right up to where Elizabeth was working. Elizabeth pretended that she was unconcerned about their presence and continued to maneuver the shoe in the fire. With the rest of the hoodlums still on their horses behind him, the leader dismounted and walked over to Elizabeth's fire pit. "Good afternoon, ma'am," he said. "My name is Mordecai Slate." The way he said his name, Elizabeth got the impression that it was supposed to mean something to her. It didn't.

"So?"

Slate's expression turned dour. "My men here are hungry, thirsty, and have a few other appetites that need to be satisfied. So we thought we'd spend the afternoon with you, enjoying your hospitality."

Elizabeth's eyes flashed as her worst fears were confirmed in her heart and mind. "I've got nothing for the likes of you," she said.

The men behind Slate hooted and hollered, laughing and making snide remarks about Elizabeth, her blacksmith's apron, and what they had in mind for her.

"Oh, I think you do," Slate said coldly. "Where's your man?"

"None of your business."

"Well, let's just see what *is* my business." Slate stepped toward Elizabeth. As he did, Setter barked furiously, distracting Slate momentarily, providing Elizabeth with just the opportunity she needed.

She didn't wait to see what Slate had in mind. With lightning speed Elizabeth O'Banyon pulled the red-hot horseshoe from the fire; and with the long-handled clamp she thrust it right into the face of Mordecai Slate. Elizabeth felt the horseshoe connect with his face and beard and saw

Slate reel back in pain as the shoe seared into his skin, branding him. Slate's hands flew to his face as he stumbled backward, tripped, and fell to the ground. Several of his men bounded off their horses to his assistance.

Elizabeth dropped the poker and bolted for the cliff behind the house, the place that Shaun O'Banyon had prepared for just such a day as this. Elizabeth ran as though the devil himself was chasing her.

She rounded the corner of the house and raced across the yard. She pulled back the bush that concealed the opening to the mine, ripped open the door, and slipped inside, locking the strong iron panel behind her.

Enough daylight streamed in from the gun ports that Elizabeth didn't bother lighting a lantern. She grabbed one of the rifles and stuck it out the gun port. One of Slate's men started firing at her. Elizabeth returned his fire, catching him dead in the chest. Her second shot dropped another one of Slate's men from his horse.

Two of them pulled Mordecai Slate under a tree, out of the line of fire, while the other man ran around the house, returning fire in vain toward the mountain. Unless he could stuff a bullet down the barrel of Elizabeth

O'Banyon's gun, he had almost no chance of hitting her.

Slate got onto his horse and growled to his men, "Get that woman and bring her to me." He rode off toward town, alone.

"You better come out of there, little lady, or we're coming in after you!" one of the villains threatened.

"Come on in!" Elizabeth called out, as she returned several volleys of fire, sending the thugs for cover again.

More gunfire pelted the mountain mine door, but nothing impacted Elizabeth. She was safe in the cleft of the rock.

One of Slate's men came out the back door of the O'Banyon home. He was carrying the heliotype photograph of Lizzie and Shaun. "Hey, boys. Do you recognize this feller?" He raised the picture toward Slate's men so they could see it.

The men grinned.

The man slipped up to a tree and hunkered behind it. He held the picture out toward Elizabeth so she could see it. "Hey, sweetheart. Look what I found. So this is your man, huh, little lady? Well, I am so privileged to be the first one to tell you that your man ain't coming home."

"He will be home soon!" Elizabeth shouted in return. "And when he comes, he'll send your sorry hides to hell."

"Well, let me tell you why I know he won't be coming." The man with the picture looked over at his cohorts and waved the photograph again. "Because the Death Raiders sent your man to kingdom come just a few weeks ago."

"That's a dirty rotten lie!" Elizabeth screamed.

"So the only memory you will have of your recently deceased husband is this photograph."

Elizabeth felt her face flush. "Put it down," she cried from the iron door.

"Come and get it!" He shook the picture in the air. "You better come out of that hole, or I'll have to destroy this pretty picture."

Elizabeth's heart sank. That was her favorite photograph of Shaun and her, the one she'd convinced him to pose for right before he'd left to join the Union Army.

"Put that picture down, or I'll blow your brains out!" she yelled.

"Oh, well, now. Aren't we the toughy?" he said as he dangled the photograph for Elizabeth to see. "How much does this picture mean to you?" He ran his gloved hand across the picture, then pulled his knife.

"I'm tired of looking at you and your dead husband. I think I'll cut him out of the picture." He held his knife up as though he intended to slice the picture in half.

Elizabeth fired. The photograph flew out of the man's hand, as he clutched the bleeding hole in his wrist. "Why you dirty, little . . . !"

Setter had been barking incessantly at the intruders in the front of the house, but now he raced toward the rear. Slate's men saw the dog and opened fire on him as he headed across the yard, weaving between the trees and the well in the middle of the backyard.

Elizabeth saw Setter streaking toward the mine and in an instant was faced with a decision. Should she open the door and risk one of the intruders reaching the mine, or should she allow the dog to stay outside and be shot? She whistled loudly, squeezed off several more rounds, and reached around to open the door, just as Setter dashed up to the mine. The iron door creaked open, the dog bounded in with bullets ricocheting off the stone and the metal door as Setter ran inside to safety. The door squeaked shut behind him just as quickly.

Elizabeth looked at Setter, who was still panting heavily. She slid down the wall and put her hands to her face. "God, please tell me that man is lying to me about my Shaun." But in her heart, she knew he wasn't. Setter came to her and began licking the tears trickling down her face. Elizabeth pulled Setter closer to her. *How can I live without my Shaun?* She stood up slowly and began reloading the rifle.

"I can't."

The sound of gunfire caught the attention of the six men galloping toward Elizabeth O'Banyon's property. Behind them came a horse-drawn wagon carrying the body of their friend.

"Sounds like someone is in trouble," Nathaniel York said to Ezra Justice.

"It sure does," Ezra replied. "Let's ride. Carlos, you stay back with the wagon. The rest of us are going to find out what's going on!"

Justice and the riders raced toward the O'Banyon farm. As they approached the horseshoe-shaped trail in front of the property, they heard the gunfire and saw Slate's men firing at the mountain cliff behind the house. Strangely, they couldn't see what or who merited such an outburst of gunfire.

Elizabeth unlocked the steel door; the

expression on her face turned from sorrow to grim determination. "Shaun, I will see you in heaven real soon. But I'm going to send some of these men to hell first."

The men shooting at the mountainside turned and saw Ezra and his men approaching. The Death Raiders had no taste for a fair fight. They mounted up and headed out the opposite direction. Just then Elizabeth jerked the door open and ran out, firing at the departing riders.

As Justice and his men drew closer, Elizabeth O'Banyon turned her gun in their direction. She spun around and fired wildly. Ezra and the men scattered. Elizabeth turned and bolted back into the mine, slammed the door, and rammed the lock into place. She leaned against the door, her head pressed against the cool surface. "Lord help me. Give me the strength to deal with this."

"Better watch out!" Ezra called to the men. "That woman probably thinks we're part of Slate's gang. Split up and take cover."

Ezra waved Roberto Hawkins and Harry Whitecloud to the left side of the house while Reginald Bonesteel moved around behind the right side of the home. Ezra and

Nathaniel York rode toward the front of the house.

They dismounted and carefully ran toward the front porch, keeping low just in case anyone was inside firing from behind the windows. They crept up onto the porch and across to the front door, slamming their backs to the wall, one man on each side of the door. Ezra nodded to Nate, Nate kicked the door open and Ezra whirled inside, his finger on the trigger of the LaMat. Slowly, carefully, he and Nate stepped into the house. Outside a few more bullets whizzed by the windows.

But inside, the house was neat and orderly except for a few pictures that were strewn on the floor. Ezra looked at Nate and shrugged. Nate picked up one of the photos on the floor and handed it to Ezra. There in the photograph was their friend, Shaun O'Banyon, smiling at them as big as life, with that familiar sparkle in his eyes. Ezra nodded as he replaced the photograph on the shelf above the mantle from the spot where it had apparently been knocked off. "I guess we've come to the right place," he said quietly.

"Looks that way," Nate replied. "Take a look at this one." Nate handed Ezra a picture of an attractive young woman with long, flowing reddish-blonde hair, and wearing a pretty dress as she leaned on a shotgun.

"Meet Lizzie O'Banyon," Ezra said with a short laugh. "Figures that Shaun would have a feisty wife. She'd have to be something else just to keep up with him. Somehow we have to get her to stop shooting long enough that we can talk to her."

"Good idea. And how are we gonna get her to figure out that we're on her side?" asked Nate.

"I don't know, Nate," Ezra said. "But we'll figure out something. You go to the right side of the house and I'll go to the left."

19

"Mrs. O'Banyon! Mrs. O'Banyon, *please!*" Ezra called from the left side of the house where he knelt on the ground behind some barrels with Roberto and Harry Whitecloud.

The sound of a bullet punched the air.

"I guess she doesn't appreciate good manners," Roberto said with a smile.

"Either that, or she just thinks that everyone is an enemy now," Harry Whitecloud offered.

On the other side of the house, Reginald Bonesteel made a more formal appeal. "Madam, we have come in peace. Please hear us out. We are friends of your husband's."

Another spate of lead filled the air, and Bonesteel ducked for cover.

"There's only one thing to do," Ezra said to Harry. "I need to get over there." He pointed to the iron door on the front of the mineshaft.

"How are you going to do that, Captain?" Roberto asked.

"I want you guys to create some distractions on this side of the house."

"What kind of distraction do you have in mind?" Roberto asked. By now, Carlos had arrived with the coffin, parked the wagon near the front of the house, and joined Roberto, Harry, and Ezra.

"I have an idea," Ezra said. "Carlos, do you and Roberto still have any of those firecrackers?"

"Sure do," Carlos answered.

"Good. I want you to string some firecrackers to one of Harry's arrows. Harry, you fire the arrow right at the cave door. Give me time to get to the other side of the house before you fire."

"Got it, Captain," Harry said.

Ezra slipped around the front of the house and joined Bonesteel and Nate taking cover on the right side. "Do we have a plan?" Nate asked.

"Yeah. Carlos and Roberto are going to hook some firecrackers to one of Harry's arrows to create a distraction. When the firecrackers go off, I'm going to make a beeline for the mountain. The firecrackers will distract her long enough for me to get to the side of the wall."

"You hope, old chap," Bonesteel said.

Ezra looked up with a faint hint of a smile. "Old chap? Should I take that literally, Bonesteel?"

"Just run fast, Captain," Bonesteel replied.

Elizabeth O'Banyon peered out the gun port, wondering what was going on. It had been quiet, and she hadn't seen anyone in quite a while. *What are they doing out there?* she wondered. *Maybe they left. Or, maybe they just want me to think that they left. Well, they're not getting me out of this cave.* "Oh, God, please don't let them burn down my house!"

As Ezra waited for Harry to fire his arrow, he said to Nate, "By the looks of it, I don't think she can get that gun barrel turned around any more than a forty-five to sixty-degree angle. If I can keep my back against the stone, I think I can get close enough to talk with her without getting shot."

"What if she has a smaller pistol that she can fire closer to the mountain? It could be risky." Nate rubbed his moustache as he pondered the possibilities.

"I'll just have to take that chance," Ezra said.

Just then a blinding flash of light and a

series of short, loud pops caused Elizabeth to jerk back from the gun port. She recovered quickly. She looked out the gun port and saw a man running across the yard. She slammed the rifle into the gun port and fired off two quick rounds, barely missing him as the man dove toward the wall.

Ezra Justice brought his back up against the stone wall and began inching his way closer to the gun ports. By the time the smoke from the firecrackers had cleared, Ezra was within a few yards of the gun ports on the right side of the mine's entrance.

"Mrs. O'Banyon!" Ezra called.

A shot rang out but skittered off the house, far from where Ezra was standing with his back flat against the stone.

"Elizabeth. Please listen to me. My name is Captain Ezra Justice, and I'd like to talk to you."

"Aye, yes," Elizabeth called out. "I'm sure that's all you want to do is talk. Just like those other men. And I'd really like to talk to you, as well. Why don't you stick your head out there a little further, and I'll give you my answer."

"My name is Captain Ezra Justice, and your husband Shaun served with me in an elite corp doing special missions for General Sherman during the war. We've been close friends for quite a while now, and I promised him that I'd come to meet you."

"If that is true, he would have mentioned you." Another shot rang out, closer to where Justice was standing but still nowhere near him.

"Elizabeth, we're here to help you!"

"Yes, yes, I know. If you'll just show yourself a wee bit more," Elizabeth O'Banyon called. "I'd like to help you, too — to meet your Maker!" Several shots tore up the ground in front of where Justice was backed against the wall.

"Lizzie!" Ezra shouted. "I am not lying to you. We *are* friends of Shaun's! Honestly, we are."

Silence.

Inside the mineshaft Elizabeth O'Banyon was taken aback.

"Lizzie, I have your locket," Ezra said. "It has your photograph in it. Either you're going to believe me or you're not, but I'm going to step out and show you the locket that your husband Shaun gave me to bring to you."

Bonesteel looked at Nate. "Is he crazy?"

Nate didn't answer Reginald. Instead, he looked up and prayed, "Lord, please let her believe him."

Ezra stepped out from behind the wall of

338

the mountain and faced the gun ports in the mineshaft door, the barrel of the rifle pointed right at his chest. He held the locket in front of the gun port so Elizabeth could see it.

Slowly . . . very slowly, the gun barrel receded from the gun port. Ezra could hear a mournful sob from behind the door.

Whether it was the name "Lizzie" or the presence of the locket and all that it implied, Elizabeth O'Banyon felt tears creep into the corner of her eyes. With the rifle still in hand, she opened the iron door and stepped outside. She walked toward Ezra, her eyes never leaving the locket, almost as if she were afraid it might disappear.

Elizabeth handed Ezra the gun and gently took the locket from his hand. "Nobody ever calls me that name," she said softly. "Not my parents, not my friends, nobody. Only my Shaun ever calls me Lizzie."

Still looking at the locket, Elizabeth tilted her gaze toward Ezra's eyes. "Is it true? Is my Shaun gone?"

"Yes," Ezra said quietly. "He is."

She gently fingered the locket, pressed it to her heart, and dropped to the ground. Ezra bowed his head and remained respectful of her private moments with the locket. The other members of Justice's group came out from behind the house until all were standing nearby, behind Ezra.

"I'm very sorry, ma'am," Ezra said. "We all are."

"He promised that he'd come back home to me," Elizabeth sobbed. "Shaun would never tell me a lie."

"He didn't lie to you, ma'am," Ezra said, "and in a sense, he has come home to you. We have brought his body back so you can bury him on your property, just as your husband asked us to do with his dying breath." Ezra paused and took another deep breath of his own. He looked around at the other men behind him before continuing. "And ma'am, one of the last things he said . . . he asked us really, to tell you that he loved you to the end. He told us to tell you that you have been his light and strength."

Ezra looked at Nate. Nate nodded and continued. "And Mrs. O'Banyon, your husband asked us to tell you that he will be waiting for you . . . in heaven."

Elizabeth O'Banyon nodded and said through her tears, "You can bet your boots I will be there with you, Shaun O'Banyon." She looked up at Ezra and the other men. "We always said that if one of us gets to heaven before the other, we'd make sure an angel watched out for the other. What I figure is that he sent several angels to watch out for me. And those angels are you."

"Well, I don't know about that, ma'am," Nate said shyly.

"It's true. I was about to charge out there and kill as many of that scum as I could before they killed me. Your riding up scared them off." Elizabeth sighed, "I'm sorry I fired at you."

"That's alright, ma'am. I guess the Lord was looking out for us, too. I can see, by the two dead men lying on the ground, that you are a real good shot."

Setter nestled in next to Elizabeth on the ground. "Oh, Setter, what are we going to do? Your master isn't coming home." Something about the dog's presence brought out Elizabeth O'Banyon's softer side, and she immediately rose to her feet. "Gentlemen, please accept my apologies." She wiped at her tears. "Come inside," she motioned toward the house, "and Setter and I will see what we can find for you to eat. There is a well right there in the yard if you want to get some water for your horses or to fill your own canteens."

Elizabeth fluffed her dress that she had been wearing all day beneath the blacksmith's apron. She was wrinkled, disheveled, and dirty, but she quickly regained her composure and led the way to the house. She hurriedly put some food on the table and then excused herself. "Please sit down and eat; make yourself at home, gentlemen. If you don't mind, I will go freshen up. I don't want Shaun to see me looking such a mess. I shall return shortly."

Justice and the men sat around the table talking quietly among themselves in Elizabeth's absence. "I guess that went about as well as one might expect," Reginald said softly.

"Nobody ever expects to get a message that you've lost a loved one," Ezra said. "Even in war most people expect their loved ones to be OK, and it hits hard to find out that the person you love won't be coming home."

When Elizabeth returned, she had washed, changed her clothes, and put up her hair. She looked strained but refreshed. Sitting down at the table with the men, she spoke easily and lovingly about her husband. Everyone had a favorite Shaun O'Banyon story, and Elizabeth wanted to hear them all. After a while she sat up straight and addressed the group. "One of those men you chased off told me that he killed my husband. Can you tell me how it happened?" she asked.

Ezra and the men all told part of the story, recounting how they had come upon part of a Confederate regiment that had pinned down a platoon of Yankee soldiers in an inescapable situation. "Your husband saved our lives," Reginald Bonesteel said, "by giving his own life. As a result, not only did he prevent Captain Justice and the rest of us from being slaughtered; he also saved the lives of a number of men in a Union infantry platoon that we were trying to rescue."

"And did he suffer much pain?"

"No, ma'am, not for long," Nate answered. "God was gracious to him and allowed him to pass on quickly."

"And he wanted to be buried here at home?"

"Yes, ma'am. He made me promise, too," Ezra said with a smile. "You know your husband better than we did. And you know when he asks you to do something, you are going to do your level-best to get it done. I'm not going to say it was easy, but I'm glad we are here and are able to honor your husband's last wishes. He was a good man, Elizabeth, and we are all better because of him."

"Thank you, Captain Justice. Now if you

don't mind, I would like to go out and talk to my husband."

"Yes, ma'am." Justice nodded.

"Ma'am, Roberto and I brought the coffin off the wagon and placed your husband on the porch," Carlos said.

Elizabeth walked to the door and, just before turning the handle, she paused to collect her courage. She then stepped outside to join her husband. The sight of the coffin took her breath away for a moment, but she quickly regained her composure, walked over, and knelt down next to her husband.

"Shaun, my love. It's going to be very difficult to go on without you, but with the Lord's help, I will. We had some wonderful memories. Remember that time . . ."

After a while, Elizabeth rejoined the men. "Tomorrow I will walk around the property and try to decide where we should lay my Shaun to rest," Elizabeth said. "Perhaps you gentlemen will have some suggestions as well, and I'd appreciate hearing them." She paused and dabbed her eyes. "I guess I never really thought much about where I'd be burying my Shaun."

"We'll be glad to help, Mrs. O'Banyon," Carlos volunteered. "I saw a beautiful spot out under that row of trees back beyond the well."

"Yes, Carlos," Elizabeth said. "Let's take a look at that spot."

"In the meantime, ma'am," Ezra paused and took a sip of coffee, "I wonder if you would mind filling us in a little more about what is going on in the town. It seems that Slate's Death Raiders has a stranglehold on the place."

"Oh, yes. You are absolutely right." Lizzie O'Banyon's eyes flared. "And Shaun will never rest until they are out of town."

"We've gotta bury two men tomorrow morning," Roberto said.

"And if they don't leave town, we will be burying a lot more of them," Ezra said.

"Their leader, that Slate fellow, he is going to have a hard time shaving for a while," Elizabeth said. "I caught his face with a hot horseshoe earlier today. It's a wonder they didn't kill me. Well, come to think of it, I guess they would have had it not been for the refuge that Shaun had prepared for me. As soon as I hit Slate with the poker, I ran for the mineshaft and locked myself in there. They fired a lot of lead, but nothing did any damage. As you know, it is a very strong fortress and rather inaccessible."

"Oh, yeah, we know all about that, don't

we, fellows?" Ezra said with a smile.

Lizzie O'Banyon smiled in return, and for a moment it was almost hard for Ezra to imagine her being the same woman who had been wielding a shotgun just a few hours earlier in the day.

"Do you think they will come back?" Lizzie asked.

"I'd almost bet on it," Harry Whitecloud said. "That bunch doesn't take rejection well. Slate will want revenge for what you did to his face. They'll be back, guaranteed."

"So, what is our plan?" Bonesteel asked.

"I think we'll ask them to leave," Ezra said flatly.

"I'm not even going to ask you what you meant by that," Nate said with a twinkle in his eye.

"Are we going to bury Shaun first?" Carlos asked.

"We have a score to settle with Mordecai Slate," Ezra said. "We wouldn't be doing right by our friend Shaun O'Banyon while those thugs are terrorizing Elizabeth and the town down the road. I think we need to take care of business first, then we'll come back and give Shaun the proper burial he deserves."

Elizabeth O'Banyon said, "The mineshaft is plenty cool, about a constant 55 degrees.

We can place the . . ." she stumbled over the words . . . "We can place the . . . I'm sorry; we can place Shaun's body in there until we are ready for the burial. But wait. What did you mean when you said that you have a score to settle with Mordecai Slate?"

Ezra looked at Nate; Nate looked at Harry Whitecloud; Harry looked at the Hawkins twins, and they all looked at Reginald Bonesteel. "Me? Why me?" Bonesteel asked.

"Because you were there, Reginald. You saw it all," Ezra said.

"What are you men talking about?" Elizabeth interrupted.

"Captain Justice is correct, ma'am," Bonesteel said. "I know who killed your husband."

"I thought you said that he sacrificed himself in battle."

"Yes, that is exactly right," Bonesteel agreed. "And the man who killed your husband first beat him and ruthlessly stabbed him to death. That man is Mordecai Slate."

"Why that dirty, good for nothin'. . . . I should have run that poker right through him today," Elizabeth O'Banyon railed, "instead of merely giving him a suntan."

"I think it's time to give the Death Raiders notice," said Ezra.

"That's Ezra's way of saying they are being evicted, one way or another," Nate said.

Ezra chuckled just a bit, which was a lot for Ezra.

"Oh, boy!" Roberto Hawkins hooted. "I'm getting some ideas already."

"Me too," Carlos chortled. "That bunch has run roughshod over that town long enough. Let's show them what it feels like. We can come up with some interesting fireworks for them!"

"Do you know where Slate and his men are staying, Elizabeth?" Justice asked.

"The people in town said that some of them are at the hotel, and some have taken over rooms at the courthouse. But I don't know for sure."

"OK, that's good enough for starters. I'm sure the fellows at The Redheaded Lady will know where to find them. They were kind enough to help us find our way to your place."

"Oh, really?" Elizabeth seemed surprised.

"Well, yes, with the help of some gentle persuasion on the part of Ezra Justice," Harry Whitecloud added.

"Oh, I see," Elizabeth chuckled.

"Well, tomorrow, let's hope we can offer some gentle persuasion to Mordecai Slate and his boys," Ezra said.

"I'll look forward to that," Elizabeth said. "I want to give Mordecai Slate the same chance he gave my Shaun."

"No, Lizzie, you better stay right here. Let us take care of Slate and his boys."

"What? You've got to be kidding, Ezra." Lizzie's face reddened, and her eyes were fiery. "That man murdered my husband. I want to make him pay."

"He will pay, Elizabeth. I promise you. But you have to stay here."

"Please, Ezra. I'll stay out of sight, I promise. Wouldn't you rather that I be with you and your men than staying here by myself. What would I do if any of Slate's men decided to return?"

"After we're done, I promise you, Elizabeth; none of the Death Raiders will ever bother you again."

20

Mordecai Slate walked out on the Clinton courthouse steps carrying a cup of coffee before breakfast, his face still throbbing with pain from the burn he'd received from Elizabeth O'Banyon. He looked across the street, glanced up, and saw a huge banner hanging from the second-story balcony of The Redheaded Lady. Slate read the words:

DEATH RAIDERS
JUDGMENT DAY! JUSTICE RIDERS

"Ezra Justice," he said. "You are a hard man to kill."

Slate turned to one of his guards and shouted, "Johnson, get the men up! Now!"

All twenty-three of Slate's men staggered to the front of the courthouse. All of them, that is, except the two men who were dispatched by Elizabeth, the two who had died in The Redheaded Lady, and the one young boy who had decided that it was better to run than die.

The men gathered around Mordecai Slate, awaiting their leader's orders. They were quick in coming. Slate pointed to the banner above the balcony. "The Justice Riders said, 'It's Judgment Day.' Judgment day for whom? I say it's time to end it for the Justice Riders. Do you men agree?" Most of the men shook their heads as expected.

One man dared to speak up. "I've had enough of the Justice Riders. I'm out of here." The man began walking toward his horse.

Mordecai Slate pulled out his gun and shot the man in the back. He then looked at the remaining men. "Does anyone else feel the same way?" he asked.

The men were silent.

"Good," Slate spat out. "Ezra Justice has been a pain in my backside for too long. And I think it is time that we solved the problem. I know where he is; he's out there at that O'Banyon lady's place, and we're going to pay them a visit. Mount up! We're going to take the battle to them."

What Mordecai Slate did not know was that the Justice Riders had already brought the battle to him.

As Slate and his men rode to the edge of

town, the entire portion of the street blew sky high right in front of their horses. The horses reared in the air, tossing Mordecai Slate and four of his men to the ground. The remaining men on horseback took off toward the other end of town. The men who had been thrown from their horses got up, drawing their guns. Just then Reginald Bonesteel raised up from behind the banner hanging from the balcony of the saloon. He aimed his Henry .44 and fired at the men in the street. One of Slate's men went down with a hole in his chest. The other three men looked around in stark terror. Just as they saw Bonesteel on the saloon balcony, another shot rang out, and a second man felt a thud in his chest.

"Get out of the street!" Slate screamed to his men. As the men ran for cover, two shots rang out in succession, taking the two remaining men down. Slate ran toward the side of the street, diving behind a set of stairs leading up to the boardwalk, just as a bullet whizzed by his ear.

Men and horses caught up in the chaos blindly charged toward the other end of the street. Just as before, Slate's men were met at the edge of town by powerful explosions in the middle of the road. The night before Carlos and Roberto Hawkins had buried explosives all across the road at both ends of town, just as Ezra Justice had instructed.

Three more men were thrown from their horses, narrowing the odds. One man lay dead from the explosion. The other two soon met their Maker, thanks to bullets from Reginald Bonesteel. No one noticed Mordecai Slate slipping back into the courthouse. The men still on their mounts turned tail and raced back toward the other end of town. Standing there, waiting for them with guns raised, were Carlos and Roberto Hawkins, Harry Whitecloud, Nate York, and Ezra Justice. Slate's men galloped straight at the Justice Riders, but Justice and his men didn't flinch. They stood in the center of the street and fired rapidly, picking off eight more of Slate's men as they approached. The remaining men pulled up hard, jumped off their horses, and ran inside the courthouse. The Death Raiders started shooting from the courthouse windows.

Dodging bullets from the Death Raiders across the street, Whitecloud, the Hawkins boys, Nate, and Ezra made their way to The Redheaded Lady Saloon. Breathing heavily, taking cover behind the walls of the saloon, the Justice Riders regrouped around Ezra.

"Is everyone OK?" Ezra asked.

"We're fine, Captain. Couldn't be better,"

quipped Bonesteel as he came through the back door of the saloon.

"What next, Captain?" Harry Whitecloud asked.

"Well, Harry, it worked with firecrackers. Let's see what you can do with dynamite."

"I like the way you think, Captain," Roberto Hawkins said, grinning widely as he dug into his pack, pulling out thick sticks of dynamite. "I've got the dynamite, Harry," Roberto said. "Now, can you get it to the target?"

"If I can't, Roberto, I'll let you run over and place it there personally."

"Oh, I'm sure you can do it, Harry," Roberto replied quickly as he deftly tied the dynamite around the shaft of the arrows.

"Where do you want me to put it, Captain?" Harry asked

"Take the door out."

"The door it is," Harry said as he raised his bow and pointed the arrow across the street. The heavy arrow released with a twang. It seemed to take forever to arch across the street, slamming at last into the heavy oak front door. Slate's men continued firing sporadically as the arrow flamed on the door. The fuse burned ever closer to the dynamite.

Across the street the Justice Riders took cover.

A loud concussion of sound echoed through the street as the door exploded with wood splintering in all directions, penetrating the bodies of two Death Raiders. Several of Slate's men who survived the explosion picked themselves up off the floor and began pounding shell fire toward the saloon.

Ezra stood near the swinging doors of The Redheaded Lady, peering out at the destruction. "Through the window this time," Ezra Justice said calmly.

Harry placed another dynamite-laden arrow into his bow, and Carlos lit the fuse as Harry started to pull back on the bow.

"Wait!" Ezra called.

Whitecloud stared at the burning fuse hanging from the dynamite. "Say when," Harry said with nerves of steel.

Justice and his men watched as the fuse burned closer and closer to the dynamite. Less than half an inch from the dynamite, with everyone in the room but Harry twitching anxiously, Ezra spoke: "When!"

Whitecloud pulled back on the bow and released the bowstring. The arrow streaked across the street, crashing through the front window of the courthouse, exploding instantly. Glass and brick blew out onto the boardwalk below as a corner of the building crumbled under its own weight.

"We've had enough! We've had enough!" Five men stumbled out of the courthouse with their hands raised.

Ezra and his men boldly walked out of the saloon and met the men in the middle of the street. He stepped up to the five men and glared at them. "Do you still want to be Death Raiders?" Justice asked.

"Not any more," one man said. He pulled off his red bandanna and threw it on the ground. The other four followed suit.

"Now get out of town and keep riding."

As the men turned to leave, Justice called to them, "Where's Slate?"

"He's in the courthouse," one of the men replied. "Slate said he'll meet you in there if you are man enough."

Ezra turned and looked toward the courthouse. He pulled out his .44 and checked the bullets in the chamber. He looked at his men and said, "This is between Mordecai and me. All of you stay out here." He returned the gun to its holster and started walking toward the courthouse.

Nate caught up with him and said, "Ezra, this is just plain dumb. Let us go in and take him out as a team. We started this as a team; let's finish it that way."

"This is long overdue, Nate; it's time he and I settled it."

Nate nodded.

Ezra walked the rest of the way to the courthouse alone.

Nate looked on in the middle of the street. "God, protect him," he prayed, as he watched Ezra step through the courthouse entrance.

Once inside Ezra squinted to see through the yellow haze that hung in the remains of the building. When his eyes adjusted to the weird light, he called out to Slate.

"Mordecai!"

Dead silence.

"Mordecai! This has been a long time in coming. We've both always wondered who was the faster of the two of us. I guess it's time we found out. You asked if I was man enough to come in. Well, I'm in. Are you man enough to step out?"

Ezra heard a shuffling sound as Mordecai stepped out from behind one of the courthouse columns.

Slate's eyes fixed on Justice. "Ezra, you gotta answer something for me. I shot you dead center back in Bentonville. I saw you go down. So tell me, how is it that you're still walking around?"

Ezra kept his right hand near his gun as

his left hand reached into his left breast pocket and pulled out the watch his father had given him long ago. In the center of the timepiece was a hole with Slate's bullet still pressed in it. "This is the reason why I'm still alive," Ezra said, holding the watch up for Slate to see.

"Well, I won't hit it this time," Slate replied with a smirk.

Slate and Ezra began circling the room counterclockwise, each watching the eyes of the other man. Both men knew that the eyes always reveal when a man is going to make a move.

"I presume you are not a Christian, Mordecai."

"No, I am not."

"Well, I think you ought to get right with Jesus."

"Do you want to tell me why?"

"Because you are about to enter eternity, and I would prefer to see you go up rather than down."

"Are you going to preach to me, Ezra?"

"If I thought it would do any good, I'd try."

"Well, it won't," Slate sneered. "And I'm tired of all this talk." The two men continued circling, waiting for someone to make the first move. For the first time Ezra saw doubt and fear in Mordecai Slate's eyes.

"Mordecai, you don't have to draw," Ezra said.

Slate stopped suddenly. "Yeah, I do!" Mordecai Slate went for his gun but not fast enough.

Ezra fanned two shots into Slate's chest as the leader of the Death Raider's gun cleared leather and fired into the floor.

For a long moment Slate stood staring at Ezra. Almost as if in slow motion, he dropped to his knees, his eyes still riveted on Justice. With life draining from Mordecai Slate and his upper body slumping toward the floor, he uttered one word — "Jesus" — just as he hit the floor dead.

Ezra looked down at him and whispered, "I hope so, Mordecai."

21

"Mrs. O'Banyon, might I trouble you for another touch of tea?"

"Why, certainly, Mr. Bonesteel," Elizabeth O'Banyon replied. "I'm glad you like my Irish tea."

"Irish?" Bonesteel asked.

"Yes, it is a special mixture that Shaun used to make. I'm glad you like it." She smiled at Bonesteel as she filled his cup with another cup of the brew.

"Irish tea," he mumbled. "I'm drinking Irish tea . . . and worse yet, I'm enjoying it!"

"Miracles still happen, Reginald," Nathaniel York said.

"I'll say," piped in Roberto.

"Well, my prayers have been answered," Lizzie said. "You boys came back safely. I can feel Shaun smiling on us. The Raiders are gone, and now we can live in freedom again. And the people in town have been so kind, offering to help in any way." Lizzie raised the teapot. "OK, last call for tea or coffee. We have a funeral ceremony to perform, you know."

The group had gathered in Elizabeth O'Banyon's living room prior to the burial service for Shaun. It was the day after the showdown with Mordecai Slate in Clinton. Despite the occasion that drew them together, they were all in cheerful moods and celebrating the liberation of the town as well as the demise of the Death Raiders.

Ezra and the men finished their coffee and tea and stepped outside. Elizabeth O'Banyon walked with them to the large tree in the east pasture, along the cliffs with a view of the house. There Carlos and Roberto had dug a six-foot-deep hole. The well-traveled coffin containing the body of their friend and fellow soldier sat on the far side of the open pit.

As the group gathered around the grave site, Setter came running over as well, holding something in his mouth. "Hey, look at this!" Roberto said. "It's your photograph with Shaun." He handed the picture to Elizabeth.

"Yes, it is," said Lizzie. "One of Slate's men tried to coax me out of the cave with the picture the other day, and he got a bullet for his trouble. I thought that he had destroyed it, but Setter found it for me. Thank you, boy!" Elizabeth patted the dog on the head. "Maybe you're an honorary Irish setter after all." Elizabeth held the photograph close to her heart as she sat down on a chair that Harry Whitecloud had carried outside for her. Setter nestled in next to her. "Let's begin," she said.

Each man told a story about Shaun O'Banyon and what his life had meant to him. Some of the stories were funny and described Shaun's propensity to talk his way out of any jam; others were more poignant, telling of times when Shaun O'Banyon did something to help someone else who had no means of returning the favor.

Finally, Ezra Justice stepped to the front of the group; and with O'Banyon's coffin behind him, Ezra took out a small, tattered Bible from inside his coat pocket. He cleared his throat and said, "Shaun O'Banyon was both a fighter and a lover of life. Some people knew Shaun only as a man of war. But those of us who knew him well understood that he carried in his heart the love of God, and he shared that love with anyone that would receive it. He was a man of simple faith who took joy in the daily adventures of life. He loved his wife — he loved you to the very end, Lizzie — and he loved his friends — even you, Reginald."

The group chuckled as they recalled O'Banyon and Bonesteel's constant bickering and teasing — O'Banyon who loved all things Irish, Bonesteel who cherished all things British. They were an unlikely pair, yet Ezra Justice assigned them together often because they worked so well together. Nobody questioned that for all their bombastic boasting, either man would give his life for the other. One did.

"The Bible says there's no greater love than a man who lays down his life for his friends. That's what Jesus did for all of us, by giving his life to purchase our freedom. He died that we might live. And in a similar way, that's what Shaun O'Banyon did. He willingly sacrificed himself for us. Because of Shaun, we are alive here today. We honor his life and will always cherish his memory." Ezra paused, fighting back the tears in his own eyes; then he said, "And the words 'Remember O'Banyon' will be a constant reminder for us to live right before our God, to cherish our friends, and to leave behind a legacy that will live on forever."

Ezra bowed his head, and the group followed suit. After about a minute of silence, with the birds chirping in the background and the signs of new life surrounding them, Ezra said, "We commit Shaun O'Banyon to you, Lord. Thank you for blessing our lives with his. May he rest in peace, and may we live in such a way that we will see him again in heaven one day. Amen."

"Amen," the others chorused.

"Remember O'Banyon," Justice said.

"Remember O'Banyon," the others repeated.

Ezra and the other men stayed at Elizabeth O'Banyon's farm for a few days, helping her to mend some fences, doing some painting and repair work that she had been wanting to get to herself. After the third day, however, Ezra called the group together after dinner.

"It's time for us to move on, Elizabeth," he said. "We've enjoyed being here with you, reminiscing about Shaun and taking a few days to be renewed ourselves. But it's time for us to go."

"I understand, Ezra," Elizabeth replied. "I appreciate you men staying as long as you have. Setter and I have enjoyed your being here. Now that the war is over, where will you be going?"

"It's hard to say right now. Most of the guys have plans to move in this direction or maybe even farther southwest. Harry wants to go back to medical school."

"Yes, he's right, Miss Elizabeth," Harry interjected. "I do want to finish my education and then return to the Sioux to help them."

"You'll be a great doctor, Harry," Elizabeth said with a smile. "Probably a surgeon. I've heard that your skill with a knife is legendary."

The entire group laughed as Harry patted the long bowie knife strapped to his boot.

"What about you, Reginald? What are you going to do?" Elizabeth wanted to know.

"I'm not certain at present, Elizabeth," Bonesteel said. "I've heard there are great opportunities for a man to make a good living in Texas. Can you imagine my British accent with a Texas drawl?"

"Wherever we go, Elizabeth," Ezra said, "and whatever we do, we will always be available to you. We are as committed to you as we were to Shaun. You are a part of us. If you ever need us, we'll be here; you have our word on that."

"Will you remain in the army, Ezra?"

"I don't know, Elizabeth. I was a farmer before the war, a plantation owner in Tennessee. That's where Nate and I are from. We're thinking of going back there and working together again. Of course, we don't know what we're going back to." Ezra took a deep breath and then continued. "If not the plantation, wherever God leads me, I will go."

"My, that's quite a statement of faith," Elizabeth O'Banyon said.

"Ha, especially coming from Ezra Justice," Nate said. "I've always teased Ezra about having plenty of faith in his head but not enough in his heart. It sounds to me like now he has both."

Ezra smiled and nodded. "Thanks, Nate. I appreciate that. I think the events of these past few weeks have really had an impact on me. I've seen faith in action, not just in theory. That appeals to me. And I guess I've also realized that it isn't so much what I know or can do on my own; but real faith is trusting God deep down in my heart, even when things don't work out so well. I know that I'll never be the same as a result of what I saw in Shaun and you, and a lot of others."

As the men hugged Lizzie O'Banyon and said good-bye, the Justice Riders realized that whatever they would do or become they would not tolerate evil, oppression, or injustice.

Ezra Justice waved one last time as he and

his men mounted their horses and headed off. "It's not good-bye, Elizabeth," Ezra called back to her. "It's 'See you later' for us."

Eventually they all would go their separate ways, but any time one of the Justice Riders received a message stating, "Remember O'Banyon" they reassembled to fight together on behalf of good people who needed their help. Wherever they went — whether to the gold mines of California, the wide open ranch lands of Texas, or the mountains of Colorado, they brought hope, peace, and justice.

ABOUT THE AUTHORS

Chuck Norris is known worldwide as an action movie and television star, but he considers his greatest honor, next to his family, as being recognized as a humanitarian. Chuck's most rewarding accomplishment was the creation of his KICK-START Foundation® (building strong moral character in our youth through the martial arts). Chuck has received numerous humanitarian awards, including the Make-A-Wish® Foundation's Celebrity Wish Granter of the Year; and Veteran of the Year by the Veterans Foundation of America. Chuck and his wife, Gena, live with their children in Dallas, Texas.

Ken Abraham is a *New York Times* bestselling author who has co-written books with Chuck Norris *(Against All Odds)*, Lisa

Beamer *(Let's Roll!),* and Tracey Stewart *(Payne Stewart: The Authorized Biography).*

Aaron Norris, a military veteran and martial arts expert, is also an actor, producer, director, writer, and president of Norris Brothers Entertainment.

Tim Grayem is CEO of The Canon Group and an established film writer.

The employees of Thorndike Press hope you have enjoyed this Large Print book. All our Thorndike and Wheeler Large Print titles are designed for easy reading, and all our books are made to last. Other Thorndike Press Large Print books are available at your library, through selected bookstores, or directly from us.

For information about titles, please call:
　(800) 223-1244

or visit our Web site at:
　www.gale.com/thorndike
　www.gale.com/wheeler

To share your comments, please write:
　Publisher
　Thorndike Press
　295 Kennedy Memorial Drive
　Waterville, ME 04901